of Atlantis

Stuart Taylor

Exciting
Stories

First published in Great Britain in 2013

Exciting Stories. 6A High Street, Chatham, Kent. ME4 4EP

Email: Austin@exciting-stories.co.uk

Website: www.exciting-stories.co.uk

Copyright © 2013 Stuart Taylor

Covers and illustrations copyright © 2013 Stuart Taylor

ISBN: 978-0-9560345-7-1

Contents

A Personal Message
from Stuart Taylor

I love hearing from my readers as much as I love writing adventure novels for them!

If you enjoyed this book, or any of the others, it would mean the world to me if you send me a short email to say hi! I always respond personally and I would like to put you on my mailing list to receive book news, special offers, and freebies.

Please scan the QR Code below with your mobile phone and click "Contact" to introduce yourself so I can thank you personally for trying my books….

Other Books by Stuart Taylor

These are available in Kindle and paperback versions at Amazon.co.uk

And Amazon.com

Chapter 1

U-boat X19

Kapitänleutnant 'Jericho' Lansberg scanned the polar horizon from the bridge of UB-X19. Taking off a frozen fingerless glove his stubbly chin rasped as he stroked it thoughtfully. Amid a steamy cloud of breath he removed a blackened cigar stub from between his prematurely stained teeth, and with calloused fingers picked a lone tobacco strand from his tongue. Turning downwind the Kapitänleutnant spat over the side of the conning tower and with the unlit stub back in its place between his teeth, he raised his binoculars to continue his one-eyed survey of the Arctic wastes.

Somewhere out there, amid blue and white ice and still black-water, was the final radio signal-buoy they needed to find to complete their Top Secret expedition.

Lansberg's concentration was broken by a voice rising from inside the conning tower.

"Permission to come up, Captain?"

"Granted. What is it Willi?"

The head and shoulders of a gangly blond youth emerged from the conning tower hatch.

"A signal from Rochelle, Captain. Our ships have sighted the British submarine again."

"Are they still gaining, Willi?"

1

"Yes, Sir. I've been tracking them from previous sightings and at their present course and speed they'll overtake us in less than five hours." The boy handed Lansberg the signal.

"Captain. There is also a second, Top Secret, message that only you can decipher. It is from Berlin, I think."

"Thank you, Willi. I'll be down in a minute. Now get below before you catch your death, Junge."

The boy saluted and folded his skinny arms and legs back through the Conning Tower hatch. He looked up before disappearing and smiled through his wispy beard, "Coffee, Captain?"

"Ja. Gut, Willi. Danke."

"Orders at last!" thought Lansberg raising his binoculars for the last time. "Now where *is* that signal-buoy? Without that Berlin could issue as many Top Secret orders as it wanted to – U-boat X19 might as well be cruising with the rubber ducks in his bathtub for all the good they would do."

Jericho Lansberg removed the cigar stub once more and was about to park it in its usual place in his inside pocket, when the submarine juddered violently and he fell backwards grabbing for the bridge handrail.

The eerie arctic silence was shattered by squawking klaxons and Lansberg's face was suddenly lit by flashing red warning lights. Frantic yells of "ALAAAARM!" carried up from below.

The bow of the boat suddenly pitched beneath the waves as the main valves blew and the aquaplanes plunged U-boat X19 into a near-vertical dive. The Kapitänleutnant catapulted forward. Half drowned and nursing a bump on his forehead, he clambered in through the conning tower hatch and clutching the ladder leading down inside the sail, reached up through a torrent of freezing sea water to seal the hatch behind him.

They'd found the final signal-buoy all right, or more accurately the signal-buoy had found them! The beacon must have triggered Berlin's new and hush-hush X19 guidance system locked away behind Bulkhead Thirteen. Whether true or not, the system was rumoured to have been developed by a professor from Göttingen University; a Jewish double agent who, escaping Germany, was now 'most wanted' by the Nazi authorities.

Below decks all hell was breaking loose. Clanks and bangs of heavy equipment breaking free and the tinkling of shattering glass and the terrified screams of men echoed up like a mad opera, from the bowels of the submarine. The boat's central tunnel-like corridor, which ran from bow to stern, would be like a vertical lift-shaft by now. Lansberg hoped his men would find hand-holds in time to save themselves plummeting to their deaths.

The secret message from Berlin would no doubt have warned of this sudden dive. Typical! Too late as usual.

After several minutes pinned face-down to the conning tower ladder, the boat began levelling and Lansberg was able to move again. If the Enigma machine had survived the dive, he would decode High Command's message. What was the purpose of this cloak-and-dagger mission? And what other nasty surprises might be in store?

Chapter 2

Most Secret

According to Lansberg's wristwatch a full fifteen minutes passed before U-boat X19 levelled to resume a stable course. He stepped smartly down the remaining rungs of the conning tower ladder to survey the wreckage strewn around the U-boat. The hull plates of the submarine creaked ominously and here and there failed joints in pipework hissed out high pressure sea water.

The submarine's depth gauge was off the scale. Everywhere was soaked and scattered with soggy papers, bits of the crew's belongings, fragments of smashed dinner plates, and spilled cups and mugs.

Dazed men nursing black eyes and swellings stumbled about with wrenches and spanners, tightening valve-glands and pipe-flanges to stem leaks that were springing everywhere.

Away from the melee, in the peace of his tiny wood-panelled cabin, Lansberg unlocked a grey metal cupboard at the head of his bunk. Inside was a wooden box, similar in size to a portable typewriter. A small key on a chain around Lansberg's neck opened the wooden box to reveal a machine that looked like a small typewriter but with certain peculiarities. The first of these was a row of four scalloped rings or rotors above the typewriter keyboard. Beside each rotor a small window displayed letters of the alphabet. Below the keyboard, at the front of the apparatus, were two panels of

4

numbered plug-sockets with connecting plug-leads that enabled the user to cross-connect the sockets in different combinations.

Captain Lansberg took the soggy top secret signal Willi had given him from his inside breast pocket. Groaning and leaning forward he reached under the mattress of his bunk, and pulled out the Enigma machine's K-book. Lansberg scanned the signal for a series of eight code-letters. Flipping through the blotting paper pages of the K-book he stopped at a page and ran his finger down one of the code columns until he found letters that matched those on the secret message. Next to the code letters was a listing of the message sender's Enigma machine's settings for the day and date the message had been sent. Lansberg adjusted his own Enigma machine to match the sender's machine's settings. He was now ready to decode and discover the contents of Berlin's signal.

Each key of the coded message he entered into the machine, produced decoded letters called plaintext. The plaintext letters quickly became words he could understand.

"Most Secret! For Your Eyes Only," the message began. "Kapitänleutnant J. Lansberg. Your position now will be somewhere within a tunnel connecting the Arctic Ocean to the lost prehistoric sea of Tethys.

"Your mission: to navigate the tunnel and the sea of Tethys to locate the portal to Atlantis and then to the survivors of the lost Atlantean civilisation. We believe a second tunnel exists that will lead you to the ruins of the antediluvian seaport of Metronis. Here you will make contact with a subterranean people – a race who survived the sinking of Atlantis. You will, *at any cost*, secure for the glorious Reich the source of the force of Vril. Unknown in the terrestrial world until now, Vril has the power to energise our newly built and most secret weapon systems allowing us to destroy once and for all the evil enemies of The Fatherland. Please be aware that Germany is not the only Power with knowledge of the force of Vril. Our spies report the British Navy have despatched a rival expedition from Portsmouth under the command of Rear Admiral Gaylord Trumper. Their exploration submersible is a copy of the design stolen from the glorious Reich by the heinous traitor, Professor Irwin Schroder. Schroder used code-name Prometheus Pimlico. Your Science Officer, SS Obersturmführer Rudolph Schneider has detailed knowledge of Professor Schroder having served with him on an expedition to Tibet in 1938.

"We can give you no further information about the prehistoric Sea of Tethys, Metronis, or the Atlanteans. The Hollerith programming cards for the final leg of your voyage are secured inside Bulkhead Thirteen with the X19 guidance machine. The combination needed to unlock bulkhead thirteen is - 666141. The Hollerith cards are sealed in a waterproof, steel chamber with a second combination lock. The combination for this lock is 6A25615A.

"Before loading the new cards into the X19's card reader, you must terminate the X19's present guidance sequence by inserting a golden card into the card reader. You should do this before attempting to load any new cards. If you do not, your submarine's nuclear reactors will rapidly reach critical mass and the submarine and your crew will be destroyed. The Golden card is stored in a waterproof crystal box that must be broken in order to access the card. Previous expeditions to this region have been launched, but none has returned. The Reich therefore relies on your success to secure our final glorious victory in this war. Do your duty. Heil Hitler!"

Chapter 3

The Prehistoric Ocean

The whine of the U-boat's engines had ceased and the drifting submarine filled with hollow clanks of dropped spanners, the chinks of tapping hammers and the crew's shouts and the hiss and plop of leaking water and the creaking of the submarine's protesting hull plates.

Captain Lansberg picked his way aft through the chaotic aftermath of the crash dive to open Bulkhead Thirteen. Entering the combination numbers using a telephone dial on an electric panel in the centre of the door, he heard several metallic clicks before the bulkhead door softly hissed and slowly opened. Lansberg stepped through the hermetically-sealed door and surveyed a dim tunnel with hatches in the floor, walls, and ceiling.

Closing and locking the main bulkhead door behind him, Lansberg reached above his head to spin the locking wheel of the ceiling hatch. He groaned pushing it open. At once a light flickered on beyond the hatch and amid the whirr of a servo motor, a set of gleaming stainless-steel ladders slowly lowered.

Climbing, Lansberg entered a domed steel chamber about three metres in diameter and bathed in softly flashing yellow light. The floor of the dome was gimballed like the dial of a nautical compass and standing on rollers in its centre was the submarine's automatic X-19 guidance system in the shape of a Volkswagen Beetle. The car's trafficators were slowly

7

blinking, showing the U-boat's present navigation cycle was almost complete.

The steel floor of the chamber dipped under Lansberg's weight then rose again to correct the displacement. The Captain walked, as if on a trampoline or springy mattress to the front of the car. He stooped and opened its boot. Inside were the guidance machine's card reader and a sealed silver box containing the mathematical navigation machine that operated each of the Beetle's wheels in turn to guide the U-boat on its voyage to Atlantis.

The card reader's hopper was empty; the cards for the previous leg of the journey having passed through the machine to be resorted and stacked in reverse order for an anticipated homeward voyage.

Lansberg squinted around the chamber for the crystal and steel boxes the message said contained the Golden Card and the sealed packs of Hollerith cards needed to take them on to Atlantis.

Beyond the car stood a control desk with various dials and flickering coloured lamps that curved around a pedestal chair bolted to the deck.

Beside the control desk a metal workbench contained drawers with racks of tools; all fixed to prevent them sliding about with the movement of the submarine. Several of the heavier items had dislodged after the U-boat's violent dive and the Captain replaced them in their holders. To the right of the workbench, within reach of the pedestal chair, was the crystal box, and inside it Lansberg could see the Golden Card glinting in rhythm with the Beetle's trafficators.

Taking an engineer's hammer from a drawer in the workbench and protecting his eyes with goggles, Lansberg smashed the crystal box, and grasping the Golden Card, he took it to the car's boot and carefully inserted it into the navigation machine's card reader. A loud hiss of compressed air announced the appearance of a finely-made steel box rising up in the centre of the workbench. A second telephone dial was in the lid of the box, and Jericho Lansberg stooped to dial in the series of combination numbers and letters. The box opened with a short pop.

Inside were several thousand punched Hollerith cards, sealed in cellophane packs, arranged in four columns. Each column of cards was labelled according to the order they were to be loaded into the navigation machine. Breaking the seals, Lansberg loaded the cards into the card reader's hopper and immediately the Volkswagen's indicators stopped flashing. A second later the car's headlamps snapped on, and slowly, accompanied by the concerted whine of more electric servos, a pair of great steel doors covering the domed chamber began sliding apart like the sleepy opening of a giant eye.

As the steel eyelids opened, the lamps of the chamber dimmed and the Beetle's headlamps shone out through the thick glass dome. Beyond the X19's conning tower, Lansberg could see a circle of blue light at the end of the seaweed cloaked tunnel.

Without warning the Volkswagen's wheels started jerking backwards then forwards, the deck-plates of the submarine began trembling as the U-boat's main engines restarted and the submarine began gliding forward on its journey once more.

The clacking of a teleprinter machine to the right of the Volkswagen caught Lansberg's attention. The machine's printout spewed out into a cardboard box behind it. The clacking stopped and Lansberg squinted at the paper. The light inside the glass chamber brightened as the U-boat approached the far end of the tunnel. Lansberg read the printout.

The Prehistoric Ocean

Armament Modifications U-Boat X19

<u>TOP SECRET</u>

TZ-240. Guided torpedoes x 12

TS-34. Port Waist Repeating Pneumatic Torpoon gun x 1

TS-34.5 Starboard Waist Repeating Torpoon

gun x 1

TS-33. Cyanide Torpoons x 48

EX-21. High Voltage Stun Pistols x 25

Torpoons? What were Torpoons? Lansberg peered out from the edge of the dome over each side of the U-boat's hull in turn. Below him were two glass bubbles similar to the one he was standing in. Two long barrelled weapons drooped from each of these waist turrets and inside were breech and trigger mechanisms and seats for gunners, or Torpoonists, to aim through cross-hair ring-sights and fire their Torpoons. Six glinting barbed spikes on nine foot steel shafts had small cyanide cylinders connected by high pressure hoses, and were loaded in rotating cylindrical magazines ready to be fired. Powerful searchlights fixed to the Torpoon launcher barrels were focused to follow where the gunner aimed and fix in their deadly beams their soon-to-be-dead targets.

The U-boat glided from the tunnel into the prehistoric sea of Tethys and into surprisingly bright blue light. So bright in fact, Lansberg had to shield his eyes from the glare. They were apparently near the surface. Looking up Lansberg saw a solid rock ceiling with, here and there and stretching off into the faint distance, grey and black stalactites piercing the surface of the water.

If they were below a rock ceiling, what was the source of the brilliant blue light? And, mused Lansberg, this was 1945. What did a modern U-boat, armed to the teeth with the latest high-tech weaponry need of what were little more than antique toys - glorified harpoons – the tools of Ned Land and Captain Ahab? Perhaps High Command were actually expecting him to bag them Moby Dick en-route?

Lansberg chuckled to himself as he read the rest of the printout.

"You find something amusing, Herr Kapitänleutnant Lansberg?"

Lansberg swung round. Emerging through the open hatch like a black spider was the Science Officer, Schneider. His fat sallow face was cream and corpse-like and his lifeless eyes reminded Lansberg of the glinting silver Death's Head staring from the black forage cap that perched to one side of the SS officer's slicked-back black hair.

"How did you get in here? I locked the Bulkhead door behind me," growled Lansberg.

"I am here to appraise you of my role in the final stage of our glorious mission, Capitan Lansberg. Your task was to get us to the caves of Atlantis – mine is then to complete the mission by taking a party of highly trained commandos into the caves to find Metronis and secure the source of the force of Vril."

"What do you mean my task *was* to get us to the caves?"

"Well Capitan, now you have successfully found the final signal-buoy, and the sea of Tethys, your task is almost over…. This U-boat is designed with a separate, fast attack submersible built into it – a submarine within a submarine if you will. You and I are standing on its bridge, Herr Capitan! Shortly I will jettison and flood the part that is no longer needed for the mission, the part that contains your crew. Then my men and I will complete the mission for the greater glory of the Reich, Herr Kapitänleutnant!" Schneider flipped open a burnished leather holster and withdrew a service Luger to point at Lansberg. "Believe me, the Fatherland thanks you heartily, Herr Kapitänleutnant. Whilst, as I explained, your role in this operation is over, mine is about to begin. I do hope you will co-operate Capitan."

"What do you mean, you murderer? You're talking nonsense Schneider."

Schneider cocked the pistol and Lansberg heard the door of bulkhead thirteen hiss open. The sounds of voices and clanging footfalls floated up through the open hatch from the corridor below.

"Sounds like the game's up, Schneider!" cried Jericho Lansberg.

"On the contrary, Herr Kapitänleutnant, your men don't know the combination into Bulkhead Thirteen, do they? And like you I locked the door when I followed you in." Schneider sneered smugly, "I think you'll find those are *my men*!"

The glass dome suddenly became shrouded in purple shadow and the Volkswagen was reduced to a humped silhouette with pale yellow glimmers for headlamps.

In the gloom, Schneider's arrogant expression changed to one of open-mouthed terror. His eyes widened and the muzzle of the cocked Luger waivered. Lansberg turned. A nightmare leviathan of seventy metres, tiny-eyed with a snaking tail disappearing into the watery distance was upon them. Beneath the rippling scaly skin of the face, the mechanics of unseen bones hideously slid into place and the creature's enormous jaws sprung apart like those of a Scrub Python about to swallow a goat.

Lansberg craned his neck to look up. Towering over them now was the gloomy cathedral roof of the gigantic mouth and all around were row upon row of crooked, broken, and yellowing teeth festooned with flapping ribbons of rotting flesh.

Chapter 4

Grump Island

Aboard the Nautilad, en route to Atlantis in the present day.

"And just what are we supposed to do now?" said Wendy as the Nautilad left the skirmish in the cavern beneath the gardens of Belchley Park to slip silently into the murky waters of the English Channel. "I'm supposed to be cleaning Mrs Pettigrew's cottage and, if the weather's fine, mowing Major Blowhard's front lawns tomorrow! And what about Bill and Toby's schoolwork? It won't be very long before they're expected to do exams. How will they ever catch up?"

"And the Simpsons are bringing in their Tortoise to have its nails manicured in the morning and I'm neutering Mrs Oats' ginger tom if I get a spare moment in the afternoon," replied Mike.

"I don't suppose the flippin cat'll mind missing that!" said Stu, stifling a snigger.

"Can I have your attention please, everybody," cried Professor Pimlico. "I'd like you all to join me for an informal reception with some refreshments in the Nautilad's saloon. And then Farouke will show you all to your cabins."

They followed the professor down a ladder from the conning tower and along a corridor forward into a large room with a faint odour of oily metal. The room was a strange mix of sumptuous, old-fashioned furnishings, exposed grey pipes, riveted hull plates, electrical wiring, fuse boxes, taps, valves and dials of one sort or another hidden in places by brightly coloured tapestries. Brilliantly coloured Persian carpets covered the deck-plates and a watertight door at the far end of a second short corridor led to a glass observation dome at the bow of the vessel.

Having recovered from the initial shock of their present and rather strange predicament, the prospect of a voyage to the lost continent of Atlantis filled everyone with a certain nervous excitement; especially Bill, Toby and Lu, and Stu (although it was quite difficult to tell in Stu's case – because he was so grumpy).

"Well, I'm not worried about missing school. No one will miss me!" bragged Stu. And he was probably right. His foster mother might miss the allowance she was paid to 'keep' him – but she certainly wouldn't miss the agro Stu caused and the nasty letters from the Education people about Stu's persistent truancy, and therefore the real possibility of jail. The police would save endless paperwork too. If Stu went 'missing' they would only have another unsolved Missing Person case to file and forget instead of the regular mounds of paperwork the boy usually caused them. The sad truth was that Stu had no real family or friends, and after thinking about that, everyone seemed to see Stu in a slightly different light - although nobody said so.

Sam Scrivener wasn't worried about the coming voyage either. His uncomplaining wife was used to him always arriving home late and his dinners being cremated to a crisp in the oven. "And this'll be the scoop of a lifetime!" he chortled patting his camera bag. "Of course the story of the Nautilad's secret underground lair and Belchley Park and the usual cranky Atlantis stories will be all over the world's TV networks and newspapers like wildfire after the raid by the police Trojan squad on Belchley Park, but no one will have an exclusive inside Atlantis story like me!"

Inside Scrivener's head was filled with the bells of cash registers from book sales, film rights, TV appearances, not to mention the celebrity of fame.

The Professor stood with his back to the door into the bow observation dome as everyone gathered for sherry and Coke, cake and, of course, Tunnock's wafers.

"My friends!" he cried, holding his sherry glass aloft, "for we will surely have to be friends in the restricted confines of this fine vessel, I am sure that this impending voyage has come as a surprise to you all."

"Flippin' shock, more like," muttered Stu.

"But we are now faced with a fait accompli. I know only too well how mankind and the nations of the world will behave when they realise there is a chance to control the fabled force known only to the ancients of Atlantis; the force that can heal or destroy and can be used to control the minds of all living things. There will be a race – a mad scramble to be the first nation to get possession of it – the first to be in a position to rule the world. It will be no time at all before the Royal Navy and the Royal Air Force of Great Britain will on our trail to find and interrogate us all to help them find the secrets of Atlantis. Other governments will despatch similar hunting parties. We are now fugitives, my friends. And we will not be safe until we reach the very gates of Atlantis."

"Excuse me, Professor! Sam Scrivener. The Piddle Weekly. Who's driving this submarine while we are all here enjoying your excellent hospitality?"

"I know who you are and the paper you work for Mister Scrivener. In view of our present circumstances, perhaps I may call you Sam?"

"Of course, Professor."

"The submarine is automatically navigated by the X19 mechanical guidance system I developed during the Second World War to travel to Atlantis. It is located on top of the conning tower from whence we came, Sam."

"Pardon me, Professor, but all I saw there was an old car."

"That is the X19 mechanical guidance system. It is guiding the submarine to our first interim destination as we speak."

"Yes. And Austin's OUR car!" chimed-in Bill proudly.

"And where might our first interim destination be, Professor?" asked Mike.

"The Admiral Trumper."

"The Admiral Trumper?" said Wendy.

"Yes, Wendy. The Admiral Trumper: the finest and, in fact, the only pub remaining on the Island of Grump. We are less than an hour away. But now everyone, Farouke will show you to your cabins."

Bill's cabin was next-door to Wendy's. He was bursting to see inside, as Farouke opened the steel door.

"And finally Young Effendi is your cabin." Farouke managed a fleeting smile.

The berth, like all of the other cabins was small and painted white. A porthole in the hull, with a tiny desk and a chair below it, was looking out on deep greeny-black seawater beyond. A single bed inside and to the right of the door had built-in cupboards underneath, and on top of a yellow duvet was a blue boiler-suit with 'Nautilad' embroidered in red on a badge above the breast pocket. A pair of lace-up boots stood beside the bed. "I hope you make yourself at home," added Farouke before handing Bill a strange looking key on a neck-chain. "Please to change into uniform and meet in forward observation dome in twenty minutes."

***

As he climbed down the ladder to the Saloon deck in his new suit and boots, Bill was pleasantly surprised at how comfortable and free the new garments felt. The fabric of the suit was extraordinarily light and the boots felt almost like bedroom slippers. He wondered why they were calling at Grump Island. His question would soon be answered.

Chapter 5

The Admiral Trumper

Entering the empty Saloon, Bill followed excited voices floating along the corridor from the Forward Observation Dome.

The Nautilad was just breaking surface and Grump Island loomed ahead. A frowning tower of sea-lashed craggy grey granite shrouded in sea spray and swallowed in flashing storm clouds at its peak.

The forward observation dome reminded Bill of a cinema in a goldfish bowl. A metal platform with a railed balcony had a row of eight high-backed armchairs bolted to it. Each of the chairs had restraints that hinged over the shoulders, like the ones on the infamous 'Vomit Comet' at Piddleton Towers amusement park, and each was able to swivel through 180° and tilt backwards and forwards to maximise the occupant's view of the submarine's progress.

The sea level created a waterline halfway up the dome and above it Bill watched the shadowy pillar of Grump Island grow as they drew slowly nearer. Suddenly, to his horror a huge lump of jagged rock slid away from the side of the island crashing into the wild waves below.

"You look very smart, Bill," said Wendy smiling up from one of the chairs as he entered. She was dressed in a similar uniform to Bill's, but the boiler suit and boots were pink.

19

"Erm. Thanks," muttered Bill blushing and casting a sheepish smile at Lu. He sat in the last vacant chair at the end of the row wanting more than anything to look at Lu in her new uniform. She was a striking girl - with a figure Bill was sure would look fantastic in the light-weight material of her suit. Bill restrained the urge to stare and was glad when they were finally joined by Farouke, who swept into the dome and bowed. He almost lost his balance when, with a harsh metallic grating like someone struggling to get a car into gear, the Nautilad jolted to a sudden halt.

"No need for alarm!" spluttered Farouke, holding the handrail and adjusting his turban, "Professor insert Golden Card – *he* will steer into dock at Grump Island."

"How will he do that?" asked Toby. "I thought we were being steered automatically by Austin."

"Yes, yes we are! But Professor sit behind steering wheel of little car Austin, to steer up to dock. What else is car steering wheel for?"

"Ask a silly question!" whispered Mike in Wendy's ear.

They watched ringside as the Nautilad glided into a cave. At once Austin's headlamps flicked on to reveal a dock with mooring bollards and a stone spiral-staircase that wound its way up into the gloom of the cave roof. The Professor manoeuvred the submarine toward the dock and with another clunk, the tortured grinding of gears and a judder, which sent Farouke scrambling for the handrail again, the Arab announced, "Ah! Professor put submarine into reverse to stop! Who will help Farouke tie mooring ropes?"

***

Bill, Mike, and Stu stood on the Nautilad's wind-blown deck as the submarine nudged gently against the dock.

Farouke slid a gangplank into place and when the Nautilad was securely tied to its mooring bollards, everyone assembled on the dock to wait for the Professor to turn the submarine's ignition off and join them.

"I see you have all attired yourselves in your new uniforms. As you will have discovered, they are light-weight and comfortable. They are made of a special material with the tensile strength of titanium that allows the body to breathe naturally. With these garments on we have no need of cumbersome deep-sea diving suits; the material is completely waterproof and warm and affords as much comfort to its wearer outside of the Nautilad as it does inside. Now, I expect you are all wondering why we have come to such a lonely place as Grump Island," said the Professor, standing at the head of the gangplank. "We are calling at Grump Island to visit an old friend of mine from the old days."

Farouke stood beaming with a knowing smile.

"That friend," continued the Professor "is Captain Podesta Blenkinsopp, R.N. retired. Capt Blenkinsopp has the distinction of accompanying me on the first British expedition to Atlantis in 1945. We will climb the staircase carved in the rock to The Admiral Trumper where, knowing Podesta, ample refreshments will be made available to you. Follow me! There are only one thousand three hundred and thirty three steps to the top. Oh, and Sam! Please take as many photographs as you wish; I'm sure Podesta will be grateful of any publicity he can get to advertise The Admiral Trumper."

Wendy grimaced at Mike as she placed her foot on the first step to begin the climb.

At the top, the staircase divided into two. One sign on the cave wall read Ladies, and pointed to a tunnel left. A

21

second sign read Gentlemen, and pointed to a tunnel leading to the right.

"Phew! I'm feeling pretty flushed," gasped Wendy after the breathless climb of one hour and seventeen minutes, "and I'm not sure I like the idea of splitting up."

"Oh, I think it'll be an adventure, Mrs Young," said Lu.

"Sadly not a great adventure," said the Professor repeatedly standing on one foot and then the other. "Just a little less embarrassing than coming with us into the Gents tunnel."

Wendy and Lu found themselves in a dark and echoey space with an oddly familiar smell.

"We're in the Ladies toilet," said Wendy sniffing the air.

"I've found a door!" cried Lu, fumbling to feel for the latch. There was suddenly the sound of gushing water.

"I think you've wandered into one of the cubicles, Lu."

"Let's try and find the door out," said Lu, backing out of the cubicle.

"Who's in there? I know somebody's in there, I heard you," came a shout from outside. "I'm armed. So no funny business!"

"We're Mrs Young and Lu," called Lu into the darkness, in the rough direction of the man's voice.

"I'm afraid we're closed," snapped the voice.

"We've come with Professor Pimlico," said Wendy.

"PIMLICO!"

"Yes, aboard a submarine called the Nautilad," said Lu, hoping whoever it was they were talking to wouldn't think her completely mad.

"So he's back!" cried the voice and a door flew open revealing a large silhouetted man holding a gnarled shillelagh in one hand and a candle in a holder in the other.

"Oh yes," said the man, his face breaking into a smile in the candlelight, eyeing the badges on their breast pockets, "I can see you came in the Nautilad, Ladies. I'm Podesta Blenkinsopp. Pleased to meet you."

He tucked the shillelagh under his left arm to shake their hands and was about to suggest refreshments when a door across the bar opened and the Podesta spun around.

"Professor!" he cried as the gentlemen entered the bar. The Professor walked calmly across the dimly lit room and hugged his old friend. The pair stood patting each other on the back. "Let me look at you, Professor," said Podesta stepping back, "You haven't aged a day!"

"You are well?" asked the Professor.

"Very well. So you're going back at last!" said Podesta changing the subject, and beckoning in the direction of the bar, "You've come for the other half of the map, I suppose."

"Yes," replied the Professor.

"Don't worry. I've kept it well hidden for all these years, just in case you ever came back."

Podesta opened a bar-flap and positioned himself behind a row of three beer pumps. He hid the shillelagh under the bar beneath an old-fashioned cash register.

"Now then. What's you poison, everyone? There's Old Dog Drool Bitter, Young Lout Lager and Old Lout Stout and for the young people, I've got the latest from America – Coca Cola! "

"Latest from America!" scoffed Stu. "What planet's he on?"

"I seem to remember the Old Dog Drool was a flavoursome beverage," cut in the Professor, "ideal for a vet, Mike!" he quipped.

"Yes, a particularly full-bodied ale for the discerning bitter drinker," agreed Podesta nodding enthusiastically and holding a dusty glass under the Old Dog Drool tap and pulling the pump back sharply. The tap made a spitting, hollow hissing, and something green and snot-like splatted into the bottom of the glass.

"Looks like the Old Dog Drool's off," announced Podesta, apologetically holding the glass aloft and studying it in the candlelight.

"Perhaps we could have tea instead?" ventured Wendy looking askance at the slime in the bottom of the glass.

Toby was peering out through a window at the rain lashing an empty car park. Weeds were growing up through the glistening tarmac and a faded sign read: The Admiral Trumper Customer Car Park. Patrons Only.

"Yes! Good idea. I'll put the kettle on," said Podesta. He disappeared through a door at the back of the bar closing it firmly behind him. After a few minutes they heard the muffled chugging of a motor somewhere outside and the lights in the bar flicked on.

"Blimey!" cried Stu. "There's an old 'Space Corp Alien Attack Force' video game in the corner. Anyone for a thrashing?"

"Ok. I'll give you a game," said Toby.

"You, Goggle Eyes? I'll mug you!"

"What's 'Space Corp Alien Attack Force'?" whispered Bill. "Must be as old as the hills, I've never even heard of it."

"Oh it is," replied Toby, "it was all the rage after 'Defender Missile Base One', about the same time as Williams Electronics brought out 'Defender' in 1980. You have to pilot a space ship through mazes and space labyrinths destroying alien ships that try to attack you. You start off as a Space Cadet on level one and end up as a Space Commander on Level Twenty. Level Twenty's almost impossible!"

"Ladies first then," chortled Stu.

"No, after you. I insist," replied Toby ignoring Stu's insult and offering him a fifty pence piece.

Stu sat himself in the game's cockpit seat behind the control consul and placed his feet on the rudder pedals. The machine lit up as he inserted the coin and pressed the 'Player One' button. The screen at once transformed into a galactic battle zone. Stu's jaw locked in a rictus of concentration and didn't relax for a full five minutes of life-and-death struggle between whooshing space-craft dodging alien fazers, and the bangs and roars of cosmic depth-charges, and the whoosh of missiles and high-voltage hums of death-rays going off. A boom and an electronic fanfare announced the end of Stu's game. He breathed out and wiped his sweaty forehead.

"Twenty three million seven hundred and sixty thousand three hundred and thirty-five. Beat that, Goggle Eyes!"

"Impressive," whispered Lu to Bill as Toby seated himself behind the monitor and pressed the Player Two button.

The machine burst into life. A minute later a whining howl of a downed space craft and a boom announced the first of Toby's lives was over.

"Oh, bad luck!" sneered Stu mockingly. "I knew you'd be rubbish!"

"I'm a bit rusty that's all," muttered Toby pressing the 'Relaunch' button for his second 'life'.

Bill was preparing himself for Toby's inevitable humiliation and Stu crowing his triumph insufferably for days in the confines of the Nautilad when Toby's fingers all but disappeared in a blur of frenetic button-pushing and joystick-wrenching.

Stu's jaw suddenly dropped, before realising Lu was looking at him and then he tried to look disinterested.

The video game began producing all sorts of new and weird noises announcing bonus this, direct hit that, fly straight into Hyperdrive, re-arm with extra Thermonuclear Thunder Mines. Soon everyone in the bar was cheering Toby as millions rolled by and his score ratcheted up relentlessly from Space Cadet to Squadron Leader and then Space Commander.

Wendy looked round when the door behind the bar squeaked open and Podesta backed into the room carrying a tray of tea things. She was sure she glimpsed zigzagging strings, like washing lines, pegged with rows of drying teabags festooning the small ante-room behind the bar.

"Not that noisy thing!" grumbled Podesta, casting a disparaging glance in Toby's direction and pouring the tea into china mugs with 'The Admiral Trumper' and a logo of a distinguished-looking naval officer from the days of Trafalgar printed on them in blue. "I'm afraid I've run out of milk."

The Admiral Trumper

A repeated booming, a dazzling flash and a much longer electronic fanfare than Stu's announced the end of Toby's game with a free bonus game at level twenty.

"Space Commander!" cried Lu. "That's so cool, Toby!"

"Yeah, you're a dark horse. Where did you learn to play like that?" said Bill.

"My dad taught me. He's Operations Manager for Piddle Automatics. They supply amusement machines to pubs and arcades. He used to take me into the workshop to test the machines sometimes when he worked overtime on Saturdays. Would you like another game, Stu?" Toby blinked innocently through his glasses

Stu said nothing and barged past him to the bar to snatch a mug from the tray.

"This tea's like gnat's pee!" he snarled after taking a swig of the watery liquid.

"That boy's so rude. Thank goodness Bill's not like him," said Wendy into Mike's ear.

"Yes he is rude, but he's really only telling the truth, my dear," sighed Podesta. "The Admiral Trumper hasn't seen a customer since the monorail to the mainland collapsed. I was sold the pub as a "hot" investment by a sharp-suited, fast-talking estate agent after the Second World War. A "guaranteed gold mine" he called it – it was going to be a Paradise Island holiday camp with holiday chalets, a dance hall, a theatre, a swimming pool, a restaurant, an adventure playground for mums and dads to leave their children with the Yellowcoats, and a pub – The Admiral Trumper. It's been more like a bottomless money-pit ever since I signed the contract to buy it. Most of the island has fallen into the sea. The Admiral Trumper is all that remains of the original island.

The Admiral Trumper

I used to be a very good submarine commander. I just wasn't cut out to be a businessman. I should have stayed in the Navy. I've lived alone here on rainwater and Gull Goulash for over twenty years!"

"And that rather conveniently brings me to the second purpose for the Nautilad putting in at Grump Island," said the Professor. "I need a good submarine commander for the voyage to Atlantis – and as you've been before Podesta, you're by far the best-qualified man for the job. Will you come?"

Podesta unscrewed the porcelain Old Dog Drool beer pump and from inside produced an old-looking roll of parchment.

"The second half of the map to Atlantis, Professor Pimlico!"

"Time to cast off then, I think Capt. Blenkinsopp."

Chapter 6

The Green Grass of Home

"Well I miss fresh green soft sweet-smelling grass!" grumbled Vole.

"And I miss snails and worms. And the saucer of nice fresh water the-nice-lady-next-door used to leave me in her front garden," added Hedgehog.

"Oh, do stop bellyaching you two!" cried Monty. "You'll just have to put up with the Human food scraps I find for you from the galley for now."

"Galley?" said Vole. "What's a galley?"

"Galley is the Human name for a kitchen on a ship, Vole," said Legit. "I distinctly remember hearing the sailors on the ship that brought me and Blossom across the wide-ocean to England moaning and groaning about their ship's galley too. I can't repeat the naughty words they used about the cook!"

"Look, you lot. I can think of at least two *nefarious Nerks* who would give their right paws to get their claws on all this Human food – remember Cody and Brabazon?" said Monty.

"How could I forget! Deluded vagabonds of the worst kind!" squeaked Vole gruffly, raising his eyebrows in a frown.

"Yes. Yes, but for now, until we get wherever it is the Humans are going to and find dry land and fresh air and fresh worms, slugs and snails, you'll just have to put up with whatever scraps I can find us."

"I hope the Humans don't stop here," said Monty, peering out of the conning tower observation dome. "It looks cold!"

Everybody looked out through the glass where Austin's headlamps were shining through the dark.

"Nothing but sea and big blocks of ice as far as you can see as usual," complained Vole. "We've been on-board this metal thing for days! Nothing but black sea and white ice. *Are* we nearly there yet, Austin?"

"I'm afraid I don't know," replied Austin. "I only get messages from inside my boot telling me what to do. Then my wheels seem to move the rollers I'm standing by themselves and the submarine goes left or right or up and down; I never know what's going to happen until it actually does."

"Sounds like we're all in the same boat then," said Legit cheerfully, trying but not succeeding in being helpful.

Vole was about to tell everyone just how he thought this adventure lark wasn't all it was cracked-up-to-be and how nothing ever seemed to happen when the submarine juddered, red lights flashed, a deafening klaxon squawked, an urgent-sounding human's voice crackled over a loudspeaker, Austin's gearbox grated, his wheels did a full revolution forward, and the ground (or deck) seemed to disappear. The Nautilad was diving (or more accurately plummeting). At once everybody started scrabbling for claw and paw holds and failing. They rolled into a tangled heap at the front of the conning tower dome, then rather than moaning about how bored he was all Vole could actually say was, "Woaaaaaaaaaaahhh!"

Chapter 7

Crash Dive!

Bill Young felt the seat-restraints tighten over his shoulders stopping him toppling forward into the submarine's salad bowl-like observation dome below.

Despite Capt Blenkinsopp's intercom warning that they'd found the final signal-buoy and everyone should grab something solid, or strap themselves in, all Bill could see hanging from the restraints, were his and Toby's terrified faces staring back mirrored in the glass. Outside was blackness. Blackness rushing up to swallow them as the Nautilad screamed ever deeper.

Silver bubbles, some big and billowing, wobbled past like fat swimmers; others, sparkling pearls of light, swarmed past them, or crashed into the nose-dome smashing into millions more pinpricks of darting light.

Bill shivered hoping they wouldn't meet anything solid coming the other way. He imagined the sub hitting rusty shopping trolleys, or bits of shipwreck, or big deep sea fishes, or worse, sharks or sea monsters. The glass of the nose-dome would surely shatter and the freezing black seawater would rush in and drown them. He stifled the thought by glancing at Toby in the next chair.

Toby's eyes were closed and his expression calm. He appeared to be meditating, but for his white-knuckled grip on the arms of his chair.

Crash Dive!

"You OK?" called Bill, his voice wavering with the intense vibration and buffeting through the Nautilad's hull.

"So far! I hope the others managed to hold on to something," replied Toby, his eyes still shut.

"Capt. Blenkinsopp said this 'turbulence' would only last for a 'few minutes' and there was 'nothing to worry about.'"

"All very well for him, but I'm going to throw up in a minute. I don't know what's up and what's down anymore."

Toby was right. They were spiralling down just like a jet-propelled corkscrew.

***

In her cabin Lu had just managed to see the disastrous streak of red lipstick zigzag across her cheek before the sub went down. Now she was hanging from the handrails on her bunk and the lipstick and most of the stuff from her bag was rolling over the wall now below her feet.

"So much for a girl making the best of herself in adverse circumstances," she thought. "This suit's very comfortable but it's hardly Paris catwalk! Still. On the plus side, it isn't hideously baggy!"

She let go of the handrail and smoothed herself down after the Nautilad eventually slowed and the shaking stopped and her makeup rolled down the wall to settle where it should be on the floor.

***

"I'm glad that's over," said Toby opening his eyes and taking his glasses from his boiler suit breast pocket.

He squinted out through the observation dome. Nothing but blackness!

32

"Yeah, but what's going to happen next, I wonder?" said Bill.

The Observation Dome loudspeaker crackled and the Professor's voice came on.

"I apologise for the rough ride everybody. The X-19 guidance system located the final signal beacon above the tunnel entrance to the lost Sea of Tethys and took over control of the vessel. Once inside the tunnel we will be safe from surface detection for the first time. Ve can now proceed on the next part of our voyage. I am sure you vill be fascinated to know that The Sea of Tethys is home to many sea creatures totally unknown in our world for millions of years. Prepare yourselves for sights you will never have seen, nor vill ever see again. Please. I have been asked to pass you over to Capt. Blenkinsopp."

"Sea creatures unknown in our world for millions of years," repeated Bill under his breath. He remembered the hideous Sea Serpent on the concealed parchment and Mike's jest about not wanting to meet it in a dark alley.

There was rustling noise and a cough as the microphone was passed over to Captain Blenkinsopp.

"Will Mike Stevens and Bill Young and Toby Wishman kindly report to me in the conning tower in five minutes. End of message."

Chapter 8

Ergolite

Deep within the Brazilian jungle an out of place mirror-glass tower glinted in the early dawn sunlight.

Behind a vast desk on the top floor, a fat man with a monocle and blond crew-cut, shorn to near baldness, sat thoughtfully running the end of a Montblanc fountain pen along a deep scar in his cheek. While he watched the antics of squirrel monkeys in the forest canopy outside, a black-windowed black Mercedes limousine pitched and lurched along a red-mud rutted track somewhere below and parked in the shadow of the office tower.

A very large uniformed chauffeur wearing mirrored sunglasses on a flattened nose, got out and walked around the car to open the nearside rear-passenger door. After several moments a tall man in a beige linen suit and wide-brimmed hat emerged carrying a slim briefcase. He mopped his face with a pocket handkerchief. Catching his unshaven reflection in the mirrored glass of the tower he tugged the brim of his hat to a jaunty angle, and in the wake of the chauffer entered the building under a stylised sculptured eagle and a legend that read: 'THE ERGOLITE ENERGY CORPORATION'.

Twenty-five seconds later the doors of a high-speed elevator parted at the top floor. The two men's footfalls echoed down a long white corridor until they stopped at a pair of teak doors where the chauffeur sat himself cross-legged, in a throne-like chair. The man with the hat announced his arrival by knocking three times on the doors.

"Enter," commanded a gruff voice from a hidden speaker while electronic bolts clacked and the doors slowly opened.

Unlike the dim greens and browns below, the room was pleasantly bathed in a pale yellow light that flowed in from the sunlit sky above the green forest canopy stretching as far as the eye could see beyond the office windows.

"How vos your journey, Herr Armstrong?" said a low voice from behind a tall-backed black leather chair.

"A little longer than expected I'm afraid, Sir. First the plane from Heathrow was diverted to JFK, and from JFK to Dallas and then from Dallas by Greyhound bus to Mexico City and from Mexico City by air freighter to La Paz where I was picked up by jeep and taken to Lake Poopo. From Lake Poopo I was blindfolded and taken by canoe along the Piranha-infested Rio Beni and from the rapids at Cachuela Esperanza, where incidentally, I had a scrape with a rogue man-eating Jaguar, I was brought here."

"Yes. Yes. Yes," said the fat man with a dismissive wave of a hand, and as the chair swivelled to face Armstrong the fat lipped mouth below the glinting monocle continued, "I am sure you know vy you are here, Herr Armstrong."

"Erm. Well yes. I think I do, Sir."

The fat man opened a drawer in the desk and flicked a switch. Several paintings on the walls slid to reveal muted flat-screen televisions tuned to BBC World News, ABC News, and CNN.

"Ve seem to haff a problem, Herr Armstrong. I think you know vot that problem is."

"Yes Sir, I think I do," replied Armstrong wondering what, if they both knew what the problem was, he was doing in Brazil.

Armstrong shifted uncomfortably from one foot to the other in front of the desk – it had been a *very* long journey.

"As *you* are Head of European Operations, I am reassured to hear that, as you British so quaintly say, 'you seem to know vot is going on in your own back garden', Herr Armstrong."

"Thank you, Sir," replied Armstrong.

Suddenly the BBC World News screen caught the fat man's interest and the set's sound was restored to normal volume.

"Mystery surrounds the sudden disappearance of rock star Tim Tempest's daughter Lulabell Singer and a previously forgotten World War Two submarine and its inventor, Belchley Park veteran, Professor Irwin Schroder," said the presenter. "Police are combing the computer files of missing Piddle Weekly reporter Sam Scrivener who was investigating the alleged corrupt dealings of senior Wallopshire Borough Council executive Gerald Grey. Grey, who is suspected of making unauthorised criminal foreign investments with money belonging to Wallopshire Council, seems also to have vanished. Any connection between the disappearances of Gerald Grey, Professor Schroder, Lulabell Singer, and Sam Scrivener remains unclear at this time. We have just heard the police investigation has been widened to trace missing country vet, Mike Stevens, widowed Piddle Wallop mother, Wendy Young, and her son William and two other schoolchildren, Toby Wishman and Stuart Briggs, thought to be friends of William Young. Police discovered the World War Two submarine, previously believed destroyed on a wartime mission to the fabled lost Atlantis, in an underground bunker after pursuing one of the missing schoolboys, Stuart Briggs on a stolen Harley Davidson motorcycle…."

The television was once more muted.

"The vorld media is full of the story, Mr Armstrong. It appears ve have lost our contact within the Vallopshire Borough Council."

"You mean Grey, the beastly little fellow with…"

"Yes, the beastly little fellow vith the shiny shoes, Armstrong. Beastly he may have been, but he vos a Worshipful Brother Green Dragon nonetheless and he did find ze lost British Atlantean Expedition submarine and its lost X19 guidance system. And, I might add, his financial donations on behalf of the Vallopshire Borough Council have been vital for the completion of our own Ergolite submarine and vill be sorely missed."

"Yes, I can see his disappearance could be seen as a bit of a 'fly in the ointment', Sir."

"You British haff such talent for understatement, Herr Armstrong!" cried the fat man, standing up and raising his voice an octave. "Ze bird hass flown, Herr Armstrong! Grey vos about to steal ze little Austin car zat contained the British X19 guidance system and ship it anonymously here to Brazil on a tramp-steamer via several fog-bound mysterious islands and a lost jungle plateau. It vos ze last component ve needed for Ergolite to find Atlantis and seize ze mystic power-crystal of Vril. Sadly Grey has failed us: 'made ze pig's ear, I think you British say."

"I can see that, Sir, but might it not be a little premature to start crying over spilt milk at this stage of the game? After all, wasn't there a German expedition to Atlantis and another submarine with an identical X19 mechanical guidance system? And there must have been blueprints, surely? Couldn't we use those instead?"

"Ze blueprints ver smuggled from Hitler's bunker by one of the brothers of the Brotherhood of the Green Dragon at ze end of ze var. Alas ze plans vere all destroyed by invading Russian troops and, as you are aware, ze expedition of ze glorious Reich," the fat man coughed. "I am sorry. Ze *German* expedition to Atlantis never returned. Ergolite vas relying on Herr Grey to steal the newly-discovered British Atlantis expedition submersible to enable Ergolite to find Atlantis and locate ze power-crystal of Vril to exploit as a new energy source."

"If only we knew where the submarine went after it left Belchley Park. But that would be rather like finding a needle in a haystack I suppose," said Armstrong scratching his head.

"Precisely! But perhaps all is not lost, Herr Armstrong," said the fat man reaching in a desk drawer for a newspaper. "There is alvays more zan one way to skin ze cat. Look at zis."

Armstrong wiped his aching eyes and scanned the headline.

"According to this report they not only found the submarine, the Nautilad, at Belchley Park, but also a wartime control room used to track its movements on the original World War Two mission. Are you thinking what I'm thinking, Sir?"

"Ja, Armstrong. Great minds sink alike. Ve might yet retrieve our chestnuts from ze fire. You must return to Belchley Park immediately and get into ze underground control room and report to us ze last known movements of ze Nautilad!"

The fat man pressed a button on his desk intercom and within seconds an olive-skinned, Indian maid pushed a trolley into the office filling it with the swirling aroma of coffee.

"Here, Herr Armstrong! To keep ze wolf from ze door! Coffee and croissants to sustain you on your return flight to Heathrow."

Chapter 9

Into the Bowels of the Nautilad

"Thank you for responding to my message so promptly," said Podesta Blenkinsopp as Bill, Toby, and Mike arrived in the conning tower.

"How can we help?" said Mike.

"I trust you survived the Nautilad's crash-dive unharmed?" said the Captain.

"Perhaps a little more warning next-time, Captain. One of the ladies smudged her lipstick!"

"Oh dear, I hope her beauty will soon be fully restored," chuckled Podesta. "Unfortunately The Nautilad is a much older lady and leaks. We too have repairs needing immediate attention. Farouke has reported that the sudden increase in hull pressure after the dive has caused the Nautilad to take on water. The Professor has told me of your combined mechanical prowess, gentlemen. I wondered if you would kindly assist Farouke with the necessary repairs?"

"Many hands make light work, Effendi," said Farouke.

Bill nodded enthusiastically. "Cool! Yes please!"

"I guess you have your answer then, Captain," laughed Mike.

"Please to follow me," said Farouke. "We go to Engine Room. I give you both conducted tour of submarine on way!"

Mike ducked as Farouke led them through a low door from the conning tower to a metal landing. Handrails and metal-stairs led down to a dark walkway, leading aft. Above and below them dimly-lit hull plates bowed-in under the water pressure outside. Here and there pin-pricks of water spurted in through loose rivets or broken joints in pipework.

"These repairs look serious," said Mike as they ducked through a second low door into a lit, white-painted room. A large globe mostly blue stood at the forward end of a chart table in the middle of the room. Various old-fashioned navigation instruments were spread across the table: brass dividers, an astrolabe, and a metal rule. In the front corner of the room below a glass cupola in the ceiling was a raised platform for one person to stand on.

"This is navigation room," announced Farouke. "Navigator stand with head inside glass bowl and use stars and sextant or astrolabe to find position of submarine."

"Is this a globe of space," asked Toby, slowly turning the sphere on its axis.

"No. It is our world, but undersea. We are here," replied Farouke, pointing to a very dark blue spot a short distance from the North Pole.

"Where is Atlantis?" asked Mike.

"I not know," answered Farouke. "I not go with Professor on first expedition. You ask him. Now we must go before submarine sink!"

They followed Farouke through another bulkhead door into a corridor lit by pale electric lamps flickering along its length. At the far end of the corridor was another door, and as they approached Bill noticed a closed door hidden in an arched alcove in the side of the corridor. The door was fitted with a telephone dial in its centre.

"Is that an intercom?" he asked.

Farouke smiled (which on Farouke looks more like a grimace). "No Effendi that is combination lock."

"Why. What's in there?" said Mike.

"Armoury," replied Farouke.

"An armoury? Are we expecting trouble, Farouke?"

"I not know, Effendi. But Farouke hear things. Professor, he has terrible nightmares. He call out in sleep. I hear things."

"What sort of things, Farouke?" asked Bill.

"Monsters and numbers. I hear him call out about monsters and numbers in sleep all the time. And sometimes pirates too. And Slaveers."

"Prehistoric monsters, Farouke? Is that what the Professor dreams about?" said Mike.

"I not know. Professor does not speak of such things to Farouke," replied Farouke, "but in his dream, Professor has much fear for lost son. I know. The name Rudi. The Professor cry out over and over again for lost son, Rudi."

"Haven't you asked the Professor about these things Farouke?" quizzed Mike.

"Farouke is only servant. Professor is master. It is not for Farouke to ask such things."

Mike patted Farouke fondly on the shoulder. "No, you're right Farouke. It wouldn't be proper for you to ask the Professor about such things."

"What weapons do we have in the armoury, Farouke?" said Toby.

"All sort, Young Effendi. I service and oil all weapons in armoury to make sure they work."

"Can you show us?" ventured Mike.

"Not now. We must repair submarine – but. You will learn all about weapons soon enough. Where we going we need!"

The second door at the end of the palely-lit corridor led into another room that reminded Bill of the gym changing room at school. The walls had slatted bench seats with numbered clothes hooks above them. At the far end of the room, either side of another bulkhead door, were wide metal lockers. Several of the locker doors were flapping open and Bill could see weighted boots and belts and brass diver's helmets and aqualung breathing apparatus inside. Between metal hose sockets that stuck out at the back, each of the helmets was painted with a number.

"What's down there?" cried Toby, pointing to a large circular hatch in the floor of the changing room.

"That is airlock. It lead to midget-subs and outside. We go this way," replied Farouke pointing to the bulkhead door between the diving equipment lockers.

"Midget subs? You mean we've got midget subs as well?" said Bill.

"Yes, Young Effendi. It means we can travel places undersea where pressure too great for diving suit. I service and oil minisubs."

"To make sure they work!" chorused Bill, Mike and Toby laughing.

"Now we go to engine room," said Farouke. "Please to put on diving equipment."

"Are we going outside?" said Bill excitedly.

"No. We wear diving suits in case engine room flooded."

Into the Bowels of the Nautilad

It took ten minutes for Farouke to show them how to secure the diving helmets to their boiler suits and connect rubber hoses from their aqualungs. The helmets were eerily silent and Bill and Toby grinned at each other through circular windows in the faceplates.

"Come in number seven, your time's up!" mouthed Bill. Toby laughed.

Speakers inside their helmets suddenly crackled and a voice said, "Please to follow me, Effendis."

The door between the lockers led down a flight of iron stairs that disappeared below gently, slopping seawater.

"The water level is quickly rising. The submarine will soon be too stern-heavy to steer. Switch on helmet torches," said Farouke through the headphones.

They clambered in their weighted boots backwards down the iron stairs below the inky surface of the water.

Toby instinctively held his breath as the water level covered his faceplate. He reached above his forehead to find the switch for the torch moulded into the crown of his helmet. It clicked and its bright light illuminated whichever direction he turned. Following the others into the darkness, Toby took the final step off the bottom of the iron ladder. The floor sloped steeply away under his boots.

The engine room was dimly lit by pallid waterproof lanterns strung sparsely here and there on the walls. Dominating the centre of the room, a huge riveted iron box was engulfed by copper cooling pipes and electric wires like spaghetti. Toby grabbed something to stop himself slipping and losing his balance on the increasingly steepening floor. Immediately everybody felt a tingly vibration through the water submerging the engine room and a muffled whine as the

Nautilad's engine started up and the propeller shaft started spinning.

"What are you doing, Young Effendi?" crackled Farouke's voice through Toby's headphones.

"I. I don't know," stammered Toby, his glasses steaming up as beads of sweat ran into his eyes. "I held onto this to stop myself falling!"

Farouke began 'swim walking' up the slope as fast as he could past Bill and Mike to reach for the lever.

"You pull override lever, Young Effendi! Submarine out-of-control!"

"I'm sorry," stammered Toby, "I didn't mean to. I didn't know."

"Don't touch anything else, Young Effendi!"

DONG-ONG-ONG-ONG! A shockwave whiplashed through the submarine as it struck something very solid and everyone flew forward past Toby.

"What the devil's going on down there?" crackled Podesta Blenkinsopp over their headphones. "There's nobody steering up here! The Nautilad's crashed into the wall of the tunnel. The forward observation dome's completely smashed!"

A woman's scream sounded somewhere in the background, "We're SINKING!"

Chapter 10

Water Water Everywhere!

"Evacuate the Observation Dome and shut the forward bulkhead door. QUICKLY!" cried the captain over the intercom.

Toby felt the engine room floor levelling as the flooding Observation Dome counterbalanced the submerged engine room.

The submarine's engines screamed struggling against its increasing weight, and after a minute and a half they heard a dull clang and a shudder and a screeching scraping noise beneath them.

"We've hit the bottom," shouted Podesta Blenkinsopp over the boat's intercom. "We are listing heavily to starboard. I can go neither forward nor backward!"

"Come," said Farouke, gesturing for the others to follow him up the iron stairs from the engine room. "There is nothing we can do here now. We go back to captain for orders."

The Saloon carpet was squelchy with seawater that poured in before the Observation Dome door had been closed off. Most of the furniture had piled up against the starboard wall. Everyone gathered in nervous silence, attempting to stand upright before the Professor and the captain.

"What do you plan to do, Captain?" asked Sam Scrivener hanging on to a hull former with one hand, his pen poised over his notebook held open against his bent knee with the other.

"Yes, where exactly are we?" said Wendy.

"Stuck in a ruddy cock-eyed, leaky, antique submarine somewhere under the ruddy Norf Pole waiting to ruddy-well drown!" muttered Stu grudgingly under his breath.

"Trust you to look on the black side," snapped Lu, shooting Stu a withering glance. "You're such an uncouth, uncool bore!"

"Come, come," said the Professor. "Bickering amongst ourselves won't help. We need to work together as a team."

"We wouldn't be 'ere at all if it weren't for your loony ideas abaat findin' some kid 'oo went missin' years ago! Do ya seriously 'fink 'e'll still be alive? You need to wake up, mate. That kid'll be pushin' up daisies after all this time!"

The Professor's usual expression of calm momentarily crumpled into despair and for a second he turned away.

"STU!" scolded Wendy, "that's too bad. Apologise!"

But before Stu could say anything, apology or otherwise, the captain cut in, "Belay there ALL of you! The Nautilad is trapped...Sinking. We need to lighten her to gain buoyancy. Then we might lift her from the bottom and move her out of the tunnel."

"How?" said Bill.

"We need to jettison everything we can that's heavy. Weapons, tools and deploy you all in the midget-subs," replied Captain Blenkinsopp.

"But there are only three midget submarines aboard the Nautilad and they take only two persons each," said the Professor.

47

"I shall stay with my boat and try for the Terrapino rebel base for repairs," said Podesta. "That means three of you will have to sit on another's lap."

"You needn't fink I'm sittin' on 'is lap," said Stu pointing at Bill.

"My apologies Toby, but you and Lulabell and Mrs. Young are quite small – you could double-up with someone else, couldn't you?"

Bill's heart beat faster imagining sharing a seat with Lu. He'd held her once before, an experience he relished repeating.

"Captain, Effendi. One question, please? If we are on bottom of tunnel and if midget-subs come out from hatch underneath Nautilad, how we open hatch to launch midget-subs?"

"We must rid ourselves of weight and hope when I blow the ballast tanks the Nautilad will rise enough for the midget-subs to escape."

"And what happens if the Nautilad doesn't rise enough for the midget-subs to escape, captain?"

"Then, Mr Scrivener, as I have only one chance to blow the main ballast tanks we shall remain trapped and die."

Chapter 11

Before They Die

"What on earth's going on?" said Hedgehog. "The silly humans are running about like headless chickens carrying things!"

"I think something's wrong. My feet are getting wet. Water seems everywhere," replied Vole.

"We're sinking," said Austin gloomily. "I keep sending navigation signals from my boot, but nothing ever happens when my wheels turn on the rollers."

"Does that mean we're going to die, Monty? I thought I'd be out walking in the fields one day and then I'd get tired and curl up asleep in the sun and never wake up – not drown in a smelly, gloomy old metal tank-thing like this," wailed Vole.

"I don't know what will happen to us, Vole. I've seen the Human, the one with the bandage who's hurt his head telling the others to collect weapons, and pots and pans, and furniture and tools and machines from the boat's workshop, and even the stove from the galley to dump at the airlocks. The Human boy, Toby, ticks everything off on a list and the two Humans called Mike and Bill, wearing the most peculiar getup I might add, abandon it all outside in the sea! Very odd behaviour!" said Monty.

"Do you think that's what Humans do before they die, then?" suggested Hedgehog.

49

Chapter 12

Bailing Out

"Let me see inventory, Young Effendi," said Farouke.

Toby handed over the clipboard. "All of the Torpoons and weapons have been unloaded. Only a couple of toolboxes from the workshop to go and the piano from the saloon according to this list," said Toby.

"I take list to Professor."

"No need, Farouke. I will look at it here," said the Professor, ducking to enter the inner-airlock chamber.

Through the porthole, outside in the murk of the tunnel, Bill and Mike's helmet-lamps swept this way and that as they lugged more and more items onto an ever-growing pile.

"My calculations indicate that if we unload my piano from the saloon, when Capt Blenkinsopp blows the ballast tanks, the submarine will float three metres above the tunnel floor."

Toby said nothing but crossed his fingers inside his pocket hoping the Professor's calculations were correct.

"Gentlemen," said the Professor into a microphone, "the good news is that you will only need to unload one item more."

Bill and Mike stood grinning in at the porthole, making circles between their thumbs and forefingers signalling they understood.

"The bad news," went on the Professor, "is that the final item is my beloved piano!"

It took Mike, Bill, and Wendy and Lulabell, the Professor, and Farouke (he was not a lazy Arab), Stu, and Sam Scrivener, three long hours (while the water level inside the Nautilad rose steadily) of groaning and grunting to get the piano down steep iron staircases, through narrow watertight doors, to get it to the airlock chamber. Luckily nobody suffered pinched fingers or crushed toes in the process.

"Now all we've got to do is push it out of the submarine through the airlock," said Mike scratching his head.

"I don't fancy lifting that thing over the threshold of the outer airlock door," agreed Bill, looking at the Professor for inspiration.

"P'raps you could tickle the ivories and play an uplifting tune, or summink. Then it might float itself out, Young?" mocked Stu.

"P'raps you could shut up!" retorted Bill, feeling his ears heating up and his fingers clenching into fists.

"We use buoyancy balloons!" cried Farouke. "We tie them to piano and fill with oxygen from aqualungs and then piano float out when airlock flooded!"

"Buoyancy balloons? What are they?" said Wendy.

"We use them if we want to lift heavy things into the submarine or take them to the surface. Especially useful for recovering treasure," said the Professor. "That's a very good idea, Farouke. Perhaps you would fetch some balloons from the midget-submarine bay?"

51

Bailing Out

On Farouke's return Mike and Bill put on their diving helmets and the Professor pressed the button that flooded the airlock. He watched sadly as steadily the water level rose.

"Ach. I vill miss my poor old pianoforte. Ve played many happy tunes together."

Bill and Mike tied four buoyancy bags to the piano's legs and after pushing them out through the outer airlock hatch into the tunnel, they blew up the bags with a spare aqualung cylinder. The ropes securing the bags to the piano started creaking and tightening.

"We need more gas in the bags!" cried Mike over the intercom. The piano slowly began creeping across the airlock deck toward the hatch as Bill squirted more oxygen into the bags. Still the ropes creaked and one end of the piano lifted over the outer hatch threshold.

"More oxygen, Bill! I'll get my shoulder behind it and push it out."

Suddenly without warning the piano tilted sharply and rising from the deck swung out through the airlock hatch.

"It's free!" shouted Bill through the helmet earphones, almost deafening Mike as the piano swung back like a pendulum and struck the hull of the Nautilad with a loud "DONG".

At once the inflated gas-bags and piano shot upwards like a rocket.

"Oooer! I think I might have overdone the oxygen a bit," said Bill leaning back to watch the heavy instrument fly up out of sight into the blackness of the tunnel above.

***

"It is now time to blow the submarine's main ballast tanks," announced the captain from Austin's driver's seat. "That is, if you're happy with your calculations, Professor? We only have one chance."

The Professor nodded, "Ja, I have accounted for every item unloaded and we should be light enough to raise the Nautilad sufficiently to deploy the midget-submarines successfully."

Everyone looked nervously around the conning tower at everyone else as the captain rested his hand on the lever that on land was Austin's handbrake but aboard the Nautilad would cause the submarine to blow out seawater from the ballast tanks and replace it with air.

"Fingers crossed everyone. I'm going to blow the main valves NOW!" said the captain throwing the lever.

At first came the sounds of clonks and clanks, and then a whooshing and hissing. The Nautilad juddered.

"Starting engines! Forward hydroplanes up thirty degrees!" cried the captain, pressing Austin's starter button, and pulling back on his steering wheel. The Nautilad's engines whined straining to shift the overweight submarine from the bottom. Then there was a twang and a clang and a bang bong, bang bong, bang, bong.

"It's no good," cried the captain, "all we're doing is hopping along the bottom!"

"We must be too heavy still," said Mike.

"Impossible!" retorted the Professor. "I have accounted for every object we have thrown overboard. The Nautilad should be light enough to rise sufficiently to deploy the midget-submarines!"

"Well I'm afraid it isn't," said Wendy.

"I must recheck my calculations," said the Professor.

"We don't have time," said Captain Blenkinsopp, "we're still taking on water. If we don't raise the Nautilad now it will be too late."

"I've got a hunch," whispered Mike to Bill. "Come on. I'm going outside the submarine. You can help with the airlock controls."

After several minutes the others could see Mike standing in the gloom outside waving up at the conning tower observation bubble. The Nautilad's intercom system crackled and his voice came on, "Try moving the submarine now, Captain."

Positioning himself behind Austin's steering wheel once more, the captain pressed the starter motor button and the Nautilad's motors started running again.

"Engines started. Forward hydroplanes up thirty degrees."

After an intense vibration through the hull and loud metallic scrapings from the bottom of the submarine, the motors began humming smoothly.

"Rear hydroplanes down five degrees," said the captain, manipulating Austin's gearstick, and gently pushing his steering wheel forward, "we're away!"

Everyone cheered and Wendy watched Mike's helmet lamp shrink to a distant pinprick of yellow light as the Nautilad began climbing slowly but surely away from the tunnel floor.

"Engine half speed. Front and rear hydroplanes neutral," breathed Podesta Blenkinsopp wiping his forehead with his handkerchief.

"We're saved!" shouted Lu, jumping up and down with Toby.

"You look perplexed, Professor," said Sam Scrivener noticing a frown spreading across the Professor's face.

"My weight calculations were correct. I know they were. I cannot understand why, when Mike Stevens left the Nautilad, the submarine became buoyant enough to lift from the seabed."

"You obviously can't add up, Mate," mocked Stu. "You were one man out."

"Oh do be quiet, Stu," snapped Lu. "If you can't say anything helpful, don't say anything at all!"

"No. No, young lady. I think what our young friend here has just said *is very* useful," murmured the Professor stroking his chin thoughtfully.

"See! I'm not a dummy, Clever Dick!"

"Oh, do shut up Stu. What do you mean, Professor? I don't understand," said Wendy.

The Professor's frown lifted.

"It means, young lady, that after Mike went outside, the weight of the submarine became the weight my calculations said it needed to be to lift it away from the tunnel floor."

"I'm sorry to be dense, Professor, I still don't understand.

"I think it means that after everything was unloaded the sub was still too heavy by the equivalent of Mike's weight," said Lu.

"Yeah. Like I said. Too 'eavy by one man!"

"Precisely! And that means we've got something aboard, more or less the size of Mike, we know nothing about," said the Professor.

Chapter 13

Man the Midget Submarines!

"Well, what do you think, boys?" said Lu, holding out her arms and twirling once around in her diving gear. A holster with a metal pistol-grip tilted insolently from the curve of her right hip and a dagger in a long scabbard was strapped to the top and bottom of her opposite calf.

"You definitely look better with that bucket 'fing on yer 'cad," quipped Stu rudely.

"The best looking deep-sea-diver I've ever seen ever," said Toby, blushing inside his own helmet and risking steaming up his glasses.

"Watch it Stu, or I'll shoot," said Lu, patting her holster with one hand and pointing her finger at Stu like a make-believe pistol with the other.

"I would advise against that, young lady," warned the Professor. "The pistols are stun-guns capable of liberating a high-tension discharge of many thousands of volts which could be quite lethal at close range."

"Silly old fart!" muttered Stu under his breath. The others suddenly creased up laughing.

"You should all be aware that everything you say into your helmet microphones is broadcast to everyone else," said the Professor sternly. "If you want to speak privately you must press the numbered buttons on your suit's wrist panel that matches the helmet number of the person you want to speak to. Now! Is everybody ready to go?"

Wendy found herself giggling.

"What are you laughing at?" crackled Mike's voice faintly from the tunnel floor.

"I'm nodding back at the Professor inside this helmet. I could nod at him all day and he'd never see!"

"Stand at the edge of the conning tower dome. I'm down on the tunnel floor. Try waving and then form a circle with your thumb and forefinger to say okay, or give the thumbs up if you want to say yes," suggested Mike.

"And thumbs down if you want to say no," cut in Bill.

"Okay," signalled Wendy through the dome.

Everybody peered down through the dome and followed suit.

Mike pressed button number four. "How did you hear me talking to your mum, Bill?"

"I was pressing button number three - talking to her at the same time," replied Bill.

"Good," interrupted the Professor. "As we all seem to be ready. Farouke! Please open the hatch to the midget submarine airlock."

Bill pressed button number five on his wrist panel, "Hello Toby?"

Toby's voice crackled over Bill's helmet-phones, "Hello."

"How do you think Farouke gets his diving helmet over that turban, Toby?"

A chuckle came back. "I don't know. He never takes it off does he? It must be a tight squeeze inside his helmet."

58

"I reckon he keeps a secret weapon or something hidden under that turban!"

"I hear that! Cheeky young Effendis! You forget to push button on wrist!"

"Sorry Farouke," replied the boys sheepishly.

The circular hatch in the floor of the diving-suit changing room slid open. Seawater lapped up to a meter below its rim and submerged lights made it look an inviting azure blue.

Parked side-by-side, their hulls bobbing just below the surface of the water were three two-seater midget submarines. Their Perspex cockpits were open just above the water-line and reminded Bill of the cockpits of old-fashioned fighter aircraft. Each sub was about five metres long with a bow shaped like a small motorboat. Their crews sat one behind the other with the pilot in the rear seat.

"The midget-subs are fairly easy to control," explained the Professor. "There are left and right pedals which operate the rudders to make the craft turn left or right and a joystick, which if pulled back makes the sub go up and if pushed forward makes it dive. The red button at the top of the joysticks fires a cyanide Torpoon. Each craft has…"

"I'm sorry to interrupt the party," crackled Podesta's voice over everyone's helmet-phones, "but we're still taking on water at an alarming rate. The depth-gauge in the conning tower is indicating that we're starting to sink again."

"Sorry, Podesta. I was explaining the midget-sub controls to everybody," replied the Professor.

"Detail Toby and Stu pilot two of the subs and you get going in the third while you still can!"

Man the Midget Submarines!

"Me a midget-sub pilot?" gasped Toby, feeling himself trembling at the thought of being in charge of the cigar-shaped machine that now looked even bigger than ever bobbing gently in the blue seawater below him.

Stu felt strangely elated too at being trusted for once, but being unused to such treatment said nothing.

Wendy pressed button number 2 on her wrist panel.

"Goodness knows what's going to happen now, Mike?" she said nervously as Stu seated himself behind the controls of the left-hand midget-sub.

"Mike? Mike? Can you hear me?"

There was only static hiss from Wendy's helmet-phones. She pushed button number 1.

"Hello?" said the Professor.

"I've tried calling Mike, Professor. He's not answering."

"Nothing to worry about, dear lady. Mike's outside. He's probably beyond the fifty metre range of the helmet-phones that's all. We'll stop to pick him up when we get underway."

"Bill!" cried Wendy, pressing button number 4, "make sure you and Lu get on Toby's midget-sub."

"Yes, mum," replied Bill wearily.

Wendy watched as Bill touched Lu's arm and said something and Lu began nodding and grinning back at him through her helmet faceplate.

Toby's heart raced. His midget-sub sank in the water as he settled himself behind the controls. He glanced through the side-glass of his helmet at Stu. The midget-sub sank even lower and bobbed up and down as Lu seated herself on Bill's lap in front of Toby.

"What on earth!" cried Lu. "There's something hard digging into my?"

Bill felt his cheeks burning with embarrassment inside his helmet.

"Sorry Lu," he replied, sheepishly handing Farouke a spanner. "Must've left it in my pocket by mistake."

"Well this is finally it!" said Sam Scrivener looking over from the front seat of the Professor's midget-sub.

"Everybody safely aboard the midget-subs?" crackled the captain's voice over the helmet-phones.

"Aren't you coming, Farouke?" said the Professor glancing up at the Arab standing beside the hatch without his helmet on.

"I stay to assist captain. I see you at other end. Good luck, Effendi."

"As you wish, Farouke. Good luck, old friend," replied the Professor. "We're all aboard, Podesta. You can release the docking clamps."

Toby's heart began pounding as, with a mechanical whine, four claw-like clamps opened and the midget-submarines dropped below the water level. Within seconds they were hovering outside a metre below the dark shape of the Nautilad's keel.

"Now you pilots, slow ahead and joysticks gently forward until we drop to three metres below the Nautilad's hull. Then you can push your throttles gently forward to dive to the tunnel floor to pick up Mike. Remember! Make sure you're well below the Nautilad before you start going forward or you'll scrape your heads off against the barnacles on the Nautilad's hull."

Toby thought his heart would burst it thumped so fast. He felt the controls of the midget-submarine responding to his feet on the rudder pedals and his hands on the joystick. His passengers' lives depended on him now. Then he realised he couldn't see beyond Bill and Lu's helmets! He pushed the joystick forward slightly and the submarine's nose slowly dropped allowing him a good view forward.

A silver bubble-trail snaked from Stu's sub's propeller diving at full speed, with Wendy clinging on, towards the pinprick of light from Mike's helmet-torch.

"Watch your speed, Stu" cautioned the Professor, "and don't get too far from the others. The range of the helmet radios is only fifty metres – less underwater. We must maintain radio contact."

"I can hear you loud and clear, Professor," responded Toby.

"Yes. And so can I. You Clever Dick, Wishman!" said Stu, and then remembering the ghastly incident with Wolf's Harley Davidson he eased back on the throttle.

"Mother-ship to midget-subs! This is Captain Blenkinsopp. I'll tell you this before you go out of range. Farouke and I will continue ahead slow. Once you've picked up Mike follow us to the tunnel-mouth in the lost Sea of Tethys. Keep broadcasting and as soon as you are back in radio range, follow us directly to the Terrapino outpost. Over-and-out. Oh! And one last thing. Good luck everyone!"

Wendy was relieved to see Mike waving as they landed nearby. Stu soon got the hang of slowing his midget-sub with its hydroplanes pointing down and its motor ticking-over to hover-park. Mike began swim-walking towards them.

Man the Midget Submarines!

Wendy clambered out of her seat, her heart nearly stopping when Mike tripped forward amid a cloud of billowing silt. Saving himself with outstretched hands he emerged from the cloud and clambered aboard the sub, his weighted boots clanking on the hull as he seated himself in front of Stu.

"Phew!" he breathed. "The bottom's quite uneven! Just like walking over a series of curved ridges – a bit like a cattle grid that's constantly moving. Very strange."

"You ready?" sneered Stu.

"Just a minute!" said Wendy clambering awkwardly to sit on Mike's lap.

"Now we're ready Stu," called Mike, making an Okay signal with his right hand when Wendy was comfortable.

"Oi, Wishman!"

"Yes?"

"Try and keep up on the way back!" laughed Stu, jerking back on his joystick and shoving the throttle lever as far forward as it would go. The nose of the midget-sub reared up and as it gained speed, Stu pushed the joystick forward and the sub levelled.

"It might be an idea to think about turning to follow the Nautilad now," crackled the Professor's voice.

"All right! Keep yer 'air on!" muttered Stu, stamping the right rudder pedal hard to the floor.

Immediately the sub veered right and its nose fell.

"Handbrake turn!" yelled Stu. "WOA! WHAT'S 'APPENIN?"

"You're going into a spiral dive, Stu!" cried the Professor. "You must do something quickly or you'll crash the submarine!"

63

Man the Midget Submarines!

"WaddoIdo?" wailed Stu, as the world started spinning around them.

"Throttle back and let go of the controls!" said Mike.

Mike and Wendy clung on as the midget-sub pitched and bucked and spun until eventually it slowed.

"Now we're dropping!" said Stu, his voice slurred from giddiness.

"Give her a little throttle and pull gently back on the stick to give up-hydroplane," gasped Mike.

The sub moved gently forward and levelled.

"Now this time when you turn, only press the rudder pedals lightly – and when you see the nose begin turning, pull gently back on the stick to feed in up-hydroplane. That way the nose will stay level and you won't go into an uncontrollable spin. Now try it," said Mike.

Nervously Stu did as he was told and cried, "Blimey! It works! Look Toby I DID A TURN! I DID A TURN!"

"Now push the stick forward slightly to level out," said Mike. "Now you try, Toby!"

Beads of sweat ran into Toby's eyes as he manoeuvred his submarine into a gentle U-turn.

"Well done Toby!" called Wendy. And Bill and Lu clapped noiselessly as through the darkness, the distant twinkle of the Nautilad's lights came into view.

"Now keep the subs in neutral-hydroplane and increase speed. We've got to catch the Nautilad as quickly as we can."

Chapter 14

Into The Light

"Midget subs to Nautilad? Midget-subs to Nautilad? Do you read me Podesta?"

The long cigar-shaped silhouette of the port-listing Nautilad loomed against a brilliant blue light, stretching into infinity before them.

"Reading you but faintly, Professor. What's your position?"

"About forty metres astern of you and gaining."

"Don't come too close, Professor. The Nautilad's stability has been badly upset by the extra weight of water she's taken on. It's a fight to steer her."

"Affirmative, Podesta. We'll maintain our present distance."

"Isn't this blue light beautiful?" marvelled Lu as the midget-submarines emerged from the tunnel.

"Just like the flowers in the Post Office trough at Piddle Wallop," mused Wendy, craning her head in every direction to see everything in this silent blue world the windows in her helmet would allow.

The Professor's voice crackled over the helmet-phones. "The blue colour is caused by the interaction of the force of Vril with certain species of plankton that exist here, Lu. It makes each tiny organism glow like a blue firefly."

Below them the milky blue darkened like faded denim to black, and behind them Bill craned to see the tunnel exit near to the top of a sheer cliff-face rearing up from the inky depths below.

"What's below us, Professor?"

"An extremely deep abyss, Bill. Nobody knows how deep. It could go to the very centre of the earth. Nobody has ever explored it."

"What would happen if the sub's motor broke down now, Professor?" said Sam Scrivener, "I ask only as a matter of literary research of course."

"It would be the same as an aircraft whose engines quit, Sam. We would part glide and part fall and no doubt eventually crash to the bottom."

"You mean we're flying, Professor?" said Lu.

"In a way, but not through the air like an aeroplane. We're flying in water over a deep canyon. The world beneath the sea is just like the world above it – there are undersea mountains, volcanoes, valleys, canyons, caves and endless rolling plains."

"Let's 'ope the subs don't pack-up then!" said Stu, determined not to look down and holding their course firmly in the wake of the Nautilad.

"What are those rocky spikes poking down through the surface of the water?" asked Toby, relaxing his white-knuckled grip on the sub's joystick to point above their heads.

"Those are stalactites, Toby," explained the Professor. "You see we are inside a gigantic rock chamber with all of the prehistoric creatures sealed inside at the time of the great catastrophe. There is no sky. Ten metres above the water surface is a solid rock ceiling. The gap between the rock and

66

the seawater is filled with a warm sea-mist and when the mist condenses on the cool rock above it, it dissolves the rock's minerals and drips to form those stalactites."

"I'm sorry to interrupt, Professor, but the oxygen gauge on Lu's aqualung's gone into the red," said Bill.

"I feel drowsy," she murmured.

Podesta Blenkinsopp's voice crackled over everyone's helmet-phones. "Farouke has fully-charged aqualungs ready for you aboard the Nautilad. I will slow the mother ship for you to pick them up from the midget-submarine bay."

"Step on it Toby," said Bill.

There was no reply.

"Toby? Toby? Look Toby we need to get Lu's oxygen changed. If you're messing about!" cried Bill, turning as best he could to peer into Toby's misted faceplate. "Toby's lips are blue, Professor! And we've started drifting downwards."

"Toby's oxygen's obviously run out too," said Mike, "Bill! You need to climb back and swap places with Toby. You'll have to steer. It's up to you to get back to the Nautilad to pick up fresh oxygen."

Mike watched nervously as Bill slid Lu forward from his lap to clamber out of his seat and face the rear of the sinking midget-sub. Toby was slumped forward.

Suddenly he murmured and his eyes flicked open.

"Must catch up with the Nautilad," he gasped pulling back the joystick and jerking the throttle lever forward. The midget-submarine bucked its nose upwards.

"Aaaagh!" yelled Bill, losing his balance.

"QUICK, STU. Bill's fallen overboard. Dive and I'll try to catch him!" said Mike.

"You dimwit, Wishman!" called Stu, setting his aquaplanes down and his throttle to full.

"Bill's lead boots and belt-weights are dragging him down," said Sam Scrivener.

"Try and undo your belt buckle and untie your bootstraps, Bill!" called the Professor.

"I can't. My gloves are too thick to undo the buckles! I'm SOMERSAULTING!"

"Hang on Bill! We're coming to get you!" sobbed Wendy.

Through her misting faceplate, Wendy managed a fleeting half-smile as Mike reached out to grab Bill as they dived past.

"Round again, Stu!" yelled Mike. "I missed him!"

Stu turned steeply to go in for a second pass.

"Slow down. I'll try and grab Bill's leg."

Stu pulled back on the throttle lever.

"Lean out as far as you can, Mike. I'll hang on to your legs," said Wendy.

The mysterious blackness of the chasm loomed up at Mike as he stretched way beyond the safety of the midget-sub's cockpit. Stu steered as close as he dare to Bill's slowly tumbling figure. Mike's glove brushed against Bill's calf as they were about to pass for a second time, and when he felt Bill's ankle his fingers instinctively closed.

"I've got him!" yelled Mike into his helmet microphone. "I've got Bill!"

"Thank goodness," whispered Wendy. "I'll pull you both back."

68

"Well done, Mike," said the Professor as Stu's submarine dived to pull up next to Toby and Lu's lifeless outlines.

"Here Bill, I'll help you swap seats with Toby," said Mike.

"Toby's too heavy to move without risking one of us falling into the abyss. He's a dead weight!" gasped Bill as they both attempted to lift Toby.

"Ruddy typical. Trust Wishman to muck everything up!" sneered Stu.

"I'll just have sit on Toby's lap," said Bill, reaching over towards Toby's arm.

Ahead and above them, the lights of the Nautilad twinkled in the distance.

"Gotcha!" cried Bill, grabbing a handful of Toby's suit to pull himself aboard the steadily sinking midget sub. Bill wedged his body clumsily between his friend's lifeless body and the sub's controls.

"What in the name of Jehovah is that?" gasped Sam Scrivener over everyone's helmet-phones.

Everybody stared. Sam was pointing up at something monstrous emerging from the milky blue, shrouding the Nautilad in its shadow.

Chapter 15

Swallowed Alive!

They watched in dumb-struck horror from the midget-submarines as the black shape turned into a huge snaking serpent of seventy metres or more slowly circling the Nautilad.

"Come no closer!" warned Captain Blenkinsopp over their helmet-phones, his voice dissolving into static hiss. The creature's fanged mouth opened and its jaws dislocated to an unnatural size before lunging to swallow the defenceless submarine whole.

Everyone gasped with shock or groaned with anguish as the monster slowly scanned left then right before slithering into the blue from whence it came.

"I 'ain't 'avin THAT!" yelled Stu into his helmet-microphone. Itch-thumbing the Torpoon button he rammed the throttle lever into its forward stops and wrenched back the joystick. Wendy and Mike clung on as the midget-sub reared like a startled stallion and took off in pursuit of the creature.

"Stop!" crackled the Professor's voice, but it was useless, Stu was possessed with an unquenchable desire to kill the creature and the others looked on helplessly as Stu's midget-sub, with Mike and Wendy, faded after it in a twisting trail of bubbles.

"What on earth do we do now, Professor?" stammered Sam.

Swallowed Alive!

"Lu and Toby are unconscious! I'm going to the surface," replied Bill.

***

The Stalactites looked like dark rock-trees growing up through the glowing blue surface of the water. Large drops of water fell from the rock ceiling in the damp blue half-light and at once Bill threw open the sub's cockpit canopy and removed his helmet to test the breathability of the atmosphere. It felt refreshing. No. It felt more than refreshing. It felt positively exhilarating!

"It's good," he announced at once releasing Lu and Toby's helmets.

"Aaaahhh!" breathed Lu, filling her lungs with the moist oxygen-rich gas and enjoying the warm drops from the stalactites splashing on her face.

Toby coughed, spat, and prized open his eyes. "Hey! Geroff my lap, Bill Young!"

"Ok. Ok. I'm going," said Bill clambering over to the front seat. He started examining the glowing sea nearby.

"Nothing here but stalactites," said Toby blinking and peering around.

"We seem to be alone," said Lu, taking off her gloves.

"We're not quite alone. You two didn't see that giant sea serpent swallow the Nautilad, did you?" replied Bill.

"WHAT?" chorused Lu and Toby.

"What about the other midget-subs?" cried Toby. "Did it get them?"

"Oh, Bill. Are your mum and Mr Stevens all right?" said Lu, touching Bill's hand.

"I don't know. The last I saw, that idiot Stu Briggs was trying to chase the thing. You know what *he's* like." answered Bill, secretly stifling fearful thoughts that his mother wouldn't survive Stu's mad dash after the monster.

"What about Farouke and the captain?" said Toby.

"We can't dive again to find anyone - your oxygen's run out…. I think we'll have to face up to the possibility…"

"What possibility?" interrupted Lu.

"The possibility they might all be dead," muttered Bill looking gloomily at 'rain' drops in a puddle of light from Toby's torch. He was thinking about Austin and wondering if their little car, correction, ex-little car, was a bad luck talisman. Everything seemed to have gone strangely wrong the moment they'd done him up.

Toby, wiped his glasses. He was about to say, "They probably *are* dead," but stopped himself.

"Look you two. It won't do anybody any good if we let ourselves get down in the dumps," said Lu.

"No we've got to stay positive," agreed Bill.

"I vote we carry on along the surface and try and find land," said Lu.

"Good idea. Put your helmets back on and open the face-plate windows. Weigh anchor, Toby!"

"I'll try sending mayday voice messages from my helmet-mike," said Bill as the midget-sub's motor began whining, and amid splashing from the propeller they started moving forward. "There's a chance others might hear if they get close enough."

"I wish we had a compass," said Toby as he steered the sub through the slalom of stalactites.

"Would it work in here?" asked Lu.

"Probably not," replied Toby gloomily.

And that was the last anyone said for several hours until the midget-submarine began rocking from side-to-side.

"I don't like this," said Toby. "Something's making waves."

"Oh, please don't let it be the sea serpent," said Lu, under her breath.

They peered around them with their helmet torches switched on. A large black stain was spreading beneath the oily- smooth surface until with a deafening roar the sea erupted into a plume of foam. Two gigantic creatures burst up from the depths in a boiling ball of teeth, spray, scales, and tails.

The midget-sub rolled violently sideways pitching Lu into the water with a splash. Her weighted boots and belt instantly dragged her below. She bent double trying frantically to undo them

The monsters were rolling toward the sub in a tidal wave of froth and blood. One, with a long scaly neck and small head that reminded Bill of an Ostrich with jaws of vicious teeth, had its foe by the throat. Blood pumped purple in the glowing blue water as its teeth cut an artery. The stricken creature, oozing blood, kicked out wildly with massive claws scraping its ostrich-necked opponent's belly into bleeding ribbons.

Both, presumably mortally wounded, then disappeared below in a billowing soup of blood and flesh.

"LU! LU?" called Bill and Toby together into the hollow silence. The stained surface of the sea had regained its oily calm around them.

"Can you see her, Toby?"

"What's that?" replied Toby, standing on his seat and pointing at something resembling a half-deflated football with a slimy crimson tail bobbing in the water.

"Ugh! It's an eyeball, Toby! One of the monsters lost an eye in the fight."

"No. Over there! Look!" shouted Toby. "Something broke the surface of the water."

"Steer towards it, Toby."

As they approached Bill yelled, "It's Lu! Quick Toby. Bring us alongside. We've got to fish her out."

"I, I don't want to worry you, Bill," cried Toby as Bill grabbed a handful of Lu's suit and pulled her head out of the water.

"Thank god! She's still breathing. What? What's up, Toby?"

"I think...I think we...We've got company," stammered Toby, staring bug-eyed as the blue glow around them darkened with every swarming carnivorous creature imaginable.

Chapter 16

The Chase

"Stop Stu!" yelled Wendy, peering out beyond the bow of diving midget-sub like someone about to be pitched by a horse over a cliff.

The black sea-serpent's tail swished slowly to-and-fro propelling it forward, and as they gained the midget-sub pitched and rolled in its wake like a bucking bronco

"Mike. I can't hold on!"

Mike pressed button number three on his wrist panel.

"It's all right. I've got you," he replied, sliding his arms around Wendy's waist.

The turbulence died down as they began 'flying' over the creature's massive black back.

"I'm gonna stick you right between the eyes with my Torpoon, you black bleedin' bastard," hissed Stu through clenched teeth.

The serpent's rippling gill-slits came into view and Stu rammed the sub's joystick forward.

"Aaaagh!" yelled Mike and Wendy together as the sub pitched forward in a vertical dive at the creature's head. The creature's long bony snout thrust forward from great bulbous eyes and ended in a pair of cavernous nostrils. Stu leaned hard on the throttle.

"Why won't you go any FASTER!" he shouted. Glancing down, Wendy could see the calloused black hide of the serpent's head had given way to milky-blue water below them.

"HANDBRAKE TURN!" yelled Stu warning the others before stamping on the right rudder pedal and pulling back hard on the joystick.

Wendy and Mike's horizons at once filled with the terrifying face of the sea-serpent as the midget-sub swung through a rapid one-hundred-and-eighty degree turn.

As if spooked, giant black lids flicked shut over the serpent's eyes and Mike and Wendy felt a quiver between their legs as the black lance of the sub's single cyanide torpoon, launched from the centre of the bow, hissing through the water at its target.

At once Stu rolled off the throttle to gloat over the monster's anticipated violent death throes when the cyanide cylinder struck and delivered its lethal payload.

"GET AWAY!" yelled Mike, watching the torpoon as it closed in on the creature's cliff-like forehead.

"Nah! Let's stick arahnd and watch it DIE," crowed Stu.

The torpoon struck the serpent's face.

"Hah!" cackled Stu, "straight in the pickle-barrel!"

His triumphal conceit was short-lived.

"The Torpoon! It's glanced off. You've missed!" screamed Wendy as the bent shaft of the torpoon spun into the darkness of unseen fathoms below.

The black eyelids at once flicked open and two luminous eyes glared straight at them.

The Chase

The massive jaws slowly dislocated and along with tons of pale blue seawater, Stu, Wendy, and Mike were sucked into black-fanged darkness.

Chapter 17

Vril

"Where do we go from here, Professor?" said Sam Scrivener pressing button 1 on his wrist panel.

"We will continue on to the Terrapino outpost as planned. That is unless the Terrapinos find us first," replied the Professor glancing at his watch and adjusting the course of the midget-submarine.

"If you don't mind me commenting, you don't seem terribly concerned about what's just happened, Professor."

"I am of course concerned, young man. It's just that I can do nothing about it now. We need help and, I might add, fresh oxygen. It might be better therefore to save your questions until oxygen is more plentiful."

"Wilco, Professor."

The Professor glanced once more at his watch, made a minor adjustment to their course and set the midget-sub's throttle to cruising speed.

"Professor?"

"Yes, Sam."

"Just one more thing. Why do you keep looking at your watch?"

"I thought we'd agreed no more questions for the time being, Sam."

"I know, Professor, I know, but judging by how quickly lives change in this place, if I don't ask now I might never get another chance."

"Ok, Sam. My watch is an Atlantean Vril-powered device. In our world it tells only time. Here, in the Atlantean domain, it draws energy from the ever-present Vril force. And one of several functions it possesses is that of an extra-terrestrial compass."

"Vril-powered?"

"Yes, I explained before about the effect of Vril making the plankton glow blue."

"You mean this force - Vril - is all around us?"

"Yes, Sam. It is free energy. How do you think our helmet-torches operate? What do you think is powering this midget submarine and the Nautilad? Have you ever seen batteries to power any of these things? No. The helmet torches and the submarines draw their power from the Vril that surrounds us."

"So you've been here before, Professor?"

"In another life, yes Sam."

"Hmmm. Free energy," mused Sam, "that's the Holy Grail Gerald Gray wanted for Wallopshire Borough Council's dustcart fleet."

"Yes. He tried to steal the Nautilad and its X19 guidance machine to find Atlantis and the source of Vril for himself."

"And the Brotherhood of the Green Dragon? Gray was a Grand Dragon. How do they fit into all of this?"

"The Brotherhood of the Green Dragon was once an ancient order of mystics, Sam. They were a sect of Atlantean priests entrusted with preserving the secrets of Vril. Later generations of the Brotherhood became spiritual links to the ancients and Vril. Nazi mystics formed themselves into a chapter of the Brotherhood. Just like Gray they wanted Vril. But not to power dustcarts!" the Professor laughed. "They wanted it for darker reasons, to power new and terrifying secret weapons. Luckily for the Free World they were defeated before they could achieve their evil aims. Just one moment. I need to check our course."

The darkness of the abyss below them gradually lightened as they approached a wide, sandy plain.

"And was Gray a spiritual link to the Atlantean ancients?"

"No Sam. Otherwise why would he need the Nautilad to find Atlantis? No. There is only one true sect of the Brotherhood remaining with a spiritual link to the secrets of Vril. And their whereabouts in our world is completely unknown."

"So how do they live in complete isolation?"

"Believe me, Sam; it is probably quite easy if you have unlimited free energy."

"Speaking of 'free' energy. One of the places Gray invested the rate-payers' money was a tin-pot energy company in Brazil."

"Yes. The Ergolite Energy Corporation," replied the Professor.

Chapter 18

Garcia Smallpiece

The put-put-put of a small outboard motor prompted several dozing black caimans to slither into the brown water of the glassy Amazon backwater. The shadowy banks of the tributary were thick with vines and broad-leaved ferns and high overhanging trees with dangling creepers. Exposed knotted roots teemed with every form of chirping, clicking, ticking insect and croaking, hissing, spitting reptile known (and unknown) to natural science.

The canoe's motor silenced and as it glided toward a decaying timber jetty, a thinly-clad Indian leaped with a rope from the bow to secure it to a post.

The boat's fat passenger grabbed the gunwales and was about to haul himself up when the cacophony of wild parrots, howler monkeys, tree frogs and insects was accompanied by a regiment of horns, trumpets, timpani, and large-lunged ladies singing from the 'Ride of the Valkyries (Act2)'. The passenger's fat hand produced a flashing mobile phone from an inside jacket pocket.

"Ja Gerde? Herr Armstrong? Ah gut! Put him on, please. Hallo, Herr Armstrong. What haff you to report? Oh. You managed to get into ze underground control room at Belchley Park. Disguised as a plumber! Ha ha! Very ingenious! And you haff logged the last known position of ze Nautilad? Seher gut. Let me write it down…"

The fat man scribbled the tunnel location on the back of an old envelope.

"Danke, Herr Armstrong. I have it now in my pocket safely and I must go. Garcia is waiting for me. Auf wiederhören!"

The fat man smiled, removing his wide-brimmed straw hat. Mopping the back of his head and forehead with a red polka dot handkerchief he prized himself out of the canoe and stumbled onto the jetty to greet Garcia.

"I am looking very much forward to seeing your progress, Garcia," said the fat man shaking Garcia firmly by the sweaty hand.

"I don't theenk you will bc disappointed, Senor. Come the Jeep ees waiting to take you to the jungle test-site."

The Jeep's engine rattled as it laboured over ruts, pot-holes, cracking fallen branches, tree roots, and logs. Every now and then nuts and fruits, hurled by mischievous monkeys in the forest canopy, would clatter or spatter on the bonnet.

The fat man clung uncomfortably to the dashboard and bounced up and down in his seat with unwanted thoughts of thigh-slapping and leder hosen as they crashed on through the jungle. To his relief, Garcia eventually stopped the Jeep under a rickety wooden structure with camouflage netting pegged over a roof of woven bannana leaves.

Several tattooed Indians in shorts and tee-shirts carrying Walther MPK submachine guns emerged from the undergrowth. Garcia at once nodded deliberately slowly, calming them with a slow downward wave with the palm of his hand.

"Come, Senor. Eet is only a short distance through those trees. Follow me."

The forest floor cracked under their steps and soon, emerging through creepers, they came to a sheer wall of grey granite.

Garcia beckoned to follow left along the base of the cliff until what sun there had been through the jungle dimmed to dusk as they walked beneath an overhanging ledge several hundred feet above.

The earthy forest floor changed and their footsteps now echoed on a hard, white-paved road disappearing into the cliff-face and lit by concrete streetlamp standards vanishing into the subterranean distance.

"It is certainly cooler here than outside," remarked the fat man, once more mopping his face. Garcia said nothing, but continued to follow the road into the cliff. The sound of running water came from ahead and soon they were inside a cavern, with sparkling strands of water cascading from a wide, fern-fringed skylight in the high rock ceiling. Festoons of the seemingly-ubiquitous liana creeper hung like Christmas rescue ropes from the edge.

It was then the fat man saw it. At first only tumbled blocks dusted by yellow shafts of sunlight; then as his eyes grew accustomed to the light, the ruins of a stepped Mayan pyramid and the gigantic cracked face of a statue, that together with the pyramid, must have fallen in through the hole in cavern ceiling at sometime past.

"This was once a holy place, Senor. A place where the natural free energies of the old-world were harvested by the ancients."

"Harvesting energy, Garcia. That is a very interesting idea."

"Si, Senor. There are hosts of such sites around the globe. Usually the meeting places of ley-lines. Can you not feel the vestiges of the old magic through your boots?"

"My feet feel cold, Garcia."

Garcia sighed. "That is because the Collector Crystal has long been stolen by tomb robbers, Senor. Now the spirits of the pyramid seek to take energy rather than give it. Your feet feel cold because the spirits are trying to steal back their energy from your body-heat in your feet."

"And the weapon, Garcia. What of the weapon?"

"Eet is complete, Senor, and aimed at the heart of New York as you ordered! It waits only for us to find a new Collector Crystal! Come let me show you."

"Excellent! My evil plans are almost complete. We must make haste, Garcia! Our man in England, Herr Armstrong, has told me the last known position of the British Nautilad before it entered the Portal to Atlantis. That is where we will find our new Collector Crystal. Make ready 'Ergo 1' for our immediate embarkation."

Chapter 19

Kidnapped!

"Where are we?" said Vole picking himself up when the Nautilad stopped moving.

"I don't know. It's dark. But at least we're alive," answered Hedgehog stroking his spines back into position with the side of his nose.

"Did you see it? Did you see that huge, great, massive, giant, black snake thing with huge, gigantic, massive bad teeth that swallowed us! We must be inside its belly," said Monty.

"Yes, I saw it. It was gigantically enormous!" agreed Vole.

Monty removed his sunglasses trying to peer through the murk beyond the conning tower dome. The darkness suddenly disappeared and they were bathed in eerie blue light.

"Someone's switched the lights on!" cried Legit, smearing the glass of the conning tower dome by pressing his wet nose against it.

"This place is no living thing!" exclaimed Monty, replacing his shades and peering out, goggle-eyed, beyond the glass of the dome at a great white chamber with bolted and riveted decks, bulkheads and ribs and cables and trusses perforated with circular and elliptical lightening holes. "No, this looks like the insides of a Titanic I once saw on Human TV."

Kidnapped!

"Do *you* know where we are, Austin?" asked Hedgehog.

He turned to his friend when no reply was forthcoming. "Austin! What's the matter?"

The others looked too. Austin was once more bouncing up and down on his springs with steam billowing from his red hot bonnet grills.

"Phew! What stink! Burning paint!" squeaked Vole, holding his nose. "Austin's about to burst into flames!"

"Meltdown! Meltdown! Golden Card!" croaked Austin. "Meltdown! Meltdown! Golden Card. Meltdown! Meltdown! Golden Card! Meltdown!"

Just then the hatch in the conning tower floor flew open and Podesta Blenkinsopp's head appeared.

"Scarper! Humans!" yelled Monty.

"Scarper where? Austin's boot's glowing red hot," replied Hedgehog, and before Captain Blenkinsopp wriggled up through the hatch, he, Monty, Vole, and Legit had scurried for the safety of the open ventilation shaft.

"Why aren't we sliding down this burrow like we slid down before when we were in here," said Vole.

"Because everything's gone topsy-turvy, since the big, gigantic, enormous massive ship-snake thing swallowed us, Vole," replied Hedgehog.

"Yes, what was up-and-down before is now side-to-side," said Legit, knowingly.

"Flat," corrected Monty, poking his nose out from the ventilation shaft.

Through the black smoke rapidly filling the dome, Podesta Blenkinsopp shielded his face from Austin's heat with his arm. He advanced gingerly towards the little car clutching the Golden Card in his right hand.

"Meltdown! Golden Card! Meltdown! Golden Card!"

"Poor Austin. I think he's melting," said Vole. "AND WHAT'S THAT NOISE?"

"I can't see much, the smoke's too thick. Wait! Men-things are coming up through the floor!"

"Men-things? What are men-things, Monty?"

"They're all over the place," continued Monty, ducking back inside the ventilation shaft to avoid being seen.

"Yes. But tell us what men-things are, Monty!" chorused Vole, Hedgehog and Legit.

"I don't really know. They look just like things I saw on Human telly once in moving pictures about a Doctor."

"Doctor who?"

"Yes! Did you all see it too? Terrific wasn't it?"

The discussion stopped abruptly with sounds of thumping and a strangled cry.

"Monty! What's happening now?"

"Why is it me who always has to put his head above the parapet?"

"'Cos you're the only one with sharp-eyes!" replied the others.

"Ok. Ok." Monty's nose twitched as once more he peered out of the ventilation shaft.

The men-things were dragging Podesta Blenkinsopp through the conning tower hatch. Slipping from his lifeless fingers, the Golden Card lay glinting on the conning tower floor and when Podesta and his captors disappeared from sight a bony claw reached from below to close the hatch behind them.

"Meltdown! Meltdown! Golden Card! Meltdown! Meltdown! Golden Card! Explosion imminent! Explosion imminent!" moaned a failing voice through the smoke.

Chapter 20

The Black Gorge

"Help me Toby! Lu's too heavy. I can't pull her out on my own!" yelled Bill as the water around Lu bubbled and boiled with snapping jaws and ripping claws.

"On my way," replied Toby, stepping like a tight-rope walker along the rocking hull of the midget-submarine to grab a handful of Lu's suit.

"On the count of ONE! PULL!" shouted Bill, and together they pulled Lu onto the sub.

"Thank you," she spluttered, spitting out a mouthful of water. "Aghh! No! Something's biting my ankle!"

"Toby! Grab Lu's leg it's still in the water.

"There's something clamped to her boot, Bill!"

"GET IT OFF ME!" screamed Lu, staring wide-eyed at a slug-like worm-thing with ivory teeth chewing determinedly into her boot.

"I'll blast it off!" cried Toby, reaching for his stun-gun.

"No!" yelled Bill, "You're too close. You'll kill Lu. Stick it with your knife, Toby."

Toby reached for his dagger. The creature, as if sensing somehow Toby's malintent towards it, reared up, bared stained teeth and sprung at him.

ZAP! A fat blue, ozone-smelling spark flashed from Bill's stun-pistol into the slug. Instantly, the glistening creature's body fluids boiled and it ballooned to treble its normal size before exploding in a sticky orange goo all over Toby and Lu.

"Wicked!" drawled Bill blowing the steam from the barrel of his stun-gun.

"Ugh! This orange stuff's foul!" said Lu, screwing up her small nose and doing her best to scrape the creature's 'blood' from her suit.

"Let's get out of here," said Toby scrambling back to man the sub's controls.

Bill didn't mind the smelly orange gunk dripping from Lu's suit as they continued their way taking extra care not to dip their feet in the water. She was safe and that was all that mattered. In fact, every now and then, to pass the time, he took pot-shots at the swarming slug-worms with his stun-gun. If his aim was true his target exploded into orange slime and they would all cheer, and as the other slugs swarmed to devour their stricken fellows, Lu would bounce up and down on Bill's lap clapping with excitement.

"I can see land!" shouted Toby.

In the distance the blue light darkened, and as they drew near the dirty-white of a cliff-face reared up from the mist in front of them.

"It's good to find land, I've just realised I'm very thirsty," said Lu. "We haven't had anything to drink since we left the Nautilad."

"Now you mention it I'm pretty parched too," answered Toby.

"We must find fresh water," said Bill touching a globule of water on the midget sub's hull and tasting it. "Yuk! It's salty."

"Let's hope there's water on land," said Lu.

They continued moving under the shadow of the cliff to where they saw a strip of beach piled with fallen boulders from the cliff.

"I don't fancy climbing that cliff," said Toby.

"We wouldn't make more than fifty feet without ropes and crampons. Best follow the line of the beach and see where it takes us," replied Bill.

"Left or right?" said Lu.

"I don't think we've got much choice. Something's pulling us to the left," replied Toby glancing down at the sub's instrument panel. "The sub's power's showing 'High' on the Vrilometer."

"Look!" called Lu, pointing out to sea. "Over there sticking up out of the water. Can you see it?"

"Yeah! It's the mast of a wrecked galleon," replied Bill.

"Wow! There's another one over there!" shouted Toby, pointing at another snapped masthead in the distance beyond the first.

"They must have run aground on these rocks," said Toby leaning over the side to peer at a jagged rock-bed beneath the clear surface of the water below them.

"Can you keep us off the rocks, Toby?" called Bill over his shoulder.

"I'll try. But this current's getting so strong I can hardly steer!"

The Black Gorge

For several hours, they lurched along the rocky coastline clinging for their lives like limpets to the submarine as it pitched and rolled in the ever roughening sea. Every now and then they sped by more hulks of mysterious dead ships, and at one point, wedged between two rock-prongs, Toby spotted the paint-peeled blue tail of a downed American fighter aircraft, broken and battered by foam fringed waves.

Soon their arms and legs ached with the effort of holding on as the breakers roared around them, relentlessly pounding the white cliff until, without warning, the current changed direction as the cliff sucked the swirling sea into a gaping black gorge.

At once Bill secured the canopy shut as first the submarine rolled, then capsized, and rolled again to right itself before swinging madly, surfing atop a high rolling wave into the dark towering jaws of the gorge.

Chapter 21

The Pirate Smegeye

"My poor head," mumbled Podesta Blenkinsopp, wincing as he came to. His head ached like someone inside was trying to break out with a sledge hammer. A purple carpeted podium surmounted with a gigantic glass throne swam into foggy view.

The steel-plated room glared white, and was brightly lit, doing nothing to help his thumping head.

He tried to move but could not. His arms were pinned. No, on second thoughts something was holding him painfully under his armpits. Turning his head, he got his first shock. His upper arms were gripped by giant, leathery brown claws. Black talons encircled his biceps and his feet dangled uselessly two feet above the floor.

The leathery claws were attached to heavily-muscled, leathery arms. Podesta was reminded of a Black Rhino, but this *thing* was no wild animal. His captor's arms were clad in highly-glossed, Japanned-black vambraces, and, as his half-closed eyes followed the massive arms upwards, he could see he was being held on each side by two enormous, armoured giants.

Podesta lifted his eyes painfully to look at one of the creature's faces. It was then Podesta got his second shock, for returning Podesta's squinting gaze was indeed a monstrous face which stared down and returned a sly smile at Podesta's obvious expression of disgust.

Beneath a long snout the creature's black lips parted revealing massive white incisors like those of a sabre-toothed tiger. The giant then looked over Podesta's head to engage its companion's attention.

It winked a huge bulbous eye and throwing back its head let out a metallic belly-laugh. In a moment Podesta's aching body was shaking like a rag doll as both his captors similarly dissolved into gales of raucous laughter.

Their laughter ceased instantly, and their heads bowed in deference as heavy metal doors behind the podium swung open and an entourage of similar armour-clad creatures entered the room.

Podesta's heart raced as dozens of greedy eyes drilled into him, their mouths slavering uncontrollably.

The hungry expressions of the creatures suddenly became deadpan, and their eyes fixed forward, when as silence prevailed, the last figure to enter the room strode in through the doors.

Podesta recognised it from old. A giant - at least a metre taller than the rest - a leader, clad in studded black leather and Ox blood thigh-length boots and carrying a hooked staff in his right claw. A low-slung wide leather belt with a gold buckle, slouched over the creature's right hip and attached to it was a boxy holster and pistol tied with a strap around the muscled thigh.

The weapon looked for all the world like an ancient flintlock with a curling comma-shaped grip and a belled muzzle that protruded from the bottom of the holster. Closer inspection revealed a soot-blackened electrode in the centre of the pistol's barrel, and Podesta knew from experience that if used in anger this weapon was a thousand times more deadly than the antique powder and ball boarding pistol it so closely resembled.

The giant's shrivelled wart-like companion Peebody Fiddler was alive and well too, occupying its usual place perching on the giant's wide right shoulder. Peebody's furled bat-wings were rendered flightless by a floppy pink, surgically attached nerve-cord that tethered it to a shaved patch on the back of the giant's neck.

"So. Captain Podesta Blenkinsopp we meet again," roared the giant, its huge barrel chest like a sounding chamber booming out its words and filling the room.

"I only wish I could call it a pleasure, Smegeye."

Podesta recoiled as the sneering giant moved to tower over him. He remembered well the stink of Peebody Fiddler. The giant's tolerance of the parasite's smell had been a source of mystery to Podesta until he'd discovered Peebody's contribution to the odd pair's symbiotic relationship.

"I can see you are starting to itch again, Master," interrupted Peebody peering keenly at a large cream-headed pustule rapidly rising on the giant's cheek.

"See to it," commanded the giant.

Peebody's beady eyes widened gleefully and it scuttled along the giant's shoulder toward the eruption. The giant's attention focussed on Podesta once more.

"Oh, it will be anything BUT a pleasure, Captain Blenkinsopp, let me assure you of that."

Podesta winced and tried to turn away as Peebody unfurled his bat-wings to expose two bony 'thumbs'.

The giant's skin popped between Peebody's bony digits and a mix of yellow-pus and blood oozed down Smegeye's cheek. Immediately the parasite creature leaped and pouting its thick lips sucked-in the slime which formed wobbly strands to Smegeye's cheek as it chewed and sucked and sucked and licked and licked and slurped before swallowing the mess with a single sickening gulp. Smegeye tilted his head back and closed his bulbous eyes in ecstasy before bellowing, "Bring in the other prisoners."

With an imperious wave of a claw he turned his back to Podesta to take his seat on the glass throne.

Peebody Fiddler let out a vulgar noise and a horrible smell and sputters of yellow droppings sprayed and slithered down the encrusted back of Smegeye's leather jerkin.

"Oh. You naughty boy. You know you're ruining my jacket, Peebody Liebling."

Podesta Blenkinsopp's stomach turned as the giant poising to sit, turned to the parasite and smiled stupidly, his snout wrinkling with lustful flirtatiousness.

The small creature responded with a high-pitched cackle, hopping from one foot to the other in a kind of grotesque dance.

The glass throne throbbed with a soft blue hue as Smegeye lowered his rear onto its seat, and as another set of doors behind Podesta opened the rhythmic squeaking of oil-less axles drifted into the room from a dark corridor beyond.

With an angry glare, Smegeye waved Podesta aside as a black iron cage on the bed of an iron wheeled wagon rumbled into the Throne Room shouldered by two massively built one eyed-men, oiled and naked from the waist up.

Podesta's heart sank. Standing at the bars of the cage were Farouke, Wendy, Mike and Stu. Stu reached for his stun gun only to find it had been taken along with his knife. He stood rattling the bars and spitting at the Cyclopes in frustration until one of the Sabre-Tooth soldiers jabbed him hard in the ribs with a rod that sparked and left a faint singeing smell in the room.

Stu collapsed in the corner of the cage gasping and flopping like a landed fish on the sawdust floor, a blackened hole smouldering in the side of his suit.

"You beast!" screamed Wendy at the Sabre Tooth as she rushed to help Stu. "What sort of a, a thing are you?"

"FOOL! DON'T damage them! There are those who will pay well for these prisoners in Metronis!" boomed Smegeye, reaching for the hooked staff. The staff pulsed in time with the throne and a wavering white hot stream of Vril tracked across the room into the eyes of the offending Sabre Tooth. For a moment the creature looked at its master with an expression of stupefied disbelief and then sadness before sinking to its knees with flames licking from its ears, snout and gaping mouth.

"Now I don't think introductions are necessary, are they, Podesta?" sneered Smegeye coolly. Podesta flinched as Smegeye brought the Vril staff to bear on him. Then flicking it in the direction of the cage growled, "Put him in with his friends. You'll have plenty of time to regale them with the gruesome fate awaiting them when we dock at Metronis, Podesta. Now throw them all in the Brig!"

Chapter 22

The Undersea Road

Sam Scrivener breathed gently as he dozed in the front seat of the Professor's gliding midget submarine.

"Wake up Sam," crackled the Professor's voice over the helmet-phones.

"Uh. Oh. Sorry, Professor."

"Don't sleep! With your oxygen level as low as it is, you might not wake up again."

"Are we nearly there yet?"

"Ha ha! You sound just like my Rudi when we...." the Professor's voice trailed away. "Yes Sam. We are nearly there. Look before you."

Sam's eyes felt like they did reading a boring book at bedtime. After a moment sleepily scanning the horizon they suddenly widened and he sat up with a jolt. The midget sub was cruising over a blue bathed sandy plain; and coming into view was an island-oasis of brightly-coloured coral that soared above them and disappeared through the quicksilver surface of the water shimmering distantly above them. Nestling within the coral Sam could just make out a white snaking road winding through an avenue of broken classical columns and statues of an ancient civilisation.

As they approached, the reds, yellows, purples and greens of the corals teemed with iridescent fish that shimmered and flashed like rainbow gems darting in and out

98

of coral tunnels and the shattered limbs of statues lining the road. Sinister black eels slithered between the boulder-foundations of the reef and slick hungry sharks swam into reef-tunnels to emerge unexpectedly elsewhere searching for their next meal.

"What is this place, Professor?"

"One of thousands of sunken cities destroyed when the ancient world ended."

"You mean?"

"Yes Sam. You know of Noah and his ark?"

"You mean the Old Testament story of the Great Flood is true, Professor?"

"Perhaps with some licence, yes Sam."

"Licence?"

"Yes. Changes to the truth to make it easier for ordinary folk to understand. The flood was not caused by the hand of some unseen god, but rather the way of life of the earth's inhabitants at that time. We tend to think of the earth peopled by primitives in ancient times, but it was not. There were abroad, at that time, highly sophisticated civilizations - peoples capable of all of the things we take for granted today, with technology far in advance of our own."

"But that's incredible, Professor!"

"Yes it is, Sam. The ancients knew of both space and time travel."

"But that's…"

"I know, Sam…. Incredible!"

"No. I was going to say impossible. Time travel's impossible isn't it?"

"No Sam it is perfectly possible."

The Undersea Road

"But how do you know that, Professor?"

"What do you notice about the block road down there, Sam?" the Professor pointed to a distant temple at the end of the road.

Sam frowned inside his helmet, scouring every visible inch of the gleaming white thread winding below them.

"Let me give you a clue, Sam," said the Professor after a long silence.

"No, Professor. I think I can guess. Yes I've got it! The white road. It's too clean! There is no debris, or seaweed, or coral covering it. It looks as pristine as if it was built yesterday."

"Perhaps not yesterday, Sam, but quite recently. You see…."

"Yes, I see!" gasped Sam recalling the huge sea serpent. "Somehow we've travelled back to a prehistoric time when monsters roamed the world."

"Precisely, Sam. A time just after Noah and the Great Flood."

"That's incredible, Professor!"

Cruising over the pristine white road, they made their way into the shadow of the towering temple gate.

Sam's drooping eyes suddenly widened, marvelling at the clear water around them filling with beautiful fair-skinned nymphs, their pink frilled gills undulating at their throats and long golden locks flowing over their backs.

Chapter 23

The Whirlpool

"Woah!" cried Lu, ducking as they swept and pitched over shallow rapids and under fallen trees spanning the low banks of the Black Gorge. They were entering a tunnel. Toby eased the sub's joystick forward to clear the low ceiling.

Soon, like a person possessed of a demon, his hands and feet were wildly pushing and pulling the joystick and stomping on the rudder pedals. Jagged rocks loomed from the darkness, seeming to block their path. Toby's lightning reflexes constantly corrected their course and the obstacles flashed harmlessly by to fade like sparks behind them. They were fighting the grip of an irresistible force sucking them faster and ever faster towards something unseen, powerful, and terrible.

Pulling down their helmet visors inside the sub's spray-lashed canopy they found it impossible to speak because somewhere in the pitch-black, an unseen watery maelstrom drowned out all but its own roaring voice.

After an eternity of buffeting and din, Bill felt Lu's small fingers tightening on his hand as they found themselves suspiciously becalmed in open water. Then they saw it, three hundred metres in front of them, as if Neptune himself had pulled the plug from his own gigantic bathtub: a massive whirlpool sucking-in fallen, broken trees, bushes and shrubbery and the waterlogged carcasses of dead animals.

The Whirlpool

After a moment of stillness, like a rollercoaster setting off downhill after climbing a peak on its track, the sub began gathering speed.

"Reverse!" yelled Bill, craning back to see Toby's red and twisted face, sweating to control the submarine.

"It's no good. We're on full reverse-power already. The current's too strong." He gasped breathlessly.

They began circling. Slowly at first, but as they drew nearer the black watery eye at the whirlpool's centre they speeded up. Bill leaned into Lu as the waters closed in over their heads. Their visors touched. Instinctively they went to kiss farewell. The light went out and Lu gripped Bill's hands as they spun down and down into blackness, down and down, and round and round into the swirling waters of the whirlpool.

Chapter 24

Into the Brig

Clang!

The heavily-riveted iron door of the brig slammed behind them. Stu staggered, his ankles manacled, and he leant panting against a corner behind the door before sliding down the cold metal wall into a heap on the floor.

"He's really sweating badly," said Wendy, mopping Stu's forehead with her hanky.

"You're worse than my mum. She used to scrub me face off wiv an 'anky," mumbled Stu deliriously.

Podesta hammered on the back of the cell door. "We need a doctor!"

"Let me have a look," said Mike, stooping to open Stu's burnt suit.

"Gerroff. I'm fine," said Stu, wincing and swiping weakly at Mike with his left hand.

"We NEED a doctor!" repeated Podesta, hammering on the door again.

"It's ok for the moment Capt Blenkinsopp. I can probably cope. Humans are pretty similar to animals. Oooh! This is nasty."

A raw, blackened hole two inches deep below Stu's ribs oozed blood.

Into the Brig

"It will never heal if it's left," warned Podesta, rattling the bars of a small window in the top of the brig door. "WE NEED A DOCTOR!"

"What do you mean it will never heal, Podesta?" asked Wendy.

"It was caused by a Vril wand. There is no medicine that you or any conventional doctor can provide that will heal a Vril wound, Mike."

"Remember Vril can heal as well as destroy, Effendi," cut-in Farouke.

"Yes of course! I remember the Professor telling us that at the reception in the Nautilad's Saloon," agreed Wendy.

Podesta looked perplexed shaking his head, "That's the theory. The healing Vril must be applied soon, before any cellular degeneration takes place. Vril will only renew what it destroys and no more. If body cells suffer further damage or die after injury caused by a Vril War Staff, healing Vril cannot restore them. The victim will always have part of their body that will never heal."

"Give that man a round of applause," growled a voice through the barred window in the brig door. "Perhaps it will remind the young pup to curb his insolence in future?"

A busy jangle of keys was followed by the clicking mechanics of an opening lock. The brig door flew open and a small pink human-like man wearing a white loincloth and carrying a cut-down version of the usual warrior Vril-Staff and what appeared a pigskin bag, was shoved into the room. The door slammed behind him.

"And you'd better patch him up good if you know what's good for you, Pimpy!" mocked the growling voice through the bars.

"I am the doctor. Where is the boy?"

"Over here, Pimpy," cried Wendy, inwardly shocked at the small man's soft feminine tone.

"Please. My name is not Pimpy," replied the doctor. "Pimpy is a cruel nickname afforded me by my Husvolken masters."

"Husvolken masters?" said Wendy.

"Please we do not have much time. I must attend the boy before atrophy affects the wound. If he is not perfect after the treatment, I will suffer."

With a skinny bow-legged gait the small creature scuttled forward to stand over Stu. He then raised his skinny arms with the small staff pointing down at Stu's wound. Tilting his head back and screwing his eyes shut the doctor chanted, "Aaeeeshaaar!" and the brig filled with a warm, rushing wind and ghostly rosy glow of flesh coloured plasma leapt from the staff's tip to fill Stu's wound.

Stu let out a low-pitched gargle followed by a long, hollow rushing intake of breath. For a moment he sat bolt upright, his eyes wide and staring. Then, he slumped backwards, a wisp of steam curling from his open suit to lie with his eyes contentedly closed, and his head cradled in Wendy's lap.

"Tha-That's miraculous! The wound's entirely healed," stuttered Mike, studying the clean, mended flesh where Stu's bloody wound had been.

"Amazing," answered Wendy, shaking her head.

Opening one cautious eye, the doctor glanced nervously at his handiwork. A slow smile lit his small features. Nodding with satisfaction he declared, "That's it! Jobby done. The great Lord Smegeye will be appeased."

105

Into the Brig

"You'd better get out now, *Pimpy*. Before your head swells wider than the door and you have stay in there with the slaves," sneered the voice from outside. The busy keys jangled and the door opened.

"Let him rest," counselled the doctor. The brig door slammed behind him and they were once more alone.

"Well I'm nobody's SLAVE! What did he mean by *the slaves*, Podesta?" said Wendy indignantly.

There was a long pause interrupted by Farouke who said, "Our chains suggest we are....In Atlantis all foreigner are slaves."

"But I don't understand?" said Mike.

Podesta then answered, "Farouke's quite correct, Mike. It's the Law in Atlantis that any creature or man straying into its borders or territories automatically becomes a slave of the Atlantean empire. That doctor was a slave too. And our friend Smegeye is a Slaveer."

"Slaveer?" chorused Wendy and Mike.

"A slave trader," explained Podesta. "He hunts and captures Xenodes and sells them in the Plaza Slave Market at Metronis."

"Xenodes?" asked Wendy frowning.

"The Atlantean word for foreigner," answered Podesta.

"You seem to know an awful lot about all this," said Mike.

"You forget. I've been here before during our Second World War, Mike."

"Our Second World War? That's a strange way to describe it."

"I agree, it is," answered Podesta, "but it's accurate none-the-less. When the Professor and I last visited Atlantis we found that somewhere on the journey we'd travelled back in time. We left our world when the Second World War was raging, and we arrived in another world, much older, in a lost ancient time."

"An ancient time with machines like this submarine-sea-serpent, Podesta? I don't remember learning about ancient Greek or Roman submarines at my school," said Mike.

"I said exactly the same thing to the Professor at the time, Mike," replied Podesta. "He told me we had gone back way beyond all the ages of Rome, Greece and ancient Egypt; to a time before the great flood, a time when Atlantis was a great military power with a Vril-based technology and extensive Vril-powered weaponry - flying machines, land-going armoured vehicles, massive siege-buster cannons. The blueprints of which the Nazis wanted steal to help them turn the tide of The Second World War in their favour."

"What about this Smegeye character? He might be a Slaveer, but he's certainly not human. What exactly is he?" said Wendy looking down at her ankles and jangling her chains contemptuously.

"NO! Definitely not human!" laughed Podesta. "He's an ancient full-blood Mobian."

"A WHAT?"

"A full-blood Mobian, members of a war-like race from the planet Morbius Magda. A planet in the outer limits of the Epsilon Fringe beyond the Carthanian System. His kind invaded earth and after generations of conquest and integration we humans are the result... But the Professor knows much more about Atlantean history than I do."

Into the Brig

"I wonder if I ever see Professor again?" sighed Farouke.

"I daht it, Mate. I reckon he's a gonner," said Stu hauling himself up to lean on one elbow. "One fing's for sure though. I bet it won't be long before we get to see this Plaza place at Metronis… And, like that Smegeye geezer said, find out the gruesome fate that awaits us!"

Chapter 25

Areenee the Oldest People in the World

"They're guiding us to that great coral arch, Professor," mumbled Sam, expending a last oxygen starved effort raising his arm to point at the beautiful Nymphs now circling the midget-sub. "What are these creatures?"

The Professor's voice crackled through the helmet-phones, "The Areenee. The Gate Keepers and the most ancient people to live on our planet, Sam."

"I thought we descended from ape men, Professor.

"You are assuming with the typical arrogance of our species that our ancestors were our inferiors, Sam. They were not. The earth was once populated by many different, and I might add, highly intelligent non-ape species."

"What happened to them, Professor?"

"Most perished. Try not to talk too much, Sam. Your oxygen is nearly empty."

"Most?"

"There are remnants of some of the races alive in our world today, but they live hidden from us in tunnels deep within the earth's crust and in particular beneath the Himalayan mountain ranges."

The Professor's attention was taken by three of the Areenee, who, alighting on the nose of the midget-sub, tapped on the canopy and pointed to a dark doorway in a rainbow-

109

coloured façade of carved columns and archways in a soaring cliff of polished coral.

The Professor gently adjusted the sub's trim to glide in through the doorway. One the Areenee, momentarily losing balance, grabbed hold and laughed impishly into the canopy. Raising its eyes, it mouthed "Phew," and waved a slender, long fingered hand in front of its perfectly-shaped smiling lips in mock relief.

The coral doorway opened out to a large submerged chamber, or tank, dimly lit by lemon-shaped lamps in rows around the walls.

The Professor shut the sub's throttle and they hovered in the middle of the room. Almost at once the sea-door of the chamber closed behind them and through his feverish drowsiness, Sam felt relief to hear a muffled rush of gurgling water as the chamber drained and the waterline steadily crept down its mural-decorated walls. When the water level was below their helmets the Professor opened the canopy and, fumbling with oxygen starved clumsiness, Sam removed and dropped his helmet and drank in lungfuls of fresh air.

"I wouldn't have lasted much longer," he gasped.

"Come Sam. Can you walk? Our hosts are beckoning us."

Wading through knee-high water they climbed four stone steps with ornate balustrades to a flagged platform and a carved linteled doorway to a dripping inner vestibule. The Areenee were waiting in the dim 'lemon'-light in front a massive, circular iron door. The rusty door had a heavy locking wheel like a ship's steering wheel at its centre. The Professor smiled to himself. A thick iron bar, shaped to fit neatly over the door's locking-wheel for extra leverage to turn it if needed, was fixed by brackets to the wall of the vestibule.

The Areenee began turning the ship's wheel anticlockwise - until with a faint hiss - it swung slowly open.

Sam went to walk through. The Areenee shaking their heads together, gently touched his arm to restrain him.

The Areenee who nearly fell placed its hand over a carved wall plaque. Lights slowly brightened and Sam and the Professor could see they were about to enter a triangular room from its apex. The base of the triangle opposite the door was in fact a defensive wall, which afforded protection to two Areenee spearmen in mercury-bright breastplates and helmets. A sinister dish-like object began smoothly and precisely tracking Sam and the Professor's movements as they followed their hosts into the triangle's centre.

"Enter Blatvok," squeaked a high-pitched oracular voice filling the room from nowhere in particular, "What have you brought us today?"

"Why, The Professor, Nikvok!" replied Blatvok, the Areenee who nearly fell.

"THE PROFESSOR!"

Everybody winced holding their hands to their ears.

"SORRY," said the voice, "I'LL turn down the volume."

Everybody relaxed and Blatvok smiled sheepishly at the Professor and Sam.

"Well don't just stand there Blatvok. Bring him in. I will tell Bigvok. There will be much feasting in Areenia tonight!"

Chapter 26

The Man from Ergolite Arrives (eventually)

Garcia Smallpiece was queasy. He was also cold. Balancing precariously on a narrow deck somewhere in the Arctic Ocean scraping ice from Ergo 1's windscreen in a howling gale was nowhere in his tropical job description.

The fat German's face came into view. He was pointing animatedly at a yellowing sea chart and beckoning the drenched Indian inside. Garcia didn't need beckoning twice: at that moment the submarine's bow dived beneath the icy waves and before drowning, Garcia jumped for his life into the nearest deck hatch.

"Look! Look! Ve are nearly there, Garcia!" exclaimed the fat German jabbing an excited fat forefinger on a red 'X' on the chart. "Here, Garcia! Ze Mayan map marks ze spot! Ve haff nearly triumphed! Ve haff nearly found ze entrance to Atlantis! Ha! World domination is within our grasp at last Garcia! I can almost feel the Vril energy radiating from the Collector Crystal as we speak."

Garcia did his best to look excited, but his frozen face permitted only 'mildly enthusiastic'.

Accompanied by the fat German's maniacal, power-crazed and villainous laughter, Ergo 1 and a cold, wet, rather miserable Garcia Smallpiece plunged beneath the Arctic waves toward the hidden entrance tunnel to Atlantis.

Chapter 27

Mysterious Rescuer

"TAKE COVER EVERYBODY AUSTIN'S ABOUT TO EXPLODE!" yelled Monty grabbing as many tails as he could to drag his friends inside the ventilation shaft.

"Poor Austin," sobbed Vole, his hairy nose twitching as a tear rolled down his face.

"Yeah. Poor Austin. I didn't know him like you guys did, but I liked him. He was a swell dude," said Legit.

"Better block our ears," warned Monty, "any minute now there's bound to be a loud bang!"

Several minutes passed and no bang came and after uncovering his ears, Vole said, "Nothing's gone bang yet, Monty. Do you think Austin exploded quietly?"

"Don't be silly Vole. How can you have a quiet explosion?"

"Well I don't know, Monty. I've never seen an explosion until I came here. How was I to know?"

"Maybe you'd better take a look, Monty?" suggested Legit, pointing with his nose at the ventilation shaft entrance.

Monty took off his shades and rolled his eyes, "Always ME! What would you lot do if I wasn't here?"

"Oh please don't say that, Monty. Not in this place. You might tempt fate and disappear," said Hedgehog quietly.

Monty edged to the ventilation shaft entrance. The smoke was gone. His beady eyes darted this way and that around the conning tower.

The Golden Card was nowhere to be seen and through a wavering heat haze, a Human or at least what looked Human, soot and oil-blacked, barefoot and in rags, was backing away from Austin's open boot. Austin was silent. The orange heat-glow from his body dulled, and quite remarkably, Monty recognised the returning shine of his newly painted bright green body.

Sensing he was being watched the ragged Human looked nervously over his shoulder. The whites of his eyes, wide with fear, stood out from his blackened face as he sloped away from Austin to kneel at the conning tower hatch and lean forward to listen for movement from below by placing an ear against the deck. Then, without a backward glance, he gingerly cracked open the hatch an inch, squinted down through the gap and detecting no dangerous sounds, opened it fully to slip below as stealthily and mysteriously as he'd arrived.

"Who was the Human?" asked Vole, after Monty explained to everybody what he'd seen.

"I couldn't recognise him, Vole. His face was completely black."

"Some Humans look like that don't they?" said Vole, twitching his nose.

"I think the main thing is your friend Austin didn't explode," ventured Legit.

"Yes! How are you Austin?" said Hedgehog.

Austin raised one tired headlamp and mumbled, "I have felt better thank you."

114

Chapter 28

Metronis

The vibration through the brig floor increased and changed up an octave. The sea serpent submarine bumped into something solid. Everyone staggered sideways.

"We've crashed!" cried Wendy, brushing the filth of the brig floor from her knees as she stood. "We're locked in! We'll all drown."

"We haven't crashed, we've landed," corrected Podesta Blenkinsopp, "the helmsman reversed the engines to heave-to, and the bump we felt was the vessel coming to rest at a jetty or mooring."

"I wonder if we've reached Metronis at last?" said Mike.

A jangle of keys in the lock came from outside.

"I fink we're all abaht to find out," said Stu.

Two of the Sabre-Tooth guards armed with Vril-War-Staff stood in the open doorway of the brig.

"Out!" barked the soldier on the right with gold embellishments on his shoulders and collar.

Their shackles made it hard to walk and Wendy's ankles were sore. One-by-one they shuffled clinking out of the brig into a gloomy corridor where two more guards waited in front of them. Sandwiched between four giants they stumbled along the dank corridor. Condensation stood in rank globules on the greasy metal walls and here and there along the way

115

they passed dark and barred doors, similar to the one in the brig. Cries and moans drifted out as they passed. From one door came a violent scuffling and a blinding red flash followed by the uncomfortably pleasant smell of barbecued meat that reminded Wendy she'd all but forgotten her last meal.

The jailor leading the party unlocked a steel door barring their way. Once through they entered a steel cubicle and were jostled and surrounded by their captors, and whisked aloft to fresh air and a deck hatch open to an azure sky.

Wendy was last to climb the steel ladder to the deck and stumbling because of her chains grazed her shin painfully against the rungs.

"BLAST THESE CHAINS!"

A helping hand reached down, and looking up, she was stunned to be greeted by Stu.

"'ang on, missus. I'll try and pull you up," said Stu gripping Wendy's wrists in a 'trapeze grip'. "Hold my wrists. You'll be safe, missus. One of my foster parents was a circus trapeze artist," he added smiling, and surprised himself most of all by lifting her out through the hatch as if she was a feather.

Podesta Blenkinsopp was right. They were bobbing and bumping against a wood-clad stone jetty. Everyone stood aghast at the sight of a pointed mountain with a dazzling black marble city clinging to its sides that soared in the sun like a funereal wedding cake glittering in a confectioner's window.

The stone jetty ran for several miles. Along it were moored masted ships with odd-looking rotary devices that Stu reasoned must be sails of a peculiar design. A gleaming white paved road ran along the jetty and after two miles it entered a

116

black iron gate between two squat square towers in a high circular city wall.

Beyond the wall the road zigzagged its way up the mountain between houses, shops, taverns, and temples. Grand statues posed at each turn as the road passed through six concentric inner walls, each with its own black gate and towers, dividing the city into seven distinct districts.

Perhaps the most mesmerizing of all, attracting everyone's gaze like a magnet, was an enormous crystal sparkling with rainbow lights cleaved from the beating sunlight at the mountain's summit.

The crystal, cradled in four outstretched claws of solid gold, poked up from the peak of a black glassy pyramid just visible from the canopy of a surrounding forest of Yew trees inside the highest of the city's circular walls.

Tearing his gaze from the fascinating crystal, Stu looked down from the Sea Serpent's deck. The jetty below was teeming with ragged people herded into ragged phalanxes by armed Sabre Tooths who force-marched them along the road to the city gates.

"Tickle 'em good, Sire!" squeaked Peabody Fiddler as Smegeye the Pirate's huge frame rumbled along the stooping ranks in an iron chariot, lashing crying stragglers with a long range electric whip.

"MOVE YOU VERMIN!" yelled Smegeye turning a switch on the whip's handle and levelling it at one stumbling old man.

Even Stu winced as the whip's snaking tentacle snapped across the curve of the old man's spine. Somehow it glued to the skin, and tore it off in a single measured ribbon leaving a profusely bleeding welt across the screaming man's back.

"Ha! Ha! Ha! That will make the dogs move faster, Master!" chortled Peabody Fiddler as the other slaves glanced nervously at their brother's pain, and picked up the pace.

"What sort of hellish place is this? Where have you brought us, Captain Blenkinsopp?" cried Wendy looking down hearing the old man's screams and the cracking of Smegeye's whip.

Turning his back on the city to face her, Podesta Blenkinsopp opened his mouth to reply.

"SILENCE!" barked the senior Sabre Tooth giant brandishing his Vril Staff, "Down to the dock, all of you! Lord Smegeye is WAITING!"

Together they filed slipping and stumbling in their chains down a rickety wooden gangplank to the jetty. Glancing back over her shoulder, the leviathan bulk of the sea serpent, looked as high as a black house to Wendy. Her ankles were red and beginning to swell. She stooped to try and stop the hobbles chaffing her fine skin.

A rumble of chariot wheels announced Smegeye's arrival.

"Welcome to Metronis," he growled. "YOU STAND IN MY PRESENCE!"

"I can't! These damn chains are cutting into my ankles!" yelled Wendy.

At once Smegeye swung down from his chariot to cast his massive shadow over her. He stood for several moments coiling his whip and hooking it to his belt.

"Let me see," he said with surprising tenderness. Wendy scowled and Mike tensed as the giant knelt and cradled her naked foot in the palm of a great claw. He looked

118

sympathetically at the redness under the irons and beckoned to the senior gaoler.

"Remove the chains."

"Look at my foot!" exclaimed Wendy, "much more of those anklets and my skin would have broken!"

Smegeye lifted her foot once more.

"Don't touch me!"

"Such exquisitely tiny feet. You are indeed a delicate prize, my dear. We must take good care not to damage you."

Mike and Stu lunged at Smegeye, only to find their shoulders clamped by Sabre Tooth claws from behind.

"I see you have admirers, my dear. Such a pity their affections will be unrequited," sneered Smegeye, his black lips twisting to flash the whites of his fangs. "Still, my dear. What I have in mind for you won't be so bad. After a time you might even grow to love your slavery."

Smegeye stooped and scooping up Wendy carried her to his chariot. He turned his head beyond Peabody Fiddler to address his men, "I will meet you at the Plaza with the other prisoners! And *if you value your lives* take special care of them. They are precious! Where there is Podesta Blenkinsopp the Professor will not be far behind. And She-We-Obey will pay handsomely to learn of *his* whereabouts!"

The Slaveer cracked his whip and the iron wheels of his chariot rumbled away down the white paved road to the marble city.

Chapter 29

Attack of the Flying Machine

"Biiiiiiiiilllllll!" screamed Lu, feeling herself lifting away from Bill's lap and thrown hard against the midget submarine's canopy. Bang! Bang! Bang! One by one the canopy hinges broke and Lu screamed as it disappeared, twisting and tumbling, into the watery typhoon. She tried hooking her legs around Bill's joystick but the whirlpool's force was too strong. In a split second, like the canopy, she was sucked spinning into watery space.

Something was wrong. Not wrong-wrong; but wrong-right. She could still feel Bill's hand holding her's. How come? She peered down and warm relief washed through her as Bill's fleeting smile entered then exited her helmet window as they tumbled together.

But where was Toby? Where was the midget-sub?

They fell through darkness for what seemed hours and then, as suddenly as the lights went out, they came on again. Now Lu saw Bill close to her. Broken oxygen hoses were flailing from his helmet. Above them, caught in a strange translucent, spiralled tube was Toby and below them the plummeting hull of the midget submarine.

If she was going to die, then at least she wouldn't be alone. Lu began savouring the final glimpses of her friends through her helmet windows. Then suddenly Bill's hand was torn from her's, and with a deafening splash the light of the tube turned to inky blue bubble punctuated darkness.

120

Water was flooding her helmet and kicking her feet she swam in the opposite direction to the doomed sub towards light.

Breaking the surface, she was coughing but relieved to see Bill and Toby a few yards away. The water level inside her helmet covered her nose and Bill swam over to help.

"Aaagh!" she gasped as he prised her helmet off, and threw it to sink out of sight. "Are we actually still alive?"

"YES! YES!" laughed Toby and Bill together.

"It's a bloody miracle! Pardon my French," coughed Lu.

"I wonder where we are?" said Toby.

Behind them the spiral column of water that disappeared hundreds of feet above, drilled into the surface of the lagoon. The water was bubbly, buoyant and warm and the current the water column caused was slowly but surely pushing them toward a distant shore.

"Come on!" said Bill. "No point in swimming against the tide, let's swim with the current."

After all of the tumult the leisurely and easy swim to shore was fun and they laughed and taunted each other to swim faster and when their feet eventually touched the sandy bottom of a warm sunlit beach, they began letting off steam playfully splashing one another and shrieking.

"Isn't this wonderful?" laughed Lu, stretching out on the sand and unzipping her suit. "It's just like being on holiday! I'm going to sunbathe."

"WOW!" chortled Toby.

"That's quite enough of *that*. You two can go off and explore a bit and give me some peace and girl-time."

"Would you like an ice cream if we come across a handy Mr. Whippy van?" chuckled Bill.

"Go on. Off with you both. And no peeking from the palm trees!"

"GIRLS!" grumbled Toby.

"Come on, Toby, let's follow the beach and see what's beyond that headland over there."

Lu watched the boys chatting and joking and playfully shoving each other in the distance.

"Right! A girl's got to pamper herself sometime," she thought, and slipping out of her suit, she ran headlong splashing in the fresh warm water for a well earned soak.

"I'm hungry," said Toby as they rounded the headland. "I wonder if there's anything to eat here?"

Bill patted his holster, "We've still got our stun-guns. Let's go hunting!"

"I vote we go inland. There's nothing much on this beach," said Toby searching in vain over his shoulder for Lu, and they turned right to head for the palm trees growing in a fringe beyond the sand.

"What about coconuts?" suggested Toby.

"We could, but too many will probably give us the shits."

Toby considered the prospect and replied, "Maybe be not then."

Beyond the palm trees they found dense undergrowth and creepers and they were about to abandon their hunt and try and bag some fish, if fish were to be found in the lagoon, when Toby shouted out.

"Bill! Come here. There's a path through the jungle!"

At once the trees were ablaze with brightly-coloured parrots, woken from dozing in the sun and startled into flight by an alien human cry.

"Try and hit one!" cried Toby.

"Nah. Waste of time. Not much fat on a parrot, Toby. Let's see where the path takes us."

The path led them inland and in places, where it burrowed tunnel-like through the jungle undergrowth they crawled on all fours.

"Tracks!" whispered Bill. "Hooves if I'm not mistaken."

"WOW!"

"Keep your voice down, Toby. You'll frighten any animals away," whispered Bill hoarsely.

"Sorry," mouthed Toby.

"I reckon these are goat tracks or pigs or something," Bill took his stun-gun from its holster and beckoned Toby to keep his head down and follow.

"It's just like that book we were doing in English. You know? Where them school kids get stranded on a desert island after their plane crashes and…."

"And the little kid with glasses gets eaten by the others!" whispered Bill, eyeing Toby under a single raised eyebrow.

"Something like that," gulped Toby.

They came to a fork in the path and Bill stooped to examine the tracks.

"This direction has more tracks. Come on this way."

Toby gripped his stun-gun in its holster and felt relieved they were sticking together.

"Shhhh! I can hear something."

From behind a cluster of boulders, through which the mud track weaved, came a grunting, snorting, snuffling. Bill adjusted the power control of his stun-gun to its lowest setting and Toby did likewise.

"I'll go over there to head off any escape," whispered Toby. Bill nodded and levelling his stun-gun he crept through the boulders.

Beyond the rocks was a hoof-churned muddy clearing at the base of a low cliff. Several wild pigs grazed or dozed below a cave half way up the rock face with a narrow ledge forming a sloping path to its entrance.

Bill jumped. A sudden loud crack came from Toby's direction. He'd obviously trodden on a fallen branch. All at once the pigs looked up. The hairs on their backs stood on end. Bill was suddenly in the path of a stampede. The lead pig, a big boar with tusks, fell in its tracks as Bill pulled the trigger of his stun-gun. The other pigs wheeled in panic and a wayward piglet succumbed to a shot from Toby's weapon. The others finding no escape turned tail and charged up the narrow ledge into the cave.

"This one's dead," said Toby, touching the motionless piglet with his foot.

"This one isn't. It's only stunned. Quick we'll take yours and run."

Big Boar's feet began twitching and its angry red eyes rolled in their sockets. The boys made off down the path to the beach dragging the dead piglet behind them. Big Boar tried giving chase but its legs buckled and it sprawled with its hooves 'galloping' uselessly in mid-air.

***

Lu was stretched in the sun when the boys returned.

"Hi!" she called, "what have you got there?"

"Dinner," replied Toby as they dragged the piglet for Lu to see.

"You can't just put it on the fire, you know. It's got to be bled and gutted and washed and loads of other yucky stuff like that."

"I don't care about that! I'm starving," replied Toby.

Gentle reader, I will not bore (or should I say boar you?) you with the gory details of what happened next, and sincere apologies to Vegans or Vegetarians, but suffice to say, "Sometime later…"

The fire they built from dry driftwood and fallen tree branches looked splendid.

"Looks just like a cowboy campfire in the movies," said Bill idly turning the branch that ran through the piglet as a spit. "Better try and light it, I s'pose."

"Oh, it's such a beautiful sunset. So romantic," said Lu.

Toby felt a gooseberry.

Bill took his stun-gun and turned up the power control.

"Here goes then," he said aiming the gun at the firewood and pulling the trigger.

Within moments the fire was blazing, and after a ghastly singeing smell, the beach filled with the aroma of barbecuing pork.

***

I think that was the best meal I've ever eaten," said Lu, washing down the meat with a mouthful of coconut milk.

Attack of the Flying Machine

The light from the fire made everything around them appear pitch-black in the moonless night.

"I feel sleepy," yawned Toby lying back in the sand and making himself comfortable. He was beginning to doze when a powerful beating pulse from nowhere made flames of the fire flicker and shrink and Toby's ears feel like he was inside a steeply climbing aeroplane, or ascending in a high-speed elevator.

"What's that awful noise?" cried Lu, sitting up and clamping her hands over her ears.

"I don't know," replied Bill. "Whatever it is I think we should take cover and get out of the light of the fire!"

"What fire? It's almost out," said Toby.

"Come on you two! Follow me," said Bill and as he ran toward the palm trees a giant flying thing appeared and swooped so low it made him sprawl headfirst in the sand. The pulsing beat was now so powerful it hurt their ears and they watched as the object tracked low along the beach and almost out of sight.

"Look out! It's coming back!" yelled Toby. They ran and crouched in the palm trees and bushes waiting for the machine's return.

The engine, for it certainly wasn't a bird of any description, appeared to be a rapidly rotating black disc. Around its circumference a ghostly green glowing ring of lights pulsed in time to the deafening noise it made. In a second the machine was hovering over the remains of the fire.

"It looks like a flying saucer," whispered Toby, not wanting whatever it was to hear them.

It was too late. The saucer was over them. The body of the machine was glossy reflecting the orange glow of the fire

126

and their wonder-filled faces looking up. The construction of the craft appeared seamlessly perfect - made in one piece without joins or rivets or welds or bolts holding it together. The palm trees bent and bushes parted in submission, and Bill, Toby, and Lu found themselves in a newly formed clearing of flattened vegetation.

"I can hardly stand," gasped Bill. "The pulsing of the machine is forcing me to my knees."

"It must be giving off some sort of force-field," said Lu, her eyelids now so heavy she was finding it difficult to keep her eyes open.

"We've got to try and make it back to the cave," said Toby breathlessly.

Together with leaden steps they made it into the undergrowth beyond the palm trees.

"LOOK!" cried Lu, pointing to the underside of the saucer. "It's got guns. It's going to kill us!"

Powered servos whined and two polished sliding doors opened. With a simultaneous click two glowing red staffs poked out and locked in position.

"Make MY day, Punk!" cried Toby, reaching to draw his stun-gun and aiming at the saucer. He pulled the trigger and a 'full stun', red plasma-track leapt from the barrel into one of the saucer's sliding gun-ports. Immediately the red shaft of the machine's weapon retracted and at once, Bill, Lu and Toby were able to move freely again.

"Well done, Toby! I reckon you stunned it," whooped Bill.

"Run!" yelled Toby, "before it gets us in its force-field again."

Crashing through shrubs and bracken they ran wildly for the beach.

The saucer, having regrouped, hummed in hot pursuit. A bolt of red lightning leapt from one of its red staffs and a palm tree in front and to Bill's left exploded. They all raised their arms protecting their faces from flying debris, but kept running toward the pig tracks. Another red lightning bolt struck a nearby boulder reducing it to smouldering powder. Nearly there? The safety of the pig-cave?

"On three we'll all turn and fire at the saucer," gasped Bill. "Ready? One, two, THREE! FIRE!"

Three red plasma streams twisted up from the jungle path into the saucer. Once more its guns retracted and once more they had a brief window in which to run.

"The boulders!" cried Toby. "There are the pig-boulders!"

Leaping through the gap in the boulders a startled pig was stopped in its tracks by a red lightning bolt from the saucer. The pig blew up to twice its normal size and, when a split appeared in its belly, exploded into millions of stinking boiling bits all over the muddy clearing.

Once more the three levelled their stun-guns at the ship but this time the saucer's weapons remained in position.

"Again!" shouted Bill. "Everybody fire again!"

This time they all scored a direct hit on one of the flying machine's gun ports, and this time the whole machine recoiled like an elephant smitten by an Express rifle.

"Quick up the rock path," shouted Bill grabbing Lu's free hand and pulling her up the narrow ledge to the cave entrance.

Toby ducked as a lightning bolt blew a four foot hole in the cliff face above him and ran as fast as his legs would carry him before thousands of stone fragments rained down behind him.

"Phew! That was close!"

"Quick, Toby. Get in the cave!" yelled Lu.

A second red lightning bolt slammed into the rock-face above the cave and a second shower of stones and boulders rained down. A third bolt and the rock-ledge in front of the cave blew to smithereens.

It was now or never. There was no time for second thoughts. A hand emerged from inside the cave. Toby leapt over the collapsing ledge and grabbed it for Bill to pull him inside.

In an instant, a ton or more of roaring rocks fell to block the cave entrance once and for all.

They were engulfed in darkness. The only light - a faint green glow from their stun-gun power dials and two red eyes staring from the cave's interior. The only sounds - their choking from airborne dust, and the body-stink of pigs, and the beat of charging hooves.

"It's Big Boar!" yelled Bill.

Unholstering their stun-guns they pulled their triggers. One by one the glimmering power dials went dark like snuffed candles.

"There's no Force left in the stun-guns!" cried Toby into the darkness.

Chapter 30

The Professor's Return

W ord of the Professor's return spread like wildfire in Areenia. Nikvok and Blatvok had wasted no time proudly presenting their find - the Professor and Sam - to Bigvok and the royal court. Now they reclined on Coralworm-silk cushions at a low table in the brightly-decorated, palace banqueting hall. The room was full, and alive with the hubbub of laughter-punctuated conversation and the clatter of plates and cutlery.

"I hope you like seafood, Sam," said the Professor. An Areenian waiter set a massive shell-shaped tureen of steaming Halibut Eye soup on the table. Sam sniffed the fishy vapours and turned a pale shade of green.

"Look! I'm sure he does, Professor!" called Bigvok from the head of the table.

Sam turned an even deeper green after the smiling waiter ladled him a shell of the foul-smelling yellow liquor, and out of politeness to his hosts, Sam drank some.

"It's like swallowing bogies," he mouthed to the Professor, trying his best not to gag. The Professor responded with a beaming smile and a nod as though Sam had just passed a hugely complimentary remark about the soup. Bigvok, Nikvok, and Blatvok all looked at each other and nodded and beamed back.

Bigvok was not, as his name suggested, big. In fact bigness in Areenia was considered clumsy with connotations of oafishness. In Areenia small was beautiful and Bigvok was small! *All Areenians were fair-skinned and not unlike their descendants, the elves of Middle Earth. I don't think I'm giving too much away telling you Areenia spawned descendants because our blue planet is now teeming with them in the form of humanity, the pinnacle, and combined evolutionary triumph of many of the races and species of the lost antediluvian world.*

Bigvok, despite his appetites for Squid Ink wine and Bladderwrack Ale and *all things* seafood, was like his fellows - slender, and in human terms handsome. The Areenian metabolism is fast. It has to be fast to build the musculature needed to swim and move easily at great depths. Athleticism and benign intellectual agility were two qualities greatly revered in Areenia.

Bigvok clapped his hands vigorously as six young Areenian dancing girls entered the hall. Like their male counterparts, Areenian women were handsome too, and the long-limbed dancers' floaty rainbow costumes did nothing to hide this.

Sam found his gaze irresistibly drawn to at least three of these beautiful creatures and he found himself quite looking forward to the remainder of the feast as their dance commenced with the arrival of the second of the seven courses.

Bigvok's pleasure too was obvious in the golden reflection from the huge gleaming Torque of office around his neck.

"A toast! To our friend the Professor's timely return!" cried Bigvok, raising his goblet of Squid ink wine.

"The Professor!" echoed the others at the low table.

"So. Bigvok. What news of Metronis?" asked the Professor.

Bigvok's golden smile tarnished. He shook his head.

"Not good. Their strategic position in the great ocean gives them almost absolute command of world trade. Their enforcement of the extortion money they call tolls for the safe passage of goods between east and west fleece within an inch the merchants and cargo carriers struggling to survive on ever-shrinking profits. The Atlanteans grow rich at the expense of others… At the expense of us, Professor."

"But surely the Areenee rule the rich undersea worlds, don't they Bigvok?"

"Indeed we do, Professor, but our forces alone are no longer a match for the military might of Atlantis. Slavery has made Ayesha strong. No one power in the world remains strong enough to challenge Her. Like a spoilt child with plenty, Atlantis is wasteful. Slavery without price makes for decadence. Why, every day Pyvok the scientist measures rises in sea-temperature that kill our corals and the microscopic links in the sea-food chain that kill our food stocks and ultimately us!"

The slender hand of the prettiest dancer daringly feathered a silky red veil across Bigvok's face. He brushed it aside angrily.

"Atlantis knows the value of nothing. They take what they want and pay nothing for it! They live by the destructive force of Vril and use it to dominate all who stand against them. We are but one. Our land-brothers, the Frengling mountain men of the East and the Lantvolken of the Western Plains, suffer too. Each of us is losing our lands and our environment to the Atlanteans."

132

"And do you know what has happened to my son, Bigvok?"

"Ah! The nub, Professor. Rudi, the reason for your return perhaps?" Bigvok's voice dropped. "Rest assured, Professor. Our spies tell us Rudi is alive. Tell me my friend. Is the good Captain Blenkinsopp with you this time?"

"He was. Our expedition was attacked and the Nautilad swallowed by a giant black sea serpent. Three midget submarines escaped from the Nautilad. Sam and I in one, but alas the other two were lost."

"I am sorry. But the sea serpent as you call it is no animal, Professor. It is an underwater ship, an underboat, the vessel of Smegeye the Pirate Slaveer. Your friends will be taken as slaves to Metronis."

"This is indeed good news, Bigvok."

"Good news? How so, Professor?" quizzed Sam.

"It means the others might yet be alive, Sam," laughed the Professor, clapping Sam's shoulder. "And speaking of those still alive, did your spies tell you anything more of my son, Bigvok?"

"Let us just say he is lucky to be alive, Professor."

"Lucky? I don't understand?"

"My daughter's brave subterfuge which allowed you and Captain Blenkinsopp to escape after the rout of Striding Landy was soon discovered by the Brotherhood."

"You mean Rudi talked?"

"No. No. My daughter…." Bigvok's voice faltered, "Rimmi talked."

There was a pause and Bigvok bowed his head. Immediately Nikvok was on his feet and blowing a whalebone horn. The dancing stopped and the room fell silent.

"Please leave us!" called Blatvok.

The dancers flitted from whence they came and the room filled with the sounds of eating utensils being downed and the swish of garments and exiting footfalls.

Bigvok drew a deep breath and closed his eyes when the room was quiet.

"My daughter was killed, Professor."

"My dear old friend," said the Professor, leaning forward to lay his palm on Bigvok's forearm.

"She was taken with the other prisoners after Striding Landy. The commanders were put to death in the Arena of Doom, but Rudi was exalted to become Ayesha's son and Rimmi spared to become a slave in the household of Ayesha."

"Her son? How can that be, Bigvok? Do you mean Rudi turned traitor?"

"No. No. Do not judge Rudi harshly, Professor. Ayesha is a powerful sorceress-queen. It is not for nothing men hail her as 'She-We-Obey'. Rudi is under Ayesha's spell. His bizarre fortune was a result of an ancient prophecy that speaks of the return of Ayesha's long lost son, Arnakk. Ayesha believed Rudi to be Arnakk. Here look at this." Bigvok passed the Professor a discoloured Atlantean coin.

The Professor turned it over and examined the Obverse.

"My goodness, Bigvok. That is an image of Rudi!"

"It might look like Rudi, Professor, but that coin is a thousand years old at least. That is the head of Ayesha's real lost son Arnakk. Legend tells that Arnakk was seduced into

134

captivity by an enemy warrior princess called Malki, and he would return to Ayesha as a prisoner to take his rightful place as her heir. After the battle of Striding Landy, Ayesha discovered Rudi among the prisoners of war. She was convinced by his uncanny likeness that he was her lost son, Arnakk, returned."

A tear filled the Professor's eye.

"I remember Striding Landy well, and Rudi's loss, my friend."

"Our last attempt to rid the earth of Atlantean tyranny," said Bigvok.

"So, Ayesha *is* over a thousand years old after all."

"Nobody knows, I must say you don't sound surprised, Professor."

"As you said, Bigvok, she is a sorceress."

"Yes, a powerful witch-queen. Anyway, after you and your crew escaped, Ayesha was in fury. It took the sorceress and the Brotherhood of the Green Dragon little time torturing other prisoners of Striding Landy to discover Rimmi's false trail that bought you and Captain Blenkinsopp the time you needed to escape to your own world. Ayesha was convinced that my lovely Rimmi was her son's seductress, her sworn enemy, the princess Malki. She vowed to make Rimmi confess and beg for death in the torture chamber."

"And did she? Did she torture Rimmi, Bigvok?"

"Yes. But in Ayesha's mind she was torturing Malki. Rimmi broke down and confessed her love for Rudi and begged for mercy. She told Ayesha the truth she did not want to hear. That Rudi was not her son. Rudi, under Ayesha's spell, swore he was Arnakk. Ayesha forced Rimmi to confess falsely that Rudi was really Arnakk and she was Malki, his

135

lover. After that, to prevent Rimmi's love from breaking her spell on your son, Ayesha had my daughter tortured and…"

Bigvok stood and turned and walked away from the Professor.

"Nobody has ever heard from Rimmi again. It must be she that was tortured and killed," whispered Nikvok and Blatvok together.

After a moment regaining his composure, Bigvok turned to address the Professor and Sam.

"The time for grieving the dead is over. The time for helping the living has just begun. You have much to do, Professor and his companion Sam. Your submarine-vessel has fallen-foul of Smegeye the pirate Slaveer. And Blenkinsopp and your friends will be taken to Metronis to be sold into slavery to work in the Mines of Tor or killed in the Circus pit or worse still taken to undergo mutation in the House of Pain. We will help you all we can, but you must hurry. Time to rescue your friends is rapidly running out."

Chapter 31

The Chamber of Terror

"Do something!" screamed Lu.

The angry red eyes widened and the cave echoed with snorts and charging hoof beats.

"Toby's right, the stun-guns are out of power," cried Bill, uselessly squeezing the trigger. The outline of Old Boar became a charging silhouette against a dull pulsating red glow from deeper inside the cave. The glow grew stronger until they could see the whites of Old Boar's eyes and plumes of wet breath from his mouth and flaring nostrils.

Instinctively Lu reached out to hold Bill's hand.

"Look at the stun-guns!" shouted Toby, "The power dials are shining bright red again!"

"Something's recharged them. Fire everybody!"

A crackling red plasma stream zigzagged through the gloom and Old Boar lit up like a Christmas tree. The cave smelled of singeing hair and cooking flesh and flickering shadows danced up the craggy cave walls as Big Boar's boiling body fat burst into flames.

"Wow!" whooped Lu. "Whatever it is that's recharged the stun guns has recharged me too. I feel GREAT!"

"Come on. This place stinks. Let's get out of here," coughed Bill. He shielded his eyes and stepped around the bloated spitting carcass on the cave floor.

"At least we don't need torches," he said as they rounded a corner where the cave narrowed to a high ceilinged tunnel. The light from the cave had turned from bright red to a constant pale yellow.

"Look. Something's been carved into the rock here," said Lu, stooping to make out what it was. "It looks like the letters 'R.S.'."

"RS could stand for Rudi Schroder?" answered Bill.

"Whoever. We'd better keep the stun-guns ready in case they're like everything else round here - unfriendly," said Toby.

As they went on, they saw the source of the eerie light was from glowing crystals embedded in the cave walls, ceiling, and floor. The crystals brightened as they approached and, like snuffed candles, went out after they passed.

"These crystals are so cool," said Lu. "I wish I had a necklace of them."

"They're certainly pretty handy if your stun-gun needs charging," replied Bill.

"Yeah, they seem to be an energy source of some kind. And *we* seem to activate them. Maybe they work telepathically? I mean when we needed the stun-guns recharged we prayed for energy to charge them and the crystals went red and the guns recharged. Then we needed light, and we thought 'we need light' and the crystals read our thoughts and started glowing yellow so we can see," observed Toby.

"Come on you two. Let's try and find a way out of here," said Bill, leading the way further into the crystal-lit cave.

The debris-strewn path began sloping down and where it did so the walls ran with water, the air temperature rose and soon the air thickened with a faint unhealthy odour of rotting.

"Smells like those pigs again," said Lu, as she pinched her nose.

"Keep your eyes peeled," warned Bill. He raised his stun-gun ready to fire.

Crouching, they entered a small dark natural doorway in the rock.

"Watch your step," said Bill, "There's a hole in the floor."

The hole supported several human thigh bones spliced together with black leather straps in the form of a cross, across its diameter. A coarse homemade rope tied around its centre disappeared into the darkness of the hole.

"Signs of civilisation?" whispered Toby.

Grunts, growls and snorts and rustlings and the sounds of things being dragged wafted up through the hole, borne on the thickening vapours of rotting flesh.

"You're not seriously suggesting we go down that rope are you, Bill Young?" said Lu.

"I don't think we have a choice, Lu. There's no other way."

Bill stepped over the hole to run his hands over the shadowy rock wall six feet beyond. "No. It's a dead end. Nothing but solid rock. The cave definitely ends here."

"But if those noises down there are pigs, how did they get up here?" quizzed Toby. "Surely they didn't climb this old rope."

"Impossible! Maybe they're different pigs?" suggested Bill.

"Or knowing this place, they're not pigs at all but something horrible!" said Lu.

"They sound like pigs to me. There must be another way down," said Toby.

"Well let's find it then. Anything's better than that smelly hole!" replied Lu.

"I agree with Toby. There probably is another way down, but what if it's in another cave altogether? We've been sealed in here by the rock fall, remember?" said Bill, "Whether we like it or not this dodgy old rope appears to be our only way forward. Now who's lightest?"

Toby and Lu looked nervously at one another, knowing full well what the next question was going to be.

"Me," replied Toby gloomily.

Bill smiled and nodded and pulling up a length of rope handed the slack to Toby.

"Sorry Toby. You first then."

Taking the rope, Toby sat nervously on the edge of the hole.

"We don't know how good the rope is. Take as much of your weight off it as you can as you go down. Wedge yourself between your feet on one side of the hole and your back on the other and sort of walk down backwards using the rope as a hand-hold," suggested Bill.

"Yeah right," said Toby easing himself over the edge and out of sight down the creaking rope.

"Poo! It's really rank down here," echoed his voice from below.

"Shout when you reach the bottom, Toby!"

"I will if the rope's long enough to reach the bottom."

They waited anxiously for five minutes.

"I do hope he's alright, Bill," said Lu anxiously.

"Hey guys! I'm at the bottom!"

"There you are. He is ok, Lu. WHAT'S IT LIKE DOWN THERE? ANY PIGS, TOBY?"

"Can't see much it's too dark! Ooer! I can hear things moving about though."

"HANG ON WE'RE COMING DOWN!"

Reunited at the bottom of the rope, they found themselves in a similar small rock chamber to the one at the top.

"Through there?" said Bill.

Toby nodded, "It's the only way."

They bent double through another low arch and found themselves in a gloomy place with a domed roof like St Paul's Cathedral. Dim daylight shone gloomily from the centre of the dome, fanning out to light a massive pit and cast eerie shadows over a dark pyramid rising from its centre. They were standing on an uneven path behind a low wall that circled the pit carved from the native rock.

"The stink's terrible in here, Bill. OH MY GOD!" exclaimed Lu, pointing to the point of the pyramid. "It's a massive pile of dead bodies."

"Ugh. I think I'm going to be SICK!" gulped Toby retching and clamping his hand over his mouth.

"Did you see that? Something moved at the top of the pile," said Bill, pointing up to where the light through the ceiling caught the fleeting movement of a crouching figure.

"Look! It disappeared down the other side of the mound. Come on. Whatever it is, it might lead us to a way out."

Drawing their stun guns they began following the pathway around the pyramid of bodies. As they made their way to the far side of the mound, their path became littered with dismembered body parts and bones and they found several caves carved into the rock wall of the cavern.

Encountering each cave, Bill would manoeuvre his way, with his back to the rock face, to the edge of each entrance. Then with his stun gun poised and in one movement, he swung to face the dark interior ready to blast anything that might leap out from inside. Each of the caves was shallow, about ten feet deep with a dead end, and each was littered with bones and old sacking formed into strange nests.

Approaching the fourth opening, they heard a low grunting. Turning his head back towards the others, Bill placed his finger across his lips for quiet. Inch by inch he approached the cave mouth. The grunting became a ripping sound and then a crunching and noisy chewing. Bill turned to face the wall and peeked around the edge into the cave.

Inside, lit dimly by residues of light from the roof-light in the chamber ceiling, something crouching was chewing and slavering like an animal. Sensing it was being watched the creature looked up. An age-lined grimy human face with a sickly cream complexion, the nose of a pig and lifeless coal-black human eyes met their horrified gaze. The eyes looked like the lifeless staring sockets of a silver Nazi death's head badge glinting on a threadbare forage cap perched on the creature's greasy, unkempt strands of black hair. The monster began sniffing the air and almost immediately its beady eyes lighted on Bill. Bill froze on the spot, waiting for what ever it was to attack. But it just stared through him. It growled revealing jaws of coarse brown-stained-tooth-stumps clogged with bits of dead flesh from a roughly severed human leg it had been gnawing.

"What's in there?" whispered Lu into Bill's ear. The creature pricked up its pink pointed ears and scuttled forward out of the darkness. It was then Bill saw the true extent of the abomination. The creature had the torso of a man. Grotesquely exaggerated musculature defined by filth ingrained in its skin was visible through holes in a tattered black Nazi SS tunic. The creature's naked lower body, legs, and trotters were those of a massive sow.

"Guten tag," grunted the creature.

"We're English," replied Bill.

"Ach! Ja! Good day then, Old Chap!" replied the pig-man edging closer to Bill, Lu and Toby. "Haff you seen Big Boar? He is the bane of my life!" A snot-bubble inflated and deflated from its left nostril, "I apologise I look a mess," it continued, sniffing and applying a hasty smear of blood-red lipstick in an attempt to smarten itself up.

"We killed Big Boar. He attacked us," said Toby.

"So there is another way out of here," added Bill.

"Ja! Natürlich…I mean, of course, Junge! Would you like me to tell you where it is? I'll come closer and whisper in your ear."

Instinctively the friends backed away.

"Ach. Don't be like that. I von't hurt you," cooed the pig-man edging closer.

"We've got company," murmured Toby, looking over his shoulder to where several other pig-men were jostling up behind them.

"FRESH MEAT!" panted the first creature, saliva dripping from its mouth. Suddenly and without warning the monsters lunged grabbing wildly at them with their filthy long-nailed hands.

"RUN!" shouted Bill taking several hurried pot-shots but missing.

"Run where?" replied Lu.

"Erm. Up there?" Bill was pointing to the circular hole in the roof of the cavern.

"What? Over all those dead bodies!" cried Lu.

"There's no other way!" said Bill, and he vaulted the low wall and scrambled over cracking arms and legs, crunching heads, breaking jaws and squishing eyeballs in the pyramid of bodies. The others followed.

"Come back!" growled the pig-man leaping like a demonic steeplechaser over the low wall and bounding up the body pile behind them. The faster they tried to run, the more the bodies broke beneath their feet. Toby's toe got stuck in a gaping mouth and he stopped momentarily to shake it off.

"Aghhhhh! THE THING! It's got my LEG!" he screamed.

"Give me your hand Toby," called Lu, and she clambered back down the slope to grab a handful of Toby's sleeve.

"Fresh meat!" bellowed the creature, its eyes rolling and its fingers grasping Toby's ankle to pull him down into the pack. For a moment a frantic tug of war ensued until Lu screamed, "Let him go you monster!" and she loosed a jagged red plasma stream from her stun gun that sent the grimacing creature pitching and rolling down the slope of bodies to lie motionless in the middle of the rock path below.

"Quick, Lu. Give me your hands," called Bill. He'd clambered out from the body pit and was reaching for her through the hole in the ceiling.

"Here. Catch this first!" replied Lu, throwing her stun gun to Bill.

"Ouch it's hot!"

Lu was about to joke and call him a wimp, but reaching up for Bill to pull her out, she decided now was probably not the right time.

In an instant Lu was beside Bill. They were in another dimly lit cavern with a single railway track that stopped at buffers at the edge of the hole and led off into the darkness of a tunnel. Twenty feet above their heads was a chimney of rock, with distant blue daylight at its end.

Bill hugged Lu and looking up she kissed him. After what seemed a glorious age Bill pulled himself away and shouted, "Oh no! We've forgotten, Toby! Quick. Give me your hands, Toby!"

Toby was desperately firing plasma streams at grasping pig-men, so enraged at the death of their comrade they charged from all sides in an all-out frenzy.

Suddenly the red of Toby's plasma faded to watery yellow and all he could do was click away on the useless trigger.

Seeing his chance, the biggest of the pig men leapt forward knocking Toby off balance. In an instant the boy was rolling down the body-mound, tangled in a morbid tango with slimy disintegrating corpses and the biting, growling, grasp of the stinking pig man.

Chapter 32

The Seer's Summons

The rest of Metronis were sleeping when young Prince Arnakk entered the garden of the Temple of the Crystal Pyramid. Shouldering the heavy gates closed behind him, he walked in moonlight towards the dark yew forest before him where a steep path wound its way to the Crystal Pyramid at the mountain's summit.

Climbing the path, the moonlight was extinguished by the dense canopy of trees, and removing the Vril pendant from its chain around his neck, he held it up. Immediately the pendant glowed bright orange lighting the forest path by a streaming yellow beam. Arnakk shivered and hurried along. The night air was chilly and Ayesha did not smile on tardiness.

Only the privileged few had access to the Crystal Pyramid: the high priests of the Brotherhood of the Green Dragon, his mother Ayesha, her servants, the handmaidens of the Crystal Temple, and on rare occasions Arnakk himself.

At the far fringe of the wood the boy prince stopped for a moment at the foot of a wide black marble staircase leading to the vast glittering pyramid. The giant crystal high above the temple was pale now the city's demand for its force had diminished.

In the crystal's resting glow Arnakk could see clearly the glassy pyramid's front begin to ripple, as if it had turned to a liquid into which someone had thrown a pebble. Hurrying up the final steps and striding over a terrace, he stepped through the centre of the 'rippling' glass which 'healed' itself to solid once he passed through.

Before him the bull-headed statue of the king of all Atlantean gods, Taurax, glowered down at him from one hundred feet. At once Arnakk knelt before the great statue, for any distant memory of Jehovah had long dimmed. After several moments of prayer he glanced over his shoulder at the sound of approaching footsteps.

A small robed and hooded messenger stopped before him, and after bowing to the statue, she turned and said, "My Lord, Arnakk. She-We-Obey awaits you."

The soft voice was powerfully compelling. This one was trained in the use of 'the voice'.

"Please. Come with me, my lord."

Arnakk rose and followed the handmaiden through a square linteled doorway in the shadow of Taurax. Together they walked fifty more paces through a roughly-hewn tunnel into a cavern with smooth orange marble walls soaring upwards to the point of a second hollow pyramid.

The vast interior was lit by a hellish red glow and in the far distance, at the far end of an ornately mosaic tiled and columned aisle, hung a high golden curtain.

"We should kneel, my Lord," cautioned the messenger in a whisper. Both knelt, and as they did so, the golden curtains slowly parted to reveal a great raised dais with a shimmering heat haze and writhing ribbons of yellow vapour rising from its surface.

"Come to me, Arnakk," commanded a distant female voice, "and tarry not lest ye burn, my son."

With the grating of stone, a narrow bridge, the width of a large man's foot-length, appeared through the heat haze, leading through the sulphurous vapours to the far side of the dais.

With a bow the messenger nodded reverently to Arnakk, and shuffled away backwards to leave the cave.

Putting one foot onto the narrow bridge, the young prince felt a scalding updraught from a lake of boiling lava seventy feet down a rocky volcanic chimney.

Stepping like a tightrope walker, one foot directly before the other and arms outstretched for balance, Arnakk heeded his mother's advice by crossing quickly without looking down or stumbling. The hem of his soldier's tunic ruffled in the eddies of searing heat and the hairs on his naked calves, below his red leather britches, curled and singed.

On reaching the far side of the bridge Arnakk paused to brush off the stinging dead skin and cremated hairs above his sandals. He peered through the thick red gloom to a flight of marble steps disappearing up though an ornately carved stone arch to a red velvet platform and a softly glowing golden throne beyond.

"Come," bade the woman's voice from the shadows beyond the arch. As Arnakk climbed the final steps, She emerged from a dark doorway behind the throne.

The young prince at once dropped to one knee before her, and she smiled and offered her slender pale hand for him to kiss.

"Come sit with me," she said pointing to a low stool beside the throne. And after seating herself, she began caressing the curve of his head and stroking his hair.

"What adventures has my handsome prince been on since last we met? I see you have the Killing Staff of a warrior now, Arnakk."

"Yes mother. Master Nicademus granted me warrior status last week," replied Arnakk proudly.

"Hah!" cried Ayesha, "my clever son! And has Nicademus blooded ye?"

"No mother. Not yet. He is taking us all to the slave auction to pick our proving-slaves next week."

"It worries ye not that ye will slay slaves to be proven, Arnakk?"

"Nay, my mother. What are Xenodes for, if not to provide sport, labour, and entertainment?"

"Spoken like a true son of Atlantis. And it is the slave auction I wish to speak with thee about, Arnakk."

"Mother?"

"Ye know of the arrival of Smegeye the pirate slaveer?"

"Of course, mother," laughed Arnakk. "Everyone does. Nicademus promised to reward all Military School graduates with a Proving Combat with six slaves of our own choosing each! I can't wait. I'll slice and chop them into pig feed!"

"Yes. Yes. I'm sure you will. But I have something more important to talk to you about, Arnakk."

"What could be MORE important than my Blooding in the Circus, mama?" replied Arnakk with a resentful pout.

Ayesha smiled and leaning forward, kissed his cheek. "Come, my Handsome Prince. Do not be sullen. Your time in the Arena with your new Killing Staff will come soon enough. I will see to it."

149

"But mama!"

Her blow to his cheek stung him into silence. He wanted to speak but knew better than to question further the High Priestess of Taurax. He flinched as the hitting hand extended a second time, but this time the cooling balm of her healing touch soothed his cheek and he looked up into her eyes now warm with love.

"You forget yourself sometimes, Arnakk," she whispered stroking his hair. He ventured to speak, but fearful of her quicksilver temper remained silent.

"Taurax has spoken a grave warning to me, Arnakk," she continued. "He has sensed evil within the bowels of the slaveer's great serpent and warns me of an Overworlder once known to me."

"Who, Mama?"

"One known as Podesta Blenkinsopp."

"Is he not but a harmless captive, mother?" said Arnakk, after plucking up courage.

"Aye, he is. But 'tis one who will be near, whose whereabouts is unknown to me. He is the menace."

"What then is the danger, mother?"

"It is beyond your ken, Arnakk. It hails from a time long ago, when two tribes of men arrived from the war-torn Overworld to steal from us our sacred Vril. Each tribe desired the force to overcome and enslave the other. These men bought with them their war, but their undersea boats and weapons were crude and easily defeated by the warriors of Brotherhood of the Green Dragon. Taurax has spoken of several who will now come. One is dangerous, and he is called The Professor. The Professor and Podesta Blenkinsopp are in league and once before, in another life, they escaped my grasp aided by the lies and deception of another. The others who come are the Professor's followers who are unknown to me. And yet others who are the descendants of the Nazi tribe."

"Then why have they returned? Surely not to relish the bitter taste of defeat a second time, Mama?"

"The children of the Nazis seek only to harness and steal Vril for their own evil ends."

"And the Professor? Does he seek Vril for evil too?"

The witch queen hung her head, slowly shaking it in sadness.

"Nay. He comes only for thee and once he has thee he means to destroy me and the crystals of Vril."

"If he thinks he will parade me through the streets of the Overworld as a trophy of your destruction, Mama, he is a deluded fool. Master Nicademus and Master Bracclades, the imperial Houscarls and - above all - I will protect thee!"

"Nay. Do not dismiss him glibly. He is a worthy opponent. He is a scholar of the ancient scriptures. He understands intimately our laws and beliefs as if he is a native of Atlantis and unlike our warriors he is versed in all three of the ancient Vril magics needed for destruction, healing and mind manipulation. He is every bit as skilled in these arts as any Atlantean High Priest."

Ayesha paused to kiss the boy's forehead.

"Now my son. This is what I want you to do."

Chapter 33

The Slave Auction

Wendy shivered despite the afternoon sun. The ornately embellished black marble buildings and god-statues of the Plaza, shone with a soft leaden lustre.

In contrast to the stately temples to commerce and gods unknown, the cobbles of the vast square on which they now walked were a hard quartz-like crystal, which after dark, radiated soft yellow light from a luminous substrate that softly splashed the columns, façades and civic ornaments of the piazza with dripping gold.

Stu limped and Farouke helped Podesta Blenkinsopp who was feeling the effects of the sun after their long forced-march from docks.

The unkind aroma of barbecuing meat wafted through the milling crowd from a nearby street vendor's stall. Wendy's stomach ached and to her embarrassment she belched loudly a reminder that none of them had eaten for ages.

"Oh. I beg your pardon," she said blushing up at Mike.

"Granted," he replied smiling.

The delicious smell reminded her of their helplessness. Back home at a fun fair or a concert or on a daytrip to the seaside she would send Bill off with money to buy a hotdog or burger as a treat. Here the smell reminded her she had no money and for all she knew no son either. Here they were prisoners herded by Sabre Tooths toward a rough wooden corral in the shadow of a squat open-fronted building with high spiked gates and a domed tower. The tower was decorated with a golden dial set with strange silver symbols inlaid around its circumference.

"Anyway, I wonder what's cooking?" ventured Mike.

"Yummy, fresh meat!" growled a passing Sabre Tooth. His Vril Staff was tucked under his arm and he offered an open waxy wrapper with an unleavened bread envelope stuffed with piping hot cubes of barbequed meat.

"Oh! Thank you," said Wendy, and as she reached to take a piece of meat, the Sabre Tooth snatched the parcel away and walked off roaring with laughter.

"Why YOU!" shouted Mike before Wendy could stop him.

The Sabre Tooth turned brandishing his Vril Staff.

"I'm sorry," cried Wendy, "he didn't mean that."

"Too late!" snarled the Sabre Tooth spitting gobs of meat and bread as he levelled his staff at Mike.

"STOP!"

A whip crack and the sea salt smell of ozone stopped the Sabre Tooth in its tracks. The Sabre Tooth dropped to his knees.

"Forgive me, sire," he mumbled touching the quartz cobbles with his forehead in front of Smegeye's enormous boots.

"Get up. Dolt! What were my orders about the female?"

The Sabre Tooth dropped his gaze in shame.

"Move on," ordered Smegeye, and the frightened line of chained slaves shuffled chinking into the stockade.

153

The instant their backs were turned, Wendy flinched at the sudden crack of Smegeye's whip. Behind them the gagging carks of the choking Sabre Tooth and a ghastly stink of burning flesh made the hairs on the back of her neck stand on end.

Wendy twined her arm through Mike's, only to be roughly separated by another snarling Sabre Tooth.

"Females over there!" it barked jabbing with its Vril staff to a tattered group of women cowering at the far side of the corral.

"MOVE!"

Looking over her shoulder, Wendy watched as Mike, Stu, Farouke and Podesta Blenkinsopp were prodded into reluctant ranks with the other scowling men.

Smegeye, hands on hips, and Peebody Fiddler stood aloft on a scaffold surveying the fidgeting pool of misery below them. With a pronounced nod, the big pirate signalled for the main gates of the enclosure to be closed and for a door at the side of the staging to be opened.

At once a clamouring crowd of well-fed Atlanteans adorned with grotesque face-makeup and silk and finery and clasping fat silk purses in jewelled fat fingers, jostled onto the platform to inspect the slaves on display.

One figure stood out from the rest. He turned his scar drawn face to Smegeye and called out, "What have you for me and the Circus today, my lord, Smegeye?"

Like Smegeye, Scarface was tall, a leader of his clan and clad in a studded leather jerkin and the lambskin britches and blade-shod ankle sandals of a Murmillo gladiator.

"Those two will be quite feisty enough for you, Bracclades," roared Smegeye, pointing at Mike and Stu with the butt of his whip.

"But this one's no more than a snotty BOY!" laughed Bracclades, descending the steps to cast his shadow over Stu, and tweak his ear.

"Ow! Gerroff you ugly great GIT!" yelled Stu, forced to dance on tiptoe by this sneering, unshaven tormentor.

"Leave the boy alone! If you want to pick on someone pick on a MAN!" snarled Mike, glowering at Scarface.

"Oh I will, Slave. I will if I see one. And be ye MAN enough to face the Wiggleon in the Arena of Doom or shall I drink your brains in broth you insolent whelp?"

"You might if you bid well enough for him, Bracclades!" laughed Smegeye.

"Who will dare to bid against Bracclades the *Lanista?* Who would deprive the good citizens of Metronis their sport in the Arena of Doom?" boomed Bracclades glowering back defiantly at the tight lipped crowd of tender-palmed bidders. "Mush, all of them! Flabby mush!"

"Silence!" came a shout from the podium accompanied by the crack of a falling hammer, "IfitpleaseseveryoneI'llstarttheauctionNOW!"

A tall thin man holding a whalebone gavel in a pinstripe toga with a bright purple silk hanky blooming from the breast pocket was standing centre stage. He rocked back and forth on his sandals waiting for hush. After a few moments, but for a few coughs you could hear a pin drop.

"Bringforththefirstlot!" cried the auctioneer, peering and pointing at Wendy with his gavel.

The Slave Auction

At once two attendants in plain brown togas ushered Wendy and stood either side of her on the stage.

"AfinefecundefemaleOverworlder!Wouldmakeanideal pleasureslave!Whowillstartmeoffat50Lanteens?"

The auctioneer's black, beady eyes swept the audience until his experienced gaze fell on a fat man wearing black lipstick, involuntarily squeezing his money pouch.

"YouSir!Makemeanoffer.Sheispleasingtotheeyewithag orgeousfigureisshenot?Comedon'tbeshythinkofthepleasureyou 'llhave,sir!"

"Fifteen Lanteens!" came a shout from the back.

"Comecomeshe'sworthmorethanthatsurely?Justlookatt hefinestronglegsandprettyfeatures!"

The fat man with black lipstick jangled his pouch.

"ThankyouSir.20Lanteenswhowillbidme25?Whowillbi dme25,whowillbidme25?" shouted the auctioneer, pointing at the fat man with his gavel once more.

"Twenty five!" came the voice from the back.

"Thankyousir!"

The fat man jangled his pouch again.

"30Lanteensfromthefloor!"

"Thirty five Lanteens!" shouted the voice from the back.

"Anyadvanceon35Lanteens?Anyadvanceon35?" cried the auctioneer, eyeing the fat man.

"I'll give you forty!" yelled a third voice in the front row.

"Anewbidderinthefront!Who'llbidme45,45,45?"

The fat man went to jangle his pouch but thought better of it.

"Anyaddvanceon40Lanteens?"

Silence prevailed.

"Anymoreforanymore? Going!Going…"

"STOP THE AUCTION!"

A body of heavily armed soldiers, blonde tresses flowing out from under pewter coloured helms, and wearing the ornate metal of Royal Houscarls, were forcing a swath through the startled audience.

The soldiers parted into ranks and Arnakk came into view. Of similar age to Bill, Toby, and Stu, he emerged in flushing armour with a tall grey haired armour-clad man of about fifty at his side. The boy stood with feet apart and slowly removed a purple horse-hair plumed helmet and tucked it under his arm.

At once everyone in the stockade dropped to one knee, every head bowed in deference.

The boy's gaze quickly combed the ranks of slaves.

"Bow," hissed Podesta Blenkinsopp to Mike, Stu, and Farouke.

A barely perceptible smile crept over the boy's lips noting the last three standing.

"Do get up, Master Smegeye. I can't transact business with a hunchback."

The boy waited for Smegeye to stand.

"Our dockside Tallymen inform us you have some Overworlders within today's shipment of Xenodes."

"Aye, Sire. Especially rare these days, simpered Smegeye"

"Oh, yes! Especially *right* rare, Your Highness," echoed Peebody Fiddler.

"Silence, Pus-Sucker, or I'll slice your legs off," growled the grey haired man at the boy's side.

Peebody Fiddler cowered behind Smegeye's head and something semi-liquid slapped on the ground.

"Rare, Master Smegeye?" retorted the boy.

"Aye, right rare, Sire."

"Commanding a *rare* price no doubt."

Smegeye shrugged and cast a sly glance in Bracclades' direction.

"Aye, Sire. And there are *other* interested parties."

Peebody Fiddler ventured a smug look at the boy from behind Smegeye's right ear.

"Don't even think about it, Pus-Sucker," snapped the boy's companion, his eyes narrowing.

"I trust the relevant transit permits have been obtained and import duties for this *especially* rare cargo paid, Master Smegeye?" said the boy.

There was a pregnant silence.

"Well?"

"We have an arrangement with the imperial Tallymen, Sire," babbled Smegeye wringing its warty claws.

"Oh?"

"Yes, Sire. They are happy for us to sell our cargo and pay the transit duties from the sale proceeds. It helps with cash-flow you understand?"

"Forgive me, Master Smegeye. But your little arrangement doesn't seem to 'help', as you put it, the royal cash-flow much, does it?"

"But it is but for the merest hint of time, Sire."

"And what, I wonder; might the amount of duty be for such a 'right rare' cargo? Rather more than an ordinary one, I daresay. What say you Master Tallyman?"

A small robed figure with a tallyboard pushed its way through the towering ranks of Houscarls.

"Tis a moot point Sire. The cargo becomes the lawful property of the Crown if it is taken beyond the docks with duty unpaid."

"Thank you, Master Tallyman. You may go."

The Tallyman scuttled off from whence he came and the boy turned to face Smegeye with both palms raised and an expression of mock helplessness.

"According to the Tallyman it appears you forfeit your cargo to the Crown on this occasion, my Lord."

"WHY YOU LITTLE...!"

The grey-haired man's hand hovered over the hilt of his broadsword.

"Tut. Tut. Remember my Mother's years of benevolent patronage if you value your life, your tongue, and your fat monopoly, Master Slave-Trader," said the boy. "And fear not. I am only interested in the Overworlders. You may keep the remainder of your booty for the Circus. Now, my Lord! Let us remain friends. I shall overlook your boorish manners this once. You may kneel and kiss my ring."

An ugly hush fell over the corral. It was finally broken by Smegeye.

"As always you are *too* gracious, Sire," he hissed through gritted fangs, and kneeling he kissed the boy's outstretched hand.

"What about the girl I've just paid 40 Lanteens for?" shouted the voice in the front row.

"SorrySirthegaveldidnotfall!Nosale!Nosale!She'sCrownproperty." said the auctioneer with a shrug of his shoulders.

"General Nicademus. I will leave you to round up the Overworlders and take them back to the palace," said the prince to his companion, "Oh, except for the one named Podesta Blenkinsopp. Take him to Doctor Grimus in The House of Pain."

The older man nodded his grey head gravely, "As you command, Sire."

Chapter 34

The Pig Man's Tale

"I'm going down to get Toby!" cried Bill, pulling himself from Lu's arms and dropping back through the hole in the chamber ceiling. Landing up to his knees in bodies, Bill aimed his stun-gun at the nearest of the pig-men, a snarling creature wearing torn navy blue overalls.

"Take that, you brute!" hissed Bill through gritted teeth, squeezing his trigger to loose a crackling bright red stream into the monster's chest.

With a scream the stricken pig-man, sheathed in a red energy-glow, fell back and grabbing wildly in the air with its human hands took down one of its fellows with it. The second pig man, as if infected by red plasma travelling through the grasping hand of the first, began glowing too.

"Here, Bill! Catch!" called Lu, tossing her stun-gun down to Bill.

"Thanks," returned Bill, and with a stun-gun in each hand he began clambering down the body-mound blasting over the heads of the remaining pig men as they fled.

Toby was in the grasp of the biggest; a monster of a thing on hind legs with one of its massive human forearms clamped tightly around Toby's throat. One of the creature's eyes was covered by a black patch and below its twitching pig nose an unlit cigar stub poked from its filthy clenched teeth. As Bill approached it snarled, dragging Toby backwards.

161

"Why don't you kill us all, Junge? It vould be kinder," said the pig man, tightening his grip around Toby's throat.

"Let him go!" cried Bill, levelling a stun gun at the pig man's eye patch. The pig man released its grip.

"Boy am I glad to see you!" spluttered Toby.

"Here take this!" Bill, handed Toby a stun gun and pulled him beyond the reach of the one-eyed pig man.

"Come on. Let's get out of here before they regroup and come after us!" said Toby. The other pig men were already recovering their nerve, and beginning to stalk them. The nearest charged and in panic Toby shot it.

Grabbing its own throat, the creature shrouded in red fire grimaced as smoke bellowed from its pig nostrils. It sank to its knees spluttering for breath and all watched in terror as, amid a throbbing glow, it went into a hideous seizure and slowly transmogrified into the dying shape of an old man.

"Toby! It's a MAN! You've killed a MAN!"

"I, I don't understand," sobbed Toby. "They're flesh-eating pig monsters aren't they?"

"Nein! Ve are men. At least ve were men before…" The one-eyed pig man's voice trailed away.

"Before what? What happened to you? Who are you? What are you?" cried Bill, shaking the muzzle of his stun gun.

"My name is Kapitänleutnant 'Jericho' Lansberg. I am Commandant of U-Boat X19 and my serial number is…"

"U-Boat?" interrupted Bill. "What do you mean U-Boat?"

"You remember old Pilsbury going on about U-Boats in History don't you, Bill?"

"Of course. But how can we be chatting to a U-Boat captain who's a cross between a man and a pig, years after the Second World War has ended?"

"Wie bitte? Excuse me? The war. It is over?"

"Yes, Captain. Today we learn about it in school," replied Toby.

"Who won?"

"I'm afraid we did, Herr Lansberg," said Bill, trying at least to soften the blow by *sounding* sympathetic.

"Don't be afraid, junge! Das ist GUT!"

"Good? You mean you're not upset?" said Bill.

"Nein! No of course not. We were submariners before the Nazis. Most of us detest the jumped-up Nazis and all they stand for."

"Stood for," corrected Bill.

"Und Hitler? Vot happened to Herr Hitler?"

"Dead," said the boys together.

"Hey BOYS! Hitler is Dead!"

The curious pig men began drawing in closer to hear the news until Bill cried, "That's far enough. Stay where you are."

Jericho Lansberg signalled for his crew to stay put.

"So why are you like...?" asked Toby, not wanting to use the pig word.

"Why are we like pigs, you mean, Junge? We were captured by the Atlanteans," replied the Captain. "You think the Nazis were bad? Boy, wait 'til you meet the Atlanteans. They are two hundred times worse! And I mean at least two hundred times worse! All Foreigners in Atlantis are made into

163

slaves. The lucky ones serve in Atlantean households as servants or entertainers, or if they have skills and can learn about Atlantean technology they become scientific assistants in the Atlantean Discovery Guilds to work for mad scientists. The unlucky ones go to the crystal mines of Tor, to extract Vril crystals. They are worked until they drop."

"And what about you?" said Bill, almost dreading the pig man's answer.

"Ve were extra unlucky! Ve were taken to the House of Pain for modification. Sometimes, you see, ze Atlanteans need slaves for specific tasks. Some need super-human strength - they would be modified by combining with bulls, or elephants or some other powerful beast for lives of intense heavy manual labour. We have been modified to scavenge. We eat the slaves who die in the mines."

"Ugh!" cried Toby. "That's disgusting!"

The pig man's one eye dropped in shame.

"Ach, I know, Junge. My mother would turn in her grave at the thought of her son in this sorry state. But pigs will eat anything from brains to old boots you know?"

"Can the process that turned you into pig men be reversed?" said Bill.

"Only Dr. Grimus in the House of Pain would know that, Junge."

"Dr. Grimus. Who's he?" asked Bill.

"She. Dr. Grimus is a voman. It is she who turns human slaves into part-animal monsters…."

"It's gone very quiet. Are you two okay?" called Lu from the edge of the hole in the chamber ceiling.

164

"Fine! We'll be up in a minute," called Bill, and offering his hand, somewhat against his better judgment, shook the pig man's big human hand.

"Well, it's been nice chatting with you, Mr Lansberg, but I think we should go now. We are trying to find my mum and our friends."

"I can't say I wouldn't like to pull you in and chew off your flesh and grind your bones," replied the pig man, gripping Bill's hand rather too firmly for Bill's liking, "but then I have the manners and appetite of a pig, you understand. You have brought us such good news about the war and, like a weight that's been suddenly lifted, we can at least be happy that perhaps the winter of human misery in our dear homeland has at last thawed. Auf wiedersehen. If I can call you my friends, good British luck finding those you seek."

***

"Those poor men," said Lu, after the boys explained to her the pig man's story. "Can we help them do you think?"

"Maybe after we've found mum and the others. The only person who might know how to turn them back into humans is Dr. Grimus."

"Sounds creepy," said Lu.

"Yeah," said Toby, "and get this Lu…*She* hangs out in The House of Pain!"

"We haven't got time to worry about the pig men now," said Bill. "We need to find the others. Come on let's follow this railway track. It might lead us out of here."

"What about up there?" cried Toby pointing to the source of the daylight.

"Think we'd need ropes and crampons to get up there," replied Bill. He gouged a glowing light crystal from the wall of the cave with his knife, and holding it aloft he started walking along the railway track.

They hadn't gone far when they all felt a rumbling through the rails. In the distance was a shaking yellow light that grew larger and brighter as the rumbling increased. They felt a warm wind and soon they saw it was a railway truck approaching them at speed.

"Quick! Over there," cried Bill, shining his crystal at a small alcove carved into the wall of the tunnel.

"I've seen little hidey-holes like this for railway workers," said Toby, remembering a ride through a tunnel lit for maintenance work on the Underground once. He couldn't resist peeking out and Bill grabbed his boiler suit and pulled him back as the tunnel suddenly bleached with light from a single crystal lantern at the front of a train of several trucks clattering by.

The trucks were spilling over with the jogging rigid limbs of corpses whose grey and ashen faces stared lifelessly into space. Huge bull-like creatures with tiny human heads on massive muscular shoulders filled footplates at the rears of the trucks, and as the train approached a bend they wrenched on brake levers making the wheels squeal and showers of sparks fly into the dark.

"More of Dr. Grimus's disgusting handiwork?" enquired Lu as they left the alcove to follow Bill's light along the railway track.

Chapter 35

Podesta's Plight

"Straight from the frying pan into the fire as usual!" said Wendy gloomily as the palace dungeon door slammed shut.

"Enjoy your stay!" guffawed a Sabre Tooth gaoler through the small barred window in the door before he disappeared and his footsteps faded down the long stone corridor.

Mike paced up and down the damp cell for what seemed hours until they heard voices and the gaoler reappeared with General Nicademus and some men from the royal guard.

"Take him," said Nicademus, pointing at Podesta Blenkinsopp. Podesta was dozing with his back propped against the cell wall opposite the door.

Before he could utter a word two burly soldiers had him under each arm and were dragging him out through the dungeon door.

"Where are you taking him?" cried Wendy as the gaoler slammed the door in her face.

"Remember his good looks, Lady. You won't recognise him when Dr. Grimus has finished with him."

"Who's Dr Grimus?" shouted Wendy after the gaoler. "Where are they taking him, Mike?"

She sank to her knees sobbing.

167

"Dr Grimus is evil and they take your friend to a bad place," said a small soft voice from outside the cell door.

Wendy peered through the barred window.

"I'm down here!"

"Oh Pimpy? Is that you?"

"That is NOT my name as you well know!"

"I'm sorry P..."

"MY NAME is Mook Wundabuck, but Wundabuck will suffice," said the little man inserting his healing Vril staff in the lock to open the door.

"Now they will know I've opened the door. Still, I shall just say I found one of you ill and called in to examine you. Yes, that should satisfy them," muttered the tiny doctor to himself.

"What are you doing here? I thought Smegeye was your master?" said Wendy as Wundabuck entered the cell.

"He is! I've been called here on a stupid fool's errand. One of the pleasure slaves from Smegeye's latest consignment offended a Housecarl. Sometimes it takes new slaves a while to adjust to their new lots in life. No doubt she refused to obey and she reaped one of the most terrible Vril wounds I've ever seen.... The wound was hours old when I got to her and she was already dead. Why they bothered calling me I can't imagine. They know Vril wounds must be dealt with quickly. Still. I suppose it is their right. Under the Atlantean terms of sale for slaves, I am duty-bound to attend the medical needs of any newly-purchased slaves until Smegeye and his villainous crew set sail on another slave-hunt!"

"You said they've taken our friend to a bad place, Mook Wundabuck?" quizzed Mike.

168

"Wundabuck will suffice," corrected the little man. "Yes. A very bad place. Very, very bad indeed! The House of Pain."

"Oh no. What's that!" sobbed Wendy, "I hate this horrible place."

"Tell us. What happens at the House of Pain, Wundabuck?" asked the vet.

"Your friend will be modified. Turned into an animal mutant. You may never see him again, or if you do, you won't recognise him."

"Oh Mike. What can we do? Poor Podesta?" cried Wendy, tears streaming down her cheeks.

Glancing right and left and then over his skinny shoulder, Mook Wundabuck whispered, "Don't lose hope! Now I must go. Walls have ears, you know? Just remember. Don't lose hope!"

Chapter 36

Bad News Travels Fast

"**P**rofessor! Professor!" echoed a voice along the tunnel outside the Professor's quarters.

"In here, Nikvok!" called the Professor. He looked up from the street and sewer maps of Metronis he and Sam were studying to find a way undetected into the palace to rescue Rudi.

"Professor!" panted Nikvok bursting into the room.

"What on earth is the matter, Nikvok?" asked the Professor.

"Terrible news. Terrible news! Captain Blenkinsopp has been taken to the House of Pain."

The Professor at once sprang to his feet.

"When, Nikvok? When did they take him?"

"Minutes ago. We've only just received the Mindgram from our spy in Metronis."

"Then we must act quickly! Before they begin the transformation process on poor Podesta," said the Professor.

Nikvok shook his head and muttered, "Poor Captain Blenkinsopp."

"Is there any news of our other companions? A man called Mike, a woman called Wendy?" asked the Professor.

"Yes. Yes. The spy reported they are all alive, but they are prisoners of Queen Ayesha in the palace dungeons.

They were safe when our spy last saw them, but who knows what their fate will be."

"What do you mean, Nikvok?" said Sam.

"They will be made slaves of course, all foreigners are made slaves. They could end up fighting for their for lives in gladiatorial combat in the great Circus, or forced to fight the dreaded Wiggleon in the Arena of Doom, or like Captain Blenkinsopp taken to the House of Pain for transmogrification. Oh it's all too terrible to contemplate!"

Nikvok! Pull yourself together and help us work out the best way to get into the House of Pain without being seen. The first thing we must do is free Podesta before they start tinkering with his mind!"

"What about the others, Professor? We can't just leave them, surely?" said Sam.

"They seem safe for the moment, Sam. It's Podesta who needs our help most urgently. Now Nikvok how do we get into the House of Pain?"

"There is but one way that I know, Professor," said Nikvok approaching the map table. "It's risky but the way I see it we have little choice. The House of Pain is not connected to the municipal sewer system precisely to stop unauthorised access in and a possible escape route out into the city for the unfortunate creatures locked inside. The only way is through a separate sewerage outlet tunnel here!" Nikvok prodded the map with his finger.

"But there's nothing marked there," said Sam.

"I know, Sam. But that's near the crystal mines of Tor, isn't it Nikvok?" said the Professor.

"Precisely, Professor. It's not shown on the map, but a secret outlet tunnel exists that leads from the House of

Pain into the Grand Macerator Pits and then on to the Sea of Tethys. The secret tunnel is, of course, guarded."

"Guarded! I don't like the sound of that," said Sam.

"There is a small Atlantean maintenance garrison outpost beneath the sea at Tethys which we should have little difficulty in overpowering."

"That sounds better, Sam," said the Professor smiling to reassure his companion.

"Oh, sorry nearly forgot! There's also a crack legion of a thousand fighting Samukanari that patrol the digesting sluices on the House of Pain side of the Macerator Pits," added Nikvok.

"In that case, I suggest you muster your forces, Nikvok. Sam and I will visit the Areenean armourer!"

"Our weapons will be no match for those of Atlantis, Professor," sighed Nikvok. "They have Vril, which is far deadlier than anything we possess."

"In that case we shall need to visit the Nautilad's armoury. I have enough Vril guns there to equip a small army."

"But where is the Nautilad, Professor? The last we saw of your submarine it was being swallowed by Smegeye's serpent, remember?" said Sam.

"Smegeye is a profiteer, Professor. He will have kept your Nautilad under lock and key to trade as booty! I'll wager your underboat will still be inside the serpent's steel belly, moored to the docks at Metronis!"

"I think I'll decline your wager, Nikvok. If Metronis was the Slaveer's destination, then I agree, my craft will be in Smegeye's serpent craft."

"Well Smegeye's serpent was certainly big enough, Professor. It shouldn't be too hard to find!" said Sam.

"Come my friends. Make haste!" cried the Professor. "I have a plan. We have much to do and little time to do it before poor Podesta gets turned into a pig!"

Chapter 37

The Vrilmen of Metronis

The room was dazzling white and hovering at its centre was a multicoloured cloud of swirling vapours that formed flickering and changing three-dimensional images.

Surrounding the cloud, ranks of Vrilmen, white-hooded members of the Brotherhood of the Green Dragon, sat cross-legged with their heads bowed in deep contemplation.

No words were exchanged, yet unspoken communication within the room was rife.

An armour-clad boy and a green-robed Shaman watched intently from outside the circle as the coloured vapours formed shape after shape depicting mind activity picked up by the Vrilmen from anywhere in Atlantis.

The shape of the small loin-clothed figure of Mook Wundabuck came into view letting himself into a palace dungeon with a Vril healing staff and speaking to Wendy, Mike, Stu, and Farouke.

"Is that not their spy, Master Mentith?"

"Aye, Sire," whispered the green-masked shaman. "The spy seems to be reassuring them not to lose hope. A conspiracy brews I suspect."

The vapours began curling in on themselves and the image disappeared. After a moment the terrified face of Podesta Blenkinsopp appeared, and then the disturbing tableau of the Captain struggling against two burly soldiers of the Royal Guard dragging him bodily from the cell. Once more the vapours swirled out of focus, until the shape of Nikvok, mouthing words like a demented silent-movie actor, ran out of the mist fading into the hideous House of Pain and the Professor's anxious face, which in turn washed into turbulence, and next into Nikvok's finger pointing at a place on a map, and lastly the submerged windows of the maintenance garrison glowing through swirling murk from the sewer tunnel outlet beneath the Sea of Tethys.

"Aha! The conspiracy, Sire! Your trap is sprung! As you cleverly predicted, their spy tells the news of Captain Blenkinsopp's incarceration in The House of Pain and immediately the Professor plans his rescue. Unless I am mistaken, the Professor means to enter the House of Pain by the underground sewer outlet."

"It appears so, Master Mentith. We calculated correctly, it seems. It appears the fool means to strike at the sewer outlet in the Sea of Tethys. In that case the Professor and his friends will find a thousand Samukanari and a concealed armada of Attack Class Fish Submarines waiting for their arrival."

"And shall we continue to intercept their mindgrams and report developments of the impending Areenee attack, Sire?"

"Of course, Master Mentith! Report to me every detail, however trivial…. Especially the whereabouts of the Professor."

"You may rest assured, my lord Arnakk," said the shaman, bowing to the boy.

Good. You and your Vrilmen have done well, Master Mentith. I shall see to it you are handsomely rewarded.

"You are most gracious, my Lord."

"Now, I must report our intelligence to She-We-Obey. The Council of War must be assembled and the wheels of our attack plan set in motion."

Chapter 38

Down in the Sewer

"**P**hew! I think we've started going uphill," said Lu as the track from the body pit began a sweeping right-hand curve.

Bill stood on tiptoe to make his light travel further but they could not see beyond the bend.

"Be on the alert for trucks," said Bill. "We don't want to be mown down."

They kept to the outer wall of the curve, craning their necks to see as far around it as they could.

"What a stink! I thought the Pigmen and the body mound was bad, but this is a gas mask job!" exclaimed Toby holding his nose.

"Smells like a sewer," said Bill, and despite their instinct to recoil from the stench and walk the other way, they plodded doggedly along the track to where it became a three-way junction with a set of rusty points. Holding up the light crystal once more, they saw beyond the points a brick-tunnel and a slow flowing canal of stinking brown sludge. The railway tracks ran beside the canal disappearing into darkness in either direction.

"Which way now?" asked Toby.

"I don't care as long as we get out of this awful pong!" said Lu.

Bill walked to the edge of the canal.

Down in the Sewer

"Be careful, Bill. Don't fall in!" cried Lu.

"Just don't strike a match!" laughed Toby.

"What on earth do you mean 'don't strike a match'? What a silly thing to say," said Lu.

"He means sewer gas is explosive," said Bill, eyeing Toby disapprovingly.

"You mean you've never set light to any of your farts, Lu?" roared Toby, and for a moment Bill's mask of disdain slipped and he let out what started off as a snigger, realising that after what they'd all seen and been through, his friend just needed to let off… steam.

"TOBY! Certainly NOT!" cried Lu.

"Didn't you know, Toby? Ladies never fart," said Bill in a mock-posh accent.

"My mum does!" said Toby. "Real corkers! It's so embarrassing when one is out shopping with the mater!"

An expression of disgust darkened Lu's face until after a pause she too took account that she was standing in a sewer and not the elegant parlour of a stately home, and without warning she bent double and let rip with a most unladylike cackle and they all dissolved into gales of laughter.

After several minutes of helplessness, Lu surfaced and said, "Please don't make me laugh anymore, Toby. My sides are bursting!"

"Better out than in, eh Lu?" laughed Toby winking, and they started roaring all over again.

The mirth petered out into sniggers and then chuckles until Bill said, "We need to decide which way to go."

178

Down in the Sewer

Toby took a fluffy Tunnock's wafer wrapper from his pocket and folding it into the rough shape of a boat tossed it into the sludge.

"Poo sticks, Toby?" laughed Bill and they all watched as after a minute the little boat began slowly moving left with the sewage.

"The city must be that way then," said Lu pointing in the opposite direction.

They began following the tracks once more with Bill lighting their way along the smoother path beside the canal. Every so often they passed more dark hidey-holes in the white glazed bricks of the tunnel walls, and Lu hurried by them, sure that pink eyes from the gloom inside were watching their every move.

To Lu's horror, further on, Bill's light crystal disturbed a flock of giant bats roosting around the edge of a chimney-like shaft in the ceiling of the tunnel and their leathery flapping filled the tunnel as they flew in all directions.

"That was close!" cried Toby, fending off a low-flying bat that brushed against his hair.

Suddenly Lu felt something crunch under her boot. She hoped whatever it was wouldn't be gooey and ooze through the hole left by the slug worm's bite. She didn't want to, but she couldn't resist looking down. The path and the walls of the tunnel were a swarming sea of every creepy-crawly imaginable. Feelers twitched and hairy clawed legs scuttled and writhing crustaceous bodies crunched beneath their steps. She wanted to scream, but she was so terrified nothing would come out.

"C-c-can't we go back?" she managed to utter as a long scaly red thing with hundreds of ticking legs began the winding ascent of her right leg.

"Oh get it off me! Please get it off!" she pleaded as the insect passed her knee.

At once Bill swiped the beast with his hand and losing its grip, the thing fell into the wriggling insect miasma on the tunnel floor.

Lu closed her eyes and throwing back her head screamed, "I CAN'T STAND THIS PLACE!"

"Come on Lu. We've got to go on. We're beyond the point of no return now," said Bill trying to comfort her.

"Agggh! Don't move! There's something about to crawl down your neck, Bill," yelled Toby, and rushing forward he splatted whatever it was under his fist.

"Ouch! That hurt."

"Sorry, Bill. You didn't want whatever it was crawling around inside your suit, did you?"

"Ooooh! They'll be inside our suits, inside our boots, in our hair and in our mouths soon," cried Lu shaking glistening wriggling insects from her boot.

Then. No sooner had she said 'in our mouths soon', the bats all flapped out of sight up the chimney-vent, and the insects disappeared to who knows where, and they were suddenly alone in eerie silence.

"Phew! I'm so glad they've gone," breathed Lu feeling a shiver up and down her spine and back again that brought her out in Goosebumps.

"Come on," said Bill, "let's get going before they come back."

They began following Bill's crystal for a good ten minutes (maybe fifteen) when Toby whispered, "Shhh! I can hear something."

They stopped and like he'd seen on a Western once, Bill knelt to place his ear against a rail.

"You're right Toby. I can hear it too. It sounds all rhythmic and crunching like marching."

"Whatever it is it's getting nearer," said Lu. "I can hear it echoing down the tunnel."

Soon the tunnel began filling with marching.

"It sounds like a whole army!" said Bill.

"Hadn't we better hide?" said Toby. "If it is an army I doubt it's friendly."

"Yes. I agree," said Lu.

"Come on then, we'll nip back to one of the hidey-holes in the wall," said Bill and grabbing Lu by the hand he began running back in the direction they'd come.

"In here," said Bill, looking over his shoulder into Lu's blue eyes. He pulled her into the dark towards him. For a moment he wished Toby wasn't with them. He wondered if her mouth would be soft and warm to kiss. A thrill ran right through him and he stifled the fantasy the moment Toby rejoined them. They waited and waited hardly daring to breathe until the sounds of crunching feet and clanking metal filled the tunnel to deafening. Soon, from within the gloom of the hidey-hole they saw the first of the 'soldiers' march by less than two feet away from them.

"What the?" gasped Lu, and Bill clamped his hand over her mouth for fear the hideous creatures might hear and raise the alarm.

And hideous they were too; a kind of giant beetle with massively thick, warty black armoured plates forming a glossy exoskeleton, jointed to allow four of their six armoured limbs to wield Vril weapons of various descriptions. Every so often they would make a creepy rustling noise as they opened their big black wing cases to stretch their black-veined lacy wings.

The friends listened as the creatures' horny mandibles chattered up and down, as they tweeted, hissed and grunted guttural conversations as they marched.

At one point one of them loosed a bright purple, crackling bolt of Vril at a single bat that foolishly emerged from a ceiling vent. The bat, no less hideous than its attacker in Lu's opinion, was instantly reduced to a damp, red airborne smudge.

The march of the beetle creatures lasted an hour and was followed closely by Atlantean Houscarls and Sabretooths. Eventually the last soldier passed the hidey-hole and, listening for the noise of clanking metal and crunching feet to fade from earshot, the children cautiously emerged from hiding.

"I wonder what that was all about?" said Toby. "Looks like there's going to be a big battle somewhere."

"Come on," said Bill, lighting the tunnel and walking in the opposite direction to the sludge. "Let's get out of here."

They soon discovered that merely brandishing their stun-guns with the Vril meters fully charged would disperse any invading insects and form a pathway through. After about an hour walking without incident they came upon a high wall with a small lagoon at its base and a 'waterfall' of sludge noisily splashing into it.

An iron ladder led to the top of the wall and an arch beside it led into a tunnel through.

"Which way?" said Toby.

"Nip up the ladder, Toby. Tell us what's up there," said Bill.

The rungs were quite widely spaced as if intended for considerably larger climbers than Toby, but on reaching the top, he could see through railings a vast reservoir with acres of sludge floating on water.

Toby instinctively ducked when he saw several of the beetle creatures patrolling walkways around the perimeter of the tank and when he felt movement through the ladder, looked down and signalled Bill to stay put on the ground.

"We must be very quiet," whispered Toby when he rejoined the others.

"Why, what's up there?" said Bill.

"More of those beetle things guarding what looks like a ginormous sludge-tank."

"Then we'll have to go this way!" hissed Lu, pointing into the tunnel, determined to squash any further discussion and get out of the stinking place as quickly as possible.

Following Bill's light they tried their hardest to silence their footfalls echoing down the smooth tunnel.

"Another dead-end!" whispered Bill as a wall confronted them.

"No. Look. It's just a right angled bend," replied Lu under her breath, walking on several steps to check.

Turning the corner, a little way on they saw a light from what must have been a doorway in the side of the tunnel. Chirping, tweeting and the hissing of beetle creatures wafted out from inside. Lu shivered at the thought of being eaten alive in the hairy horny serrated jaws of the vile creatures.

At Bill's signal they edged along the wall towards the doorway, and as they approached they smelled the aroma of roasting meat in the tunnel. With the revolting sewer smell Lu had quite forgotten she was starving, but now in cleaner air the smell of meat was almost too tempting to resist.

Bill at once extinguished his crystal light by putting it in a pocket and peeked around the edge of the doorway.

Inside was a kind of Beetle common room, brightly lit, with half a dozen funeral-black creatures sitting, some with several legs crossed, in armchairs around a low table with plates of steaming meat and strangely labelled bottles of drink. They were playing what appeared to be a card game of some kind.

Picking a moment when the players seemed particularly absorbed, Bill tiptoed across the doorway and waited for a similar point in the game to beckon the others to follow.

When they judged they were a safe distance away, Lu exclaimed, "What was that they were eating?"

"Smelled like roast chicken to me," drooled Toby.

"Don't!" cried Lu. "I'm so hungry my stomach thinks my throat's been cut."

"We'll steal some food at the next opportunity," said Bill reassuringly.

"I hope so," grumbled Lu, "or I'm going to pass out."

Down in the Sewer

"What was that noise?" whispered Toby. He was looking back over his shoulder when he said it, and to their horror, several of the beetle creatures were coming out from the doorway into the tunnel.

"Don't even breathe!" whispered Bill, as he slipped into the shadows out of sight.

"Now what?" said Lu, running her hands over a cold steel door that halted them in their tracks.

"I reckon we'll have to go through," said Bill, and he reached for a long lever protruding from a slot in the wall.

"Wait!" hissed Lu. "What if there are more beetle things behind the door?"

Two more beetle creatures joined their companions in the tunnel.

"I think we'll have to take that chance," said Bill, and he pulled the lever with all his might.

The lever refused to budge. Bill gave it a second try. This time a grating sound was followed by a loud CRACK and the lever came away in Bill's hand.

At once the beetle creatures turned. Their mandibles chattered, their antennae twitched, and they began advancing on the children.

"Do something!" yelled Lu.

"Look! The doors!" cried Toby, as with a loud rumbling the doors started to slide open.

"Come on you two, follow me!" shouted Bill, and launching the broken lever like a javelin back down the tunnel, he grabbed Lu's hand and pulled her through the widening gap.

Chapter 39

Garcia's Progress

Garcia Smallpiece peered through Ergo 1's windscreen as he steered and marvelled. Many of the species they'd encountered since emerging from the cold Arctic tunnel were from a prehistoric age and Garcia recognised most of them from wall paintings inside the Mayan pyramid.

Could it be they'd travelled back in time? Was the Arctic tunnel a portal into a bygone age? The wall paintings couldn't tell him that, but they could certainly tell him the looming undersea channel they'd been through was the way into Metronis!

They had surfaced and were now sailing in bright sunlight along a wide canal surrounded by desert. The water's surface sparkled and in the distance they saw a mountain with a black marble city clinging to its sides that glittered in the sun.

Garcia's eye was irresistibly drawn by the mountain's outline to its peak shrouded in strangely glowing cloud.

Tearing his gaze away, he glanced down behind him. Having given Garcia his orders, the Fat German was snoring his head off in a hammock in the back, "taking a well earned rest," as he called it. The arrogant pig! How dare his kind come from defeat in Europe and presume to order his people about!

Is if on cue, the Fat German sucked in a rushing deep breath, slobbered, and woke up. Hurriedly wiping a dribble from the corner of his mouth, he snorted, opened his eyes, and stretched and yawned.

"Are ve nearly there yet?" he mumbled, sitting up, and reaching in his breast pocket to replace his monocle. "Ah! Zat is better."

"Look señor!"

The Fat German struggled out of his hammock to join Garcia at the windscreen. Both men were dumbstruck. The glowing clouds at the mountain's summit had moved away leaving a single pinprick of dazzling white light.

Eventually Garcia mumbled, "Ze crystal! Eet is like ze sun, señor!" and he turned away to avoid being blinded.

"Zat iss our prize! Dive, Garcia! Ve must not be detected."

Garcia pulled a red lever to the right of the wheel to partially flood the main tanks. The submarine glided to continue its journey just below the canal's surface.

"Gut," said the Fat German removing his monocle and replacing it inside his jacket, "I need a rest now. Let me know when we are nearer our destination, Garcia."

For two pins Garcia would have slit the fat pig's fat throat there and then, but he needed him to get the Vril crystal from the mountain and then load it into Ergo1 for the journey home. "Sí señor," he replied flatly, looking out through the periscope, and planning the Fat German's demise after the crystal and the death ray were both his.

From his hammock in the back, the Fat German eyed Garcia (with his good eye) in the driver's seat with one hand on the wheel, turning the pages of a magazine with the other, and, now and then, checking their course through the periscope. As he closed his eye, pretending to sleep, the Fat German planned Garcia's demise. Now the death ray was complete; as soon as he was in possession of the crystal, the greasy engineer would be of no further use. Then he would strike.

Chapter 40

Attack on the Underwater Garrison

Blatvok glanced across at Nikvok sitting at the controls of the Areenean Squid Sub bound for the sewage outlet in the Sea of Tethys.

It could be worse, he told himself; he could actually be in charge. That dubious honour fell to Nikvok, who, as the yellow glowing eyes of the maintenance garrison windows came into view through the murky water, flicked a switch on the control console to address the rest of the fleet.

"Calling all underboats! Calling all underboats. Objective is now in sight. Prepare to jettison your midget subs. Rendezvous point at Zeta. Prepare to attack. Prepare to attack!"

Within minutes the sea around them was alive with the tiny glowing headlights of dozens of armed midget submarines similar to those from the Nautilad.

"Come Blatvok," said Nikvok, grinning, "it is time to go."

They were soon speeding to meet the midget submarine task force at Zeta, the code name for the meeting point above the outlet garrison from whence the attack would be launched.

Blatvok looked in wonder at all of the Areenean forces poised to attack. The sheer numbers of hovering midget subs, bristling with torpoons and swimming mines, bolstered his confidence. Surely no maintenance garrison, even armed with Vril weapons, would stand a chance against them?

Blatvok, like Nikvok and his fair-haired Areenean comrades, rode naked into battle having no need for suits or oxygen; breathing freely through gills beneath the waves. Their venom weaponry, although no match for the destructive power of long range Atlantean Killing Staffs, in skilled Areenean hands and at close quarters would deliver their lethal poison payload with silent and equally deadly efficiency.

Underwater, the Areenean chosen means of communication was by emitting clicks and high-pitched sometimes ultrasonic sing-song calls like dolphin and whale-song. Indeed in certain strategic situations Pods of Orca might be called on as Areenee front-line allies to spearhead terror attacks.

Blatvok listened as Nikvok issued orders to the Areenee forces in whale song.

"Come Blatvok," he said turning to face his comrade in arms from the sub's front seat. "This attack needs stealth. We swim the rest of the way."

Armed with his trusty throat sickle, Blatvok followed Nikvok to lead a thousand torpoon and gut knife wielding Areenee from the hovering midget subs, to congregate around the sewer outlet.

With a downward stroke of his arm Nikvok signalled for a single swimming mine to be released.

Blatvok watched as the device came into view through the murk, a large breast-stroking headless steel turtle with scimitar-shaped paddles.

The swimming mine entered the sewer outlet, and Nikvok beckoned Blatvok to join the other Areenee clinging flat against the cliff-face above the outlet to avoid the imminent explosion.

WUMP! And a blast of bubbles, rock chunks, bits of rusty grating and dust belched from the outlet. Several Areenee lost their grip as the shockwave travelled through the rock-face sweeping them away.

Minutes passed before the water was silent enough for Nikvok to order the advance of Areenee warriors to swim through the billowing silt cloud into the dark tunnel.

An inborn sonar, similar to the 'radar' of bats, meant navigation through dense silt or dark presented little problem to the Areenee, and Blatvok followed closely in Nikvok's wake through the shattered remains of a great iron grill across the sewer entrance.

"Be vigilant," warned Nikvok as they approached a lighted patch in the dark 'fog' that was an airlock. Stepping on to the threshold, Blatvok unholstered his throat sickle. The fine feeler hairs on the back of his neck were standing on end and he shivered in anticipation of a skirmish with the Atlantean maintenance crew inside.

The airlock was big enough for ten warriors. The outer doors closed behind them leaving the main attack force swimming outside. The water level began dropping, and Blatvok felt uneasy that whatever lay beyond the inner doors might easily overwhelm them.

The inner doors eventually opened to reveal a large tool store with pumps, shovels, diving gear and digging equipment. A door beyond the tool store led to an eerily-deserted control room.

Control panels flickered, screens blinked, a chair lay on its back, and on a desk an abandoned drinking vessel of something steamed gently to itself.

"There's nobody here," declared Nikvok, clapping his companion on the shoulder. "That was easy!"

"Perhaps a little too easy?" replied Blatvok.

Chapter 41

Door to the Enchanted Forest

The jagged end of the broken lever flew to its mark piercing the thorax of an advancing beetle-creature. For a moment the creature's companions stopped as it teetered on its feet, but seeing their attentions would now be a waste of time, they continued with weapons and armour rattling at a faster pace towards the doors.

"Stop them or they'll follow us through!" screamed Lu.

"There's another lever here," cried Toby from several feet beyond the doors.

"Pull it!" yelled Bill, and Toby leaned back on the lever which like the one on the other side of the doors refused to budge at first.

"For goodness sake don't break it or they'll be through!" shouted Lu, wrapping her arms around Toby from behind to exert more force on the lever. With a groan the lever at last moved and like the first began a deep rumbling as the doors started closing.

One of the beetle-creatures dropped on all six legs and made a determined sprint at the doors. Seeing the gap was now too small to get through, it lunged the final feet and reaching through grabbed Bill's arm in one of its horny claws. Bill was slammed against the back of the doors with his arm sticking through the closing gap. At once Toby and

Lu grabbed Bill's free arm and a macabre tug of war started between Toby and Lu on the inside and the beetle creature on the outside with Bill dragged back and forth between them.

The creature was not giving up and beyond the doors its claws screeched and skidded on the rock floor of the tunnel as it pulled hard on Bill's arm, until Lu took a pot shot at it with her stun gun through the gap in the doors. The creature let out an angry hiss and a high-pitched squeal of pain before releasing Bill's arm. With a sickening crunching crack, the doors snapped shut on its grabbing limb.

The creature's severed leg clattered to the floor at Bill's feet and he jumped back to avoid the bony claws snapping open and shut with a dying reflex action.

"Come on," said Bill, shaking his arm to get the circulation going. "Let's go before the others find a way through."

They followed a gravel path until they were walking through a green wood. The trees were alive with birdsong and every now and then their path was crossed by tropical birds, some tiny darting dots of colour, others with big rainbow wings and long flowing tail feathers. Soon they crossed a small hump-back bridge over a babbling stream and it wasn't long before the gravel petered out to dry mud path. It was then the trees became thicker and Lu was sure she saw rabbits, or some kind of animal, vanishing into the undergrowth. As it became darker they unholstered their stun guns in case they encountered more beetle-creatures or anything else nasty. Suddenly the usual noises of the forest were added to by a new one.

"Sorry," said Toby, "that was my stomach gurgling."

"When was the last time we had any food?" said Lu suddenly.

"Ages ago. When we ate Big Boar," replied Bill.

And no sooner had the words left Bill's mouth than the wonderful aroma of Sunday roast came wafting through the trees.

"Oh! That's heavenly!" cried Lu, standing still for a moment to savour the gorgeous smell of roasting chicken.

"Roast lamb!" said Toby. "My mouth's watering already!"

"Smells like beef to me," said Bill.

"Well whatever it is it smells fantastic. I bet there's a camp with whatever it is roasting on a spit? Come on," said Bill, beckoning the others to follow.

They came to a junction of paths, and as if by instinct they followed the right-hand fork, then shortly after, they came to a tee-junction and this time they followed the left-hand path. After several turns and forks, Lu was losing count. She looked back over her shoulder and began to suspect they were getting hopelessly lost; the path behind them seemed to disappear into ferns and bushes with no hint of a way back.

"We should have left a trail or something," said Lu.

"No need," said Bill. "Look, there's a clearing ahead."

"Yes, but how do we find our way back if we need to?"

"We don't need to," said Bill. "This is where the cooking smells are coming from. Look there's a cottage on the far side of the clearing."

"Yes, why should we want to go back, Lu? We didn't know where we were in the first place," said Toby.

"Ok. I see I'm outvoted. I just don't feel comfortable with this, that's all."

"Don't be such a sticky beak, Lu," said Bill. "There's such a thing as looking a gift-horse in the mouth, you know?"

Despite the boys' bravado, they did approach the cottage with some caution by skirting the clearing inside the fringe of the trees.

Drawing nearer they saw a white, weather-boarded cottage, its walls bowing and crooked with age. A wonky porch, smothered with purple clematis, sheltered a lopsided green front door and a winding red brick path led from the door to a gate in a low stone wall that surrounded a country garden of sweet-smelling yellow roses and wild flowers.

"You two wait here," whispered Bill. "I'm going to have a quick look through the windows."

Lu and Toby watched from the trees as Bill made his way, crouching, to the garden gate and then to each of the downstairs windows. Nobody seemed to be in. The front door opened when he tried it and the strong aroma of roast beef wafted out to hook him. He waved the others to join him.

"I'm not going," said Lu.

"Why not?"

"This whole thing's creepy, Toby. Look at that cottage. Doesn't it look familiar?"

Toby looked and said, "Nope."

"Wishing Well Cottage?"

Toby looked again.

"Now you come to mention I s'pose it does a bit."

"A bit? More than a bit, Toby. I've been riding Bramble up and down the driveway of Wishing Well Cottage for three years now since dad bought the Big House. That place, whatever it is, looks just like Wishing Well Cottage. This whole thing could be some kind of trap. Don't forget what the Professor told us - that, that Vril stuff can be used to control people's minds. How do we know someone isn't trying to control our minds right now?"

"Whatever. I'm jolly well hungry. My mind's being controlled by my stomach right now! I'll bring you back a doggy bag," said Toby and adopting a similar crouching gait to Bill, he made his way over to the cottage.

"Where's Lu?" said Bill.

"She's not coming. She thinks this could all be a trap and our minds are being controlled by someone. She reckons this place looks like Wishing Well Cottage!"

"Cobblers!" replied Bill, "Wishing Well Cottage has got a green front door for a start."

"I know. I tried to tell her."

"Women! Come on, she'll just have to go hungry that's all."

"That's a bit harsh, Bill. I said I'd take her back a doggy bag."

"Do what you want. Let's find that food."

They entered a high-ceilinged room that buzzed with flies. Rows of desks were arranged in front of a podium on which a single, larger desk stood with a white-board on the wall behind it. Posters around the walls depicted scenes through different periods of history.

"This is old Pillsbury's classroom," said Bill.

Door to the Enchanted Forest

A door at the far end of the room opened and a small bald headed man with thick spectacles entered carrying a pile of exercise books.

"And that's old Pillsbury!" whispered Toby, looking over his shoulder for a way out. The door they'd entered through was gone!

"Ah! Young and Wishman. You're both very keen! Class doesn't start for another half-an-hour. Sit down. I expect you'd like some nice roast chicken while you wait? Just a minute I've got your homework essays here." Pillsbury dumped his books and stood behind them resting his hands on their shoulders. "Your work wasn't up to its usual standard, Wishman. I'm afraid you've only got a C+! Oops! Nearly forgot. No eating in class. Sorry boys, roast chicken's OFF!"

The split second the boys entered the front door the delicious smell of roast chicken disappeared, and to her horror the Wishing Well Cottage Lu thought she knew so well turned into a frowning grey stone castle.

Trust a woman's intuition! She'd been right all along. Wishing Well Cottage had been nothing but an illusion. Something controlling her mind had, at least for the moment, lost its grip.

The prison now before her was probably quite real she reasoned and the boys were inside it. She had to do something!

Taking out her stun gun and setting the power meter to maximum stun, she followed the boys' tracks across what was now a black, rocky clearing towards the high walls. Nearing the fortress, the cries and screams of those inside jarred at her through its threatening barred windows. The green front door was now a high arched doorway leading into a stuffy dungeon corridor crawling with flies. Feeling uneasy at the noise her steps made echoing down the damp tunnel, she began tiptoeing up to a large gothic door.

A lock in the centre of the door had a huge iron key protruding from it, and, with heart pounding, she felt the many tumblers fall as she turned it.

Nothing could have prepared Lu for the sight that met her paralysed gaze when the door creaked open.

Chapter 42

The Pincers Close

A search of the sewer maintenance outlet revealed no trace of the resident engineering crew apart from the telltales of a hasty retreat and a meowing marmalade cat. The cat's loyalty, Nikvok discovered, was easily bought with a fresh bowl of fish scraps and some water. As the smiling cat gently buffeted the backs of Nikvok's legs filling the control room with loud purring, Blatvok and the remainder of the advance party bustled in from searching the rest of the installation.

"Nothing," reported Blatvok, stooping to stroke the cat.

"What about the main sewer tunnel?" said Nikvok.

"We haven't searched it yet, but no immediate signs of life there either."

"In that case we'll proceed to phase two of the operation. Get a search detail together and enter the sewer tunnel, Blatvok. I'll summon the main attack force to set up a stronghold here and then I'll follow you with a legion of warriors to the House of Pain."

***

The image of Nikvok and Blatvok and a happy marmalade cat mingled into coloured chaos in the swirling vapour cloud in the centre of the White Room.

"Should we proceed to phase two of our attack, Master Mentith?" asked one of the hooded Vrilmen brothers kneeling before the green-robed shaman.

"Are our forces in position, Brother Minion?"

"Yes Master. We have them completely surrounded."

"Good. I shall inform Lord Arnakk. Await my order before launching the attack."

Chapter 43

Midnight at the Crystal Temple

Climbing the high wall into the gardens of the Crystal Temple with only a grappling hook, ropes, and crampons, and without being seen, had proven no easy feat for the Fat German and Garcia Smallpiece. They were dressed in long black cloaks which caught up on everything, and masks, and wide-brimmed hats. Now concealed by shadow in thick undergrowth in the ancient Yew Forest beneath the Crystal Temple, they stared in disbelief as three saucer flying machines glided silently overhead.

They followed their progress until the saucers lost height to become obscured by the trees.

An unexpected warm rush of air blowing twigs and dust from the forest floor indicated something was happening beyond their sight.

"Come, Senor," whispered Garcia, flicking on a small torch and beckoning the wheezing German to follow him into the wind in the likely direction of the flying saucers.

After several minutes Garcia extinguished the torch as they approached the forest edge.

In a clearing beyond the trees each of the flying machines now stood on four bright metal legs with open hatchways visible in their bellies. A group of armour-clad figures, bathed in pale light, and led by a boy, were walking towards the base of a giant black pyramid.

202

"Look, Garcia!" gasped the Fat German tapping the Indian engineer needlessly hard on the shoulder. He was pointing a fat finger a hundred feet up at the fabulous crystal gently shedding light at the pyramid's peak. Garcia said nothing, staring open-mouthed as the glassy black wall of the pyramid began rippling like water and the armour-clad figures seemed to walk straight through it. The wall, having swallowed them, smoothed to its former glassy solidity.

The Fat German's eyes were glowing with menacing greed beneath the brim of his black hat and with shaking hands he gripped Garcia's biceps.

"Come, Garcia. Vhy do you look so glum? Ve must act qvickly. Ze crystal! At last she is within our grasp!"

"Eet is much beegger than I thought, Senor. I don't see how we can get it down from ze top of the pyramid let alone take it away with us."

"Pah! Mere detail. Trust an engineer to sink off trifling practicalities!"

"But."

"Nein! No buts, Garcia," snarled the Fat German pulling a Luger from under his cloak. "You vill sink of a vay to get zat crystal back to Brazil or I shall haff no choice than to kill you, my friend."

"Not eef I keel you first, Senor," hissed Garcia, deftly sliding a Bersa Thunder 380 pistol from under *his* cloak.

"Hah! Ve haff a Mexican standoff, Garcia."

"Si, Senor. I suggest we both put our guns away and think of a way to get ze crystal down from the pyramid."

Suddenly something behind them cracked a dead branch and rustled the bushes.

203

"Vot was zat?" cried the Fat German.

Garcia flicked on his torch and shone it towards the noise.

"I can see nothing, Senor. Eet is probably an animal."

The Fat German turned back to point up at the crystal and said, "And you seriously mean you vant me to get all ze vay up there, Garcia?"

"I can't manage it on my own, Senor."

An expression of panic flashed across the Fat German's face.

"I can't possibly get up there. Climbing ze vall to get in zis place nearly killed me, Garcia! No ve must find another way."

Garcia thought for several minutes, glancing absent-mindedly in the direction of the rustling noise.

"Nada, Senor. One way or another we must reach ze actual crystal to get it down."

"Can it be reached from inside ze pyramid do you sink, Garcia? Maybe ve can walk through ze walls too? Maybe there is an elevator up to ze crystal?"

"I will go and see, Senor," said Garcia stooping to leave the cover of the trees and make towards the nearest flying machine.

"Vait for me," called the Fat German hot-footing in Garcia's tracks, not wanting to leave the remotest chance of the engineer making off with the crystal without him.

They were soon in the shadow of the first flying machine looking up into its hatch. A muted whine signalled a lowering ladder.

"We might be able to fly to the crystal, Garcia?"

Midnight at the Crystal Temple

Climbing the ladder's lower rungs, Garcia stretched and peered gingerly inside the saucer.

"What can you see?" hissed the Fat German standing on eager tiptoes.

"It's like nothing I have seen before, Senor. Here. See for yourself," replied Garcia. He stepped back off the ladder to make way for the German.

"I see vot you mean," agreed the Fat German sticking his head and shoulders through the hatch. "I wonder vot that is?" And before Garcia could stop him, the Fat German was wriggling up inside the flying saucer and beckoning the engineer to follow him.

From the shadows of the forest the beady eyes of 'the animal' that rustled the bushes, watched Garcia and the Fat German intently, and driven by the same insane greed to own the glittering crystal, began stalking towards the belly of the flying saucer.

Chapter 44

The Council of War

"Are you all in agreement?" said Ayesha to the line of high-ranking military men kneeling before the throne with their foreheads touching the ground. "Rise, Arnakk. What is the decision of the War Council?"

"Our forces are in place. We must attack, O Great One," replied the boy prince glancing down at Nicademus kneeling beside him.

"And are you unanimous in this?"

"Oh yes, O Great One," chorused the kneeling men.

"And are you aware two Overworlder boy-children, previously unknown to us, have entered the House of Pain at Doctor Grimus's behest?"

The room fell into uncomfortably silence.

"WELL? Which of my so-called Generals is in command of our soldiers guarding the House of Pain?"

"M-me? I mean I am, O Great Queen. " croaked the armour clad man second in from the right.

"How is it that you knew nothing of these Overworlder children?"

"I, I."

"It should not be for Doctor Grimus to report such intrusions by mindgram. Her research to create the ultimate super-being is far too important for that. There should be NO such intrusions! No thanks to your incompetence, Dr

Grimus is repairing your bungling by consuming these children. Tell me. ALL OF YOU! How many other such Overworlders might there be at large in Atlantis?" An awkward silence ensued. "I take it from your silence you do not know."

Ayesha signalled to others unseen and pointed to the unfortunate man, kneeling second in from the left.

A burly gang of slaves, naked from the waist up, marched from the darkness and grabbed the man and frogmarched him struggling through sulphurous vapours to the edge of the fiery volcanic chimney. He cried out as searing heat scorched his flesh until, amid hysterical laughter, Ayesha shrieked, "Throw the dog into the pit!" and the slaves tossed the man like a screaming rag doll into the bubbling lava lake below.

Several of the generals made to get up.

"STAY WHERE YOU ARE!" commanded Ayesha, and leaning forward on her throne she eyed each of them in turn, including Arnakk.

"Arnakk! You will destroy the Professor's submarine craft. He will never escape Atlantis again!"

***

"Someone's coming up ze ladder! We'd better hide Senor."

Garcia and the Fat German ducked in the shadows of some stacked crates of Vril-weapons behind the control deck of the flying saucer. They watched as the blackened bedraggled head and shoulders of a human appeared in the hatchway to climb aboard. The figure was that of a fairly short man, wearing the torn remains of a grey suit and smelling of oil. He winced as he climbed the final rungs of the ladder in his bare black feet. The organ stop whites of his eyes popped out from his blackened face and scanned the gloom of the flying saucer.

"HALT!" cried the Fat German, drawing his Luger from his cloak. "Hande hoche! Who are you?"

"Don't shoot! I'm a friend."

"What is your name and what do you want?"

"I, I, I'm…" stammered the black-faced man, "Cripes! There are people coming!"

"Get inside QUEEK Senor or you will geeve us ALL away!" said Garcia moving to the edge of the hatch and reaching to give the stranger a hand.

Huddling behind the crates the three interlopers listened as an old soldier and an armour-clad boy seated themselves on the control deck.

The boy extended his hands over a featureless sloping board in front of the seats and the machine came to life. Lights flicked on, a panoramic view around the outside of the craft wrapped around the pilots, the boarding ladder raised, and the craft began rising into the air.

The Fat German's face dropped as the crystal and the black pyramid swung rapidly behind them as the boy set the flying machine's course to the docks.

***

Blatvok was astounded, when after climbing down the iron service ladder to lead his search detail into the main sewer tunnel, he found himself face to face with a thousand hissing beetle-creatures charging with a thousand Vril Killing Staffs.

In the control room Nikvok peered idly out through the control room windows. In a moment tears were streaming down his face.

The Areenee Midget sub squadron intended to land his reinforcements was completely outnumbered by a task force of Atlantean Attack-Class Fish Submarines, their large calibre Vril canons trained and ready to annihilate his comrades.

Chapter 45

Return to the Nautilad

"Cheer up Vole," said Hedgehog, "What's the matter?"

"I was just thinking about Piddle Wallop and the garden at Wishing Well Cottage, and green fields and the woods and the stream and the apple orchard and Owl and Mr Blackbird and Ma Blackbird and the Twins and the Post Mistress's horse trough filled with beautiful flowers…. And. And I think I'll die soon. I hate this metal place with its greasy smells and fires and bangs and funny-looking nasty people, and us and Austin trapped inside here forever. There's no fresh air and no sun. And I'm starving. There are no tasty snails to eat. Why it's like a huge metal coffin and I think I shall die," said Vole.

"Yes, I agree," said Legit. "I've been thinking a lot about Blossom lately." He sniffed and a tear rolled down his nose. "You know what, you guys? I don't think I'll ever see her again. I might as well be dead too."

"Hey! Hey! What is all this?" cried Hedgehog crossly, glaring at Vole. "Stop feeling sorry for yourselves! Are you telling me you're giving up? Throwing in the towel? Haven't you learned anything, Vole? What would have happened if you'd given up on me when I was in trouble and when Austin was in the Giant Steam Crusher? Something good will happen soon, you'll see. We're NOT giving up!"

And no sooner had Hedgehog said that, than Monty yelled, "Woah! What's happening? The ground's moving again! Everything's going un-topsy-turvy!"

Everyone slid and skidded and teetered drunkenly towards the edge of the glass dome to peer outside as they felt the floor levelling.

"Look! The great white Titanic chamber outside is filling with water!" cried Monty.

"Hey, guys! We're starting to float!" laughed Legit. "Ha ha, Vole! Maybe we're going home after all?"

"We ARE going home! I'm sure of it! Look Legit! WE ARE GOING HOME HURRAH!" cried Vole as they felt a sudden thrumming and the low vibration of a motor through their feet. Bright warm sunlight flooded the white chamber as the great jaws of the giant sea serpent slowly opened.

They glided forward, until the Nautilad bumped gently along the side of the dock.

"What's happening now?" said Vole.

"We've stopped," replied Legit flatly.

"You mean we're not going home now?" mumbled Vole, looking decidedly dejected.

"Look! There's a gangplank. And a flying thing's landing over there! People are climbing down a ladder and they're coming aboard," said Monty, watching as a boy dressed in glinting armour strode along the dock with an older soldier beside him. A platoon of waiting soldiers stood to attention; gave a strange salute and followed boy up the gangplank onto the deck.

"Are the Humans coming back?" said Vole. "Is it the one in rags with the black face?"

211

"No. I don't recognise this lot," replied Monty. "Besides, I can't see them anymore."

There was a sudden breeze which stopped as the steel door from the deck into the conning tower was slammed shut.

The animals waited with baited breath as the sound of footfalls climbing the conning tower ladder floated up through the hatch in the conning tower floor.

"HIDE! Someone's coming!" shouted Monty.

"I've got a very bad feeling about this," said Vole before jumping back down the ventilation shaft.

***

"Behold Metronis!" cried the Professor, looking back at Sam from the front seat of the midgct sub.

Before them stretched the single ribbon of shimmering blue water that led to the distant black city, and the mountain with a single dazzling crystal flashing from its summit.

"The crystal, Professor?" began Sam, pointing to the glittering stone in the distance.

"Yes, Sam. The source of the Atlanteans' power and the future cause of their undoing," replied the Professor, adjusting the midget sub's trim to cruise out of sight beneath the surface of the water.

"What a thought," said Sam, "a source of free energy…."

"Yes. And it is a tragic fact that it is not in the Human psyche to share a blessing like Vril among all nations to benefit everybody equally. In our world each nation would try to steal it to gain the upper hand over its neighbour. Simply put, Sam, the owner of the crystal owns the world."

"And in this world that is the Atlanteans, Professor?" crackled Sam's voice in the Professor's helmet-phones

"Yes, Sam and they rule it ruthlessly."

"What will you do if you find your son, Professor?" asked Sam. "If he is under the Witch Queen's spell, I mean."

"I will try and free Rudi from her curse once and for all, Sam. And there are only two ways to do that. The first is to kill her. And the second is to rob her of Vril."

"Which means destroying the crystal and the force of Vril forever, Professor?" said Sam.

There was a long pause but eventually the Professor answered, "Yes, Sam. It would."

They continued on in silence until the long dark shape of Smegeye's Sea Serpent submarine loomed above them.

They followed the immense plated hull below its keel for several minutes, such was the leviathan's size, until they reached the giant mouth at the submarine's prow.

"Look, Professor! The Nautilad! It's floating in front of the sea serpent!"

"Quiet, Sam."

"Are you all right, Professor?" said Sam, noticing an unexpected look of angst on the Professor's face.

"No more talk. They might be listening to our minds. I'm feeling the presence of terrible evil."

They continued under the dark keel of the Nautilad until they came to a hazy patch of circular blue light and the Professor manipulated the aquaplanes and rudder to steer the

213

midget sub up through the hatch into the diving suit changing room.

***

"Something's wrong. Can't you feel it, Master Nicademus?" said Arnakk as he and the General clambered into the Nautilad's glass conning tower dome through the deck-hatch.

"Only the Professor's stink in this woeful pile of junk, Sire."

The boy closed his eyes and breathing in deeply said, "Evil! I sense evil here, Master Nicademus! He is here! I sense it. Search the underboat from bow to stern and tell the men to leave no crevice unexamined. We have the opportunity to catch the villain. The very future of Atlantis is at stake!"

Chapter 46

Horror in the House of Pain

Lu gagged at the smell billowing from the opening door in the bowels of the prison fortress. She felt herself drifting, as if anesthetised, into a warm, comfortable trance and she pinched herself hard enough to cause a bruise on her arm before fumbling in her pockets for a handkerchief to cover her nose and mouth.

The dark chamber beyond the door was slippery with glistening tracks of slime from a grotesque snail-creature, all pink with weeping warts and leaking lesions and advancing on Toby. A gigantic probing proboscis was tentatively feeling its way as it slowly but surely sniffed him out.

"Do something Bill!" cried Lu from the doorway.

Bill slowly turned only to reveal the same blank wide-eyed expression as Toby.

"Bill!" screamed Lu again, but Bill seemed powerless to resist the vile scene unfolding before them.

The snail now had Toby completely engulfed in the funnel-like proboscis and slowly it began sealing him inside a huge translucent wobbling fleshy bag. Within a moment Toby's immobile shape, a silhouette stretching the skin sack into the shape of his outline, was all that remained of him.

At almost the exact moment the sack sealed the narcotic gas ceased and Bill jerked back into life. To his horror, the dark outline of a long black barb began sliding out from the pink pulsating body of the snail towards Toby's stomach. At once the boy's sedated figure began thrashing and kicking wildly inside the bag as the snail injected him with its venom and a pale green digesting fluid began slowly filling the bag.

In a second Bill and Lu had their stun guns trained on the snail.

"Aim for the shell," cried the familiar voice of Podesta Blenkinsopp from a barred cell across the chamber.

With a deafening crackle, two dazzling red plasma streams darted from the stun guns into the monster's shell.

A loud belching noise filled the room; Bill and Lu ducked as razor-sharp fragments of the busting shell spun in all directions. For a split second the bag inflated and Toby was shot out in a foul smelling burp and a flood of gloopy gunk.

"TOBY!" cried Lu, running over and kneeling beside him. Toby's gloop covered specs slid to one side and slowly he opened and closed one eye.

"*She's* injected him with paralysing venom," said Podesta Blenkinsopp from his cell. "He needs a Vril Doctor to heal him."

"Who is *she*, Captain?" said Bill, walking over to Podesta's cell door. "Stand back Captain!" A plasma bolt from Bill's stun gun blew the lock off and the door flew open. Bill recoiled at the sight of the captain standing in the shadows with a snub pig nose, pig ears, and trotters.

"She," replied the captain with a grunt, "was the fiendish Doctor Grimus. It was she who turned everyone in this place into part human, part animal monsters."

"Yes she's totally evil!" whinnied a voice from the cell next-door. "Will you let me out too, please?"

216

"Stand back then," said Bill and he blew the lock from the second cell door and a creature with the torso, arms and head of a man and the palomino body and legs of a horse trotted out swishing its silvery tail this way and that.

"How do you do? The name's Sidney," said the creature extending its hand for Bill to shake. "Your friend looks very poorly."

"The guards will be here at any minute. We've got to get you all out of here," interrupted Podesta Blenkinsopp.

"Lu. You try and lock the door," said Bill. "Is there another way out of here, Captain?"

"Not that I know of. The way you came in is the only way out."

"There are soldiers in the corridor outside!" cried Lu from behind the door.

"Here Captain. You'd better have Toby's Stun Gun. I think we'll have to fight our way out!" said Bill, handing the weapon to Podesta Blenkinsopp.

The captain's face crumpled and he replied, "I can't use it Bill. Look! My hands have been turned into useless pig's trotters."

"Give it to me," said Sidney. "I've still got my hands, I'll help you fight."

"Free us and we'll help too!" chorused dozens of voices from other cells in the building.

"Reinforcements! News travels fast!" laughed Podesta Blenkinsopp.

"They've got a battering ram!" cried Lu, taking several steps back from the door and aiming her stun-gun to shoot the first guard who crossed the threshold.

Bill and Sidney busied themselves blasting the locks off the other cells and within minutes the chamber was filled with dozens of the victims of Dr Grimus's fiendish experiments: pig-men, bull-men, centaurs like Sidney, crocodile-men with hugely deformed jaws and rows of devilish teeth - all armed with chair and table legs, bits of chains and anything else heavy or sharp they found that could be used as weapons.

"QUIET! Everybody!" cried Bill, trying to make himself heard over the babble in the room. "Form two groups behind each side of the door. When they break in Lu, me and Sidney will take out as many of the leaders as we can with our stun guns. Then everyone else charge the ones behind!"

Everyone took up their positions and holding their breaths, counting the battering ram beats, they waited for the chamber door to splinter off its hinges.

Chapter 47

Battle in the House of Pain

The door to Grimus's chamber burst from its hinges with a deafening BANG and the rending of splintering wood. For a moment the soldiers stood squinting as their eyes became accustomed to the gloom of the chamber. Seizing the moment, Lu, Bill, and Sidney (who had formed a rank in the centre of the room) opened fire with their stun guns. Thick red plasma tracks burst into the first lines of guards who exploded inside their armour. The remaining soldiers, now in disarray, fell back, desperately seeking cover from the withering stun gun fire and the charging animal mutants enraged by their horrific treatment at the hands of Dr. Grimus.

Lu winced at the screaming, when saliva flowed with blood as men were chewed and spun by giant crocodile men, ripped open by tiger mutants and beaten with makeshift clubs and cleaved by axes and blades of charging pig-men, ox-men, and rearing centaurs.

"LOOK OUT, BILL!" screamed Lu as a lone Atlantean guard burst through the melee into the chamber brandishing his Vril killing-staff. A bolt of brilliant purple Vril leapt from the staff and a bull-man fighting at Bill's shoulder exploded into atoms. The retaliation from Bill's stun gun was swift and its red lightning blew the Vril staff from the marauder's hand. The disarmed guard watched in disbelief as the hand that held the vaporised Vril staff withered into a smoking cinder and in the next second he was grabbed from behind in the bloody jaws of a crocodile-man.

The battle raged on for what seemed an age, but was only twenty minutes. It ended as the remaining Atlantean guards were overcome by sheer numbers and locked into cells with unbroken doors.

"We really must get going," said Podesta Blenkinsopp. "The others are prisoners in the Royal Palace. There's a Vril doctor there called Pimpy. He should be able to help Toby."

"It won't be long before more guards come," added Sidney. "You'd better put your friend on my back. I'll carry him as far as the palace."

A sly-looking alligator-man then said, "We will barricade the door and wait to hold off any Atlantean guards that come. That should give you time enough to escape."

"Thanks," said Bill, shaking the alligator warmly by the claw.

"Toby looks awfully pale," said Lu as she did her best to make Toby comfortable on Sidney's back.

"We'd better make haste. The effects of the venom may become incurable if it's left too long," cautioned Sidney, looking back over his shoulder.

"I think we should cover Toby with a blanket or something. It'll look pretty suspicious a centaur carrying a body of an unconscious Xenode through the streets of Metronis!" said Bill.

"There's a blanket in my cell," said Sidney. Lu fetched the blanket and spread it gently to conceal Toby, leaving him a place to breathe at its edge.

"We're off then! We'll need to disguise ourselves if we're going through the city," said Bill, and together they picked their way through the battle carnage in the corridor collecting discarded helmets, shields, swords, and pieces of body armour and sackcloth.

Once outside in the sunshine, they dressed as a raggle-taggle detail of Atlantean guards and made their way towards the black city and Ayesha's palace.

Chapter 48

Beneath the Arena of Doom

"Halt!" yelled a guard as they approached the towering walls and main gate of Metronis. "State your business."

"We are bringing a prisoner to the Palace Dungeons," replied Bill, pointing to the Toby-shaped lump under the blanket on Sidney's back. The guard approached and lifted the corner of the blanket carelessly.

"He don't look very 'ealthy'?" the sentry replied, in a jaded tone.

"No. We've come from Dr Grimus. We're taking him to the Vril doctor called Pimpy," cut in Podesta Blenkinsopp.

"You look like a shower from her outfit. Sure you're not one of her experiments?" smirked the guard. "Well you're a bit late. All the Vril doctors will be at the Circus by now. Mind you, it beats me why they bother with doctors at the Arena of Doom. None of them gets out alive. They never do. It's a fix!"

"Who won't get out alive?" asked Bill.

"Typical! Hello? Which planet are you on!" laughed the sentry. "The Overworlders of course. They're feeding some new Overworlders to the Wiggleon today."

"Maybe we should go straight to the Circus then?" said Lu.

"Der! YES! You're wasting your time going to the Palace. And by the looks of *him* you need a doctor quick. Watch my lips! They'll all be at the Arena of Doom today!"

Lu only just stopped herself asking the guard for directions to the arena. Any Atlantean who had to ask the way to what seemed the most popular venue in Metronis would surely arouse suspicion.

The road went three ways inside the city wall and Lu hoped they'd pick the right one. She looked pleadingly at Sidney and when the sentry wasn't looking mouthed, "Which way?"

The centaur shrugged his shoulders and mouthed back "I don't know."

She looked at Bill. He didn't know either. "Ok everyone, this way," said Bill taking the right hand road.

"Ha, ha, ha! The rumours are true! You lot *are* escapees from Grimus's *failed* experiments. Are you cross-eyed? You're going the WRONG way! It's THIS way!" cackled the sentry pointing down a road leading in the opposite direction.

Sheepishly they all turned and before the guard was completely beyond earshot they heard him call, "How long have you lot been away on the 'Farm'?"

The street soon began crowding with Atlanteans heading toward the tall outline of the distant arena. As they approached, Lu could see the building looked exactly like a newly-built version of the Coliseum in Rome. People began forming separate queues at ticket doors signed above with strange Atlantean hieroglyphics.

The longest queues by far were those peopled with the poor, and these were slow-moving. Other lines with off-duty soldiers and more prosperous-looking citizens were short and slick.

Bill led Sidney to the faster-moving queue and his heart beat faster as they approached the ticket booth. Sitting behind a lighted arched window set in the wall was a dwarf-like creature with arms that bristled with coarse black hairs and ended in two-pronged claws instead of hands. The claws snapped and clicked collecting money and giving out change with the staccato precision of a machine.

Standing in the dark corridor in front of the ticket office was a monstrous soldier who shoved spectators towards their designated areas within the arena after they'd bought tickets from the hairy-dwarf. When the soldier saw Sidney and Podesta Blenkinsopp, he forgot his shoving and strode over to confront them.

"What's the meaning of this?" he demanded, shoving the centaur.

"What the meaning of what?" replied Lu innocently fluttering her eyelashes.

"Jed's teeth! Are you STUPID? Bringing mutants to the arena. AND IN PUBLIC!"

"We've got an injured man," said Bill, lifting the corner of the blanket to reveal Toby's ash-white face.

"Then what are you are you doing here? If he needs a doctor take him to the Sanatorium with the wounded Glads and Overworlders."

"Where?"

The soldier grabbed Bill's shoulder and dragged him out of the passage into the street. Bill gripped the handle of his stun-gun.

"Moron! That building," growled the soldier pointing at a single storey building with a orange-tiled roof that abutted the back of the arena. "Take your rabble over there."

Even outside, the Sanatorium smelled of sawdust and blood and reminded Podesta of the weekly trip to the butcher's shop he and his mother would make when he was a child. Two guards stood at the doors, which opened and closed frequently as wounded gladiators were stretchered in and out to be seen by scurrying, red-robed doctors and uniformed nurses.

"There he is," said the Captain, peering through one of the windows.

"Who?" replied Bill.

"I think his name's Pimpy. He's the Vril Doctor who cured Stu."

"Stu was sick?" said Lu.

"Wounded by a Sabre Tooth's Vril staff. Don't worry. He's quite all right now. Their doctors seem almost miraculous."

"Can you attract his attention, Captain?"

Podesta tapped on the window with his trotter. The small figure attending to a wounded man looked up, but did not look back through the window at Podesta. Podesta tapped again. For a second time the doctor looked up, this time with a puzzled expression. Podesta tapped for a third time, slightly harder, and this time the doctor looked round. For a moment his eyebrows raised and his eyes widened in fleeting recognition, then seeing what Dr Grimus had done to Podesta an expression of sadness spread like a cloud over his face.

Bill and Podesta watched as the dwarf-like figure's mouth formed the word, "Aaeeeshaaar!" and a rosy glow fell over the wounded man and within a second the patient was on his feet and bending forward and scowling in the small doctor's face. Bill jumped as the newly restored gladiator cuffed the doctor smartly over the right ear and walked out of the Sanatorium. Rubbing his ear and looking rather crestfallen, the doctor signalled to Podesta and they watched as the small figure disappeared in the bustle of the Sanatorium.

A few minutes later he was standing in front of them. "I'm sorry to see you've met Dr Grimus. I'm afraid there's nothing I can do to reverse what she's done to you," he said.

"No. We have a wounded boy, Pimpy," replied the Captain.

"Why did that gladiator hit you?" asked Lu.

"It is the custom for a patient to give their doctor a clip round the ear if the treatment is a success. It represents the patient's final exorcism of death. And my name is NOT Pimpy. I am Mook Wundabuck, but Wundabuck will suffice."

"We're very sorry, Wundabuck, but my friend has been poisoned by Dr Grimus," said Bill, and he lifted the blanket for Wundabuck to see Toby. "Can you help him?"

"Did she ensnare him to devour? Did her stomach sack swallow him whole?"

"Yes," replied Lu, "and then she injected him with a horrible black barb thing."

"How long ago?"

"Six hours?" said Bill, hoping that Mook Wundabuck would tell them it was not too late to save Toby.

226

"This will be touch-and-go. The paralysis is advanced. Grimus's venom is very fast-acting."

"Correction. *Was* fast-acting. We killed her and broke out from the House of Pain several hours ago," said Bill.

"Then they will be hunting you. Leave a lookout and lay the boy out of sight at the back of the Sanatorium," said Wundabuck. Lu stayed with Podesta Blenkinsopp.

Presently they heard a cry of "Aaeeeshaaar!" and an intense rosy glow lit the gloomy gap where Toby lay. Nothing then happened for several tense minutes, until the matter-of-fact words, "That's it! Jobby done!" signalled Wundabuck's Vril-cure had worked. Lu was relieved when the others reappeared with Toby rubbing his eyes as if woken from a deep sleep and she ran to throw her arms around him in welcome.

Mook Wundabuck waited nervously for his customary clip-round-the-ear but to his relief it never came, only a dazed handshake from Toby and a kiss on his cheek from Lu.

"Do you know what happened to my friends?" asked Podesta Blenkinsopp.

"They are here," replied the doctor. "The boy named Stu and your friend Mike will both face the Wiggleon at this afternoon's games. The others will be kept here to be slaughtered by the new graduates of the Military Academy as proving slaves next week."

"What about a woman called Wendy?" asked Bill anxiously.

"She is here also. She is your mother, boy?"

Bill nodded. "Can you help us get them all out, Doctor Wundabuck?"

"Not dressed as a troupe of unconvincing soldiers, I can't," replied the doctor. "You will blend in better dressed as Gladiators; we have lots of old armour in the Spoliarium. I'm sure the previous owners won't mind you borrowing them." Wundabuck then chuckled before going on. "Then you can pretend to be Glads we've cured in the Sanatorium. How do you propose getting your friends out, may I ask?"

"With these," said Bill, holding up his stun gun. The power dial was glowing vivid red showing the weapon was fully charged.

Sidney returned Toby's weapon. "Here. It will be more deadly in your hands, Young Overworlder."

"I remember those. They are the crude weapons of Overworlders," said the doctor. "Did you get them from the Professor?"

"Yes," said Lu, "you know him?"

"Everyone in Atlantis knows the ancient legend of the Professor. Has he returned?"

"We don't know," said Bill, and together they all took turns to tell Mook Wundabuck the story of Karnak House, the Nautilad, and how they'd arrived in Atlantis.

"So, the old prophecy unfolds," said Mook Wundabuck, his last words suddenly drowned by a loud brassy fanfare and the roar of spectators from inside the Arena of Doom.

***

Bill felt uneasy about wearing a dead gladiator's armour, especially as some of it still ran with the evidence of its owner's demise.

They were pulled by Sidney on one of the rickety two-wheeled carts used to carry the wounded from the dingy pens which housed slaves and gladiators waiting to fight.

Amid clangs of clashing bronze and the unearthly scream of something not of this world that sent shivers to their marrow, the tunnel walls of the arena's basement shook with roars, cheers, and applause from the excited crowds in the seats above.

"Stop here please, Sidney," said Mook Wundabuck as they approached a wide stone arch in the wall. Bill could hardly contain his joy seeing Wendy through the bars huddled in a corner next to Farouke. Wendy was sobbing and instinctively Bill looked for Mike and then for Stu. Both were missing.

"I have two freshly-healed Glads and a pigman ready to fight," said the doctor to a burly turnkey who lumbered out from the shadows to unlock the cell, muttering to himself and nodding. Toby glanced nervously through his helmet visor at Bill. Bill returned Toby a knowing a wink and as the gaoler's keys jangled and the door squeaked open he drew his stun gun. With the power meter set to heavy stun (Bill thought the gaoler looked thick-skulled), he fired a yellow plasma bolt into the turnkey's sloping forehead.

"Ugh!" grunted the turnkey, peering up and going cross-eyed before sagging to his knees and toppling forward on to his face.

"Come on Mum!" shouted Bill. He pulled off his helmet to show his face. Toby did the same, and at once Wendy's face lit up and her tears were banished by laughter and she ran into Bill's arms. Another roar from the crowd in the arena swamped their efforts to speak.

In a second the arena fell into eerie silence.

"Mike!" cried Wendy. "They took Mike and Stu to fight the Wiggleon. Something's just happened to them. I just know it!"

"Follow us, Mrs Young," said Toby manfully, and after Lu picked up the jailor's heavy iron key ring, they unlocked a second gate, and together with Farouke they unhitched Sidney from the cart and ran up a flight of stone steps to the arena.

Chapter 49

The Wiggleon

They stood in a whitewashed antechamber with a large red-painted symbol on the back wall that Bill assumed was an Atlantean numeral. The chamber smelled of a latrine and the all-too-familiar iron bars faced in on the arena.

Wendy screamed. A monster the size of an armoured double-decker bus standing on end towered over Mike who crouched wounded against the arena's high perimeter wall on the far side of the ring. The creature's massive jointed scorpion tail was poised for the kill and it snatched away Mike's shield and broadsword with huge, black lobster claws.

"Help him," cried Wendy, her voice drowned out by the bloodlust roars of the crowd.

The Wiggleon's great human head, with flying black plaited tresses held by silver clips, stared wide-eyed at the box in the auditorium reserved for Ayesha and Arnakk.

"Mercy or death? GIVE ME THE SIGN!" he roared contemptuously, shaking an enormous human fist at the crowd. Gobs of his spit flew in all directions as he brought down a huge sandaled foot to thunder down through the tunnels of the hypogeum deep below the wooden arena floor.

"DEATH! DEATH! DEATH!" chanted the crowd.

"Quick! Gimme your stun gun, Wiseman," snarled Stu, reaching through the bars to Toby. He was bleeding from a nasty head wound and limping in battered armour.

"Good luck!" said Toby passing Stu his pistol.

"We need to get through this gate!" cried Bill, rattling the bars angrily.

"I have an idea! Wait here," said Mook Wundabuck scuttling back down the stairs into the labyrinth of tunnels beneath the arena. "There is a room with levers that unlock gates and make things work in the arena," he called, his voice floating back up the stairs behind him.

At length they heard a rhythmic squeaking of metal parts and the barred gate rumbled sideways. Suddenly they were in the arena looking up at towering ranks of bloodthirsty spectators who responded to their entrance with wild cheers and applause, anticipating more gruesome deaths to come.

In a flash the Wiggelon paused and turned its back on Mike to face them.

"I will kill you!" it roared, and with astonishing speed for a creature of such size it charged them.

"Have some of this!" cried Stu, loosing a bright red plasma stream at the monster.

"Fool!" cried the Wiggleon. "Do you think your pea-shooter weapon will harm ME!"

The plasma stream found its mark, but with a boo and then a goading roar from the crowd, the Wiggleon kept coming.

Bill and Toby fired their stun guns and the crowd went wild as the Wiggleon reared up and stabbed the sand-covered arena floor with its sting a foot away from Bill's right leg.

Bill drew his gladiator's broad sword and sliced at the bony joint connecting the bulbous sting to the Wiggleon's tail. With the clicks of closing joints the Wiggleon side-stepped and the blade hit solid bone and vibrated painfully from Bill's grasp to land in the sand several yards away. With two or three sharp tugs to pull its embedded sting from the wood-floor beneath the sand, the Wiggleon turned on Wendy.

"Get on my back!" called Sidney, and with four bounds Wendy leapfrogged over the centaur's croup and loins to land on its back a split-second before the Wiggleon's sting dug deep into the floor where she'd been standing.

With her arms around Sidney's human waist he galloped away towards Mike "Are you all right?" said Wendy, dismounting the centaur and kneeling beside the country vet.

"I've felt better," said Mike, wiping a trickle of blood from his forehead.

"Let me," said Wendy, dabbing the gash with a clean corner of her tunic.

Mike pulled her towards him to kiss her lips and said, "I've got to help the boys." Wincing, he picked up his shield and broadsword, and staggered up behind the monster which was still trying to free its sting from the wooden floor and fend off a frontal attack from the boys with its claws. The crowd roared with delight as Mike, praying the sting would stay jammed, jumped on the tail and ran up the massive bone joints like a ladder to cling on the Wiggleon's massive neck.

With the crack of splintering wood, the sting came free and whipped this way and that before plunging right through Stu's left thigh.

"Aaaagh," screamed the wounded boy, rolling about on the floor in agony. The crowd screamed with delight as the Wiggleon swivelled its enormous head, snapping and grabbing at Mike with evil rows of teeth filed into evil points. Mike could smell the creature's foul breath in his face as its jaws encircled his shield arm. In desperation and with what little strength he had left, Mike drew back his broadsword and plunged it into the Wiggleon's right eye.

The blade pierced the soft eye-matter in a torrent of blood and jelly and Mike jiggled and poked the sword until he felt the back of the socket give way and the blade slide effortlessly into the creature's brain.

As if to accompany the crowd's shrieks of delight the Wiggleon screamed and threw back its head, ripping the hilt from Mike's grasp and tottering while it hopelessly tried to remove the sword with its snapping claws. Then loudly exhaling its final breath it collapsed with a thud in a twitching heap.

In a matter of moments the crowds began booing and hissing and throwing seat cushions and rubbish into the arena. Other gates rumbled open and a cohort of Atlantean Houscarls, brandishing Vril Killing staffs, began filing into the arena.

Podesta Blenkinsopp and Farouke stumbled as the arena floor beneath them opened and they fell headlong into a caged chamber. A pattering of tiny running feet echoing along a dark tunnel heralded the arrival of Mook Wundabuck.

"Call the others!" he cried from the tunnel. In a moment everyone was staggering and stumbling wounded and bleeding from the arena into the open trap door.

"You look in a bad way. I will attend to you later," said Wundabuck, bundling everyone into the animal-smelling tunnel. "Follow me! Quickly!"

The sounds of roars and snarling big cats filled the tunnel and after a minute everybody emerged into a stinking animal house where starving lions prowled the floors of soiled cages waiting for their release and the promise of an easy meal of plump slaves in the arena.

"I hear men coming, Effendi!" cried Farouke, cocking his head listening to running feet and clanking armour inside the tunnel.

"Wait outside," ordered Wundabuck, pushing everyone through a street-door. He wrenched a lever that operated a mechanism that opened a gate from the lion's cage into the tunnel.

Closing the animal house door on the screams behind him, Mook Wundabuck joined the others outside. The light was starting to fade into evening, as it did rapidly in Atlantis, and the little Vril doctor surveyed the panting band of exhausted friends before him.

"Blimey! That bleedin' place was nearly as bad as Millwall versus Gillingham at the Den!" groaned Stu. The sting had gone completely through his leg and the Wiggleon's venom harmlessly expelled outside of his body.

The next half-hour was spent healing everybody's wounds and once restored to their former health, Mike said, "We need to find the Professor and Sam and get out of this place."

The Wiggleon

"In that case, I shall be pleased to guide you all back to the docks where the Professor's underboat is moored," said Mook Wundabuck.

Chapter 50

The Streets of Metronis

They had emerged from the animal house into a deserted alley piled with boxes and garbage from back entrances and running with rats.

"How are we going to get back to the docks without being recognised? Won't the guards remember us at the city gate?" said Wendy.

"We need to lose this armour, for a start," said Mike. "And Sidney, you must follow us from a distance. They'll be expecting us to be with a centaur, and…um…Well, you do stick out a bit like a sore thumb, my friend."

Sidney nodded his agreement, and after the armour was hidden behind some boxes of broken amphorae Mook Wundabuck said, "I have a suggestion. We will pretend that you are a party of Smegeye's slaves infected with plague and I am escorting you back to the Serpent underboat for disposal at sea."

"Disposal at sea?" exclaimed Lu.

"Don't ask," answered Bill, taking Lu's hand and squeezing it gently.

"You must take earth and make a paste with spit to smear into your faces; especially under your eyes and fingernails. Make your arms and hands look as dark as you can. No guard will challenge us and risk catching the pestilence; it is a most horrible death. When we do encounter guards, cough and retch and stagger as if you are ill."

What should I do?" Podesta Blenkinsopp asked, wondering but not mentioning whether he would be welcome on the homeward voyage as a fully transformed pig man.

"You and I shall go together my friend," said Sidney, patting the unfortunate captain on the shoulder and offering him his hand. "Here there's room on my back for two."

"Come. We must hasten to the docks if you are to escape this place," said Mook Wundabuck, pointing to the sky where flocks of birds were leaving the city. "Behold! I feel bad things are about to happen."

Dawn's golden glow silhouetted the plain outlines of the Metronian houses by the time they reached the black, barred gates of the city and there was no need to feign exhaustion.

"Who goes there!" barked a guard from the shadows.

"Do you want to wake all of Metronis?" answered the Vril Doctor. "I am Dr. Wundabuck from the lofty serpent slave vessel moored without."

"State your business. Who are these people?"

"They are new slaves infected by pestis. I am taking them back to be quarantined for disposal at sea."

"My wife and child coughed out their guts in blood during the last pestilence. Your kind should be shot. Bringing foreign diseases to Metronis for profit."

"Your story saddens me, friend; but 'tis the labour of Xenodes that clothes your back and puts food in your belly."

"Always an answer," snapped the soldier emerging from the guardhouse and opening a pedestrian door in the gate. "Go and good riddance!"

Wendy sighed with relief when the heavy door to the city slammed shut. Stretching before them was the white road to the dock, the Nautilad and she hoped, freedom.

Chapter 51

The Presence of Evil

The Professor steered the midget sub to park it in its bay in the diving suit changing room hatch. His deep feeling of unease persisted as he and Sam removed their helmets and dismounted the sub.

"Set your stun gun to 'maximum stun', Sam."

Sam followed the Professor's lead and swept the room with his gun before walking over to the door into the Nautilad's main corridor.

"Can you still feel evil, Professor?" said Sam.

"It is almost suffocating," the older man replied.

"Search in here!" commanded the voice of an Atlantean soldier beyond the door.

"Hide!" hissed the Professor, and the pair split to take cover among lockers and spare diving gear.

"I heard something move in there, Captain," said one of the soldiers.

"Keep your voices down and set your staffs to stun only. Give me a Pommandier, Auxiliary," ordered the captain in a low voice.

The nearest of the six members of the search party reached in a leather pouch and handed the captain a grey spherical object the size of a cricket ball. The others pulled down visors to cover their faces.

Sam Scrivener crouched behind a locker and watched as someone outside turned the door-handle. A hand tossed what looked like a ball into the changing room. Sam's bow-string reflexes squeezed the trigger and a yellow stream of plasma leapt from his stun gun into the back of the door. The ball bounced three times and the Professor yelled, "A Pommandier! Put your helmet…."

It was too late, a sweet-smelling purple cloud filled the changing room, and Sam felt himself drifting into a warm comfortable sleep.

**

The bucket of cold water came as a rude awakening.

"Oh my poor head," groaned Sam and he tried to massage his forehead but found his hands bound behind his back. "Hey! What is this?" he cried tugging at the ropes.

"If you struggle the bindings will tighten," said an Atlantean soldier standing over him.

They were in the Professor's Salon. Sam looked around for the Professor, but he was nowhere to be seen.

"Your confederate woke an hour ago," said a senior-looking soldier leaning in to peer into Sam's face. "Come. I will take you to him."

Sam was unsteady on his legs for several minutes and when they arrived at the foot of the conning tower ladder his head was bagged in a black hood and his hands freed.

"Up!" said the soldier.

Sam felt his footing gingerly until he got used to the rung-spacing, and when he eventually reached the conning tower his hands were tied again and the hood removed. The sun shone through the dome and, blinking, Sam discovered

241

he had a commanding view of the Metronis docks. A boy wearing bright armour was on the far side of conning tower deck and Sam presumed he was the Professor's lost son, Rudi. It wasn't long before the Professor was bundled up through the hatch, similarly bound and hooded.

The boy turned and ordered the Professor's hood be removed. He seemed unwillingly fascinated by the Professor from the moment their eyes met.

"Kneel!" he commanded. "You are in the presence of royalty, Wizard,"

"I am?" answered the Professor, kneeling meekly.

"Do you not know to whom you are speaking? I am Prince Arnakk of Atlantis. Second only to She-We-Obey, Queen Ayesha!"

"You remind me of a little boy I used to know," said the Professor.

"Insolent DOG!" shouted Arnakk. "Untie him and give him a Vril staff, Nicademus. I choose this xenode to be my proving slave!"

"I will not fight you," said the Professor quietly.

"You are a coward as well as a terrorist."

"No, Rudi. I am your father."

"Rudi? LIAR! You stinking Liar! My father died a hero at the Battle of Striding Landy." A crackling red glow suddenly enveloped the boy's Vril staff.

"I will NOT fight you, Rudi!"

Incensed, the boy charged and with a two handed stroke brought down the glowing Vril staff towards the Professor's skull. In a split second the Professor's Vril staff lit with an almost blinding white sheen and parried the blow amid a flash and a shower of sparks. The boy recoiled, rotated the staff clockwise to his right, and sliced at the Professor's middle. Once again the Professor parried the blow and jumped back to avoid a stabbing thrust at his heart. The boy then grimaced as from nowhere a red liquid line of blood ran from a wound on his exposed bicep.

"They're going to kill each other," whispered Hedgehog from the ventilation shaft.

"It's terrifying. Their faces look just like the boy who shot you with the stone, Hedgehog," replied Vole, shielding his face from flying sparks with his paws.

"Can't you stop to this!" said Legit. "Im so nervous, I think I'll skunk in a minute!"

"NO!" squeaked Vole and Monty together, and Hedgehog said it quietly because hedgehogs rarely raise their voices.

For a fleeting moment the boy's concentration faltered while he recollected a faint and disquieting memory. A memory from where? Was it from a previous life? Whatever this memory's origin, the boy recalled the voice of an animal; a conversation with a bat called Botulus. That was it! And trouble of some kind. Disturbed by the memory of a new-found and weird ability to talk to and understand animal-kind, the boy's guard dropped, and with a blinding blood red flash that seared into his vision; the dazzling white lightning of the Professor's Vril staff flew downwards and the boy's hand, still clutching his Vril staff, clattered bloodlessly on to the deck.

"RUDI! My SON!" cried the Professor throwing down his Vril staff and running forward to catch the fainting boy before he fell.

"Seize him!" yelled Nicademus, and three Houscarls lunged forward and grabbed the Professor from behind, pulling him away.

"Get a Vril doctor! Quickly!" ordered Nicademus, cradling Arnakk in his arms.

***

The now chaotic vapours in the White Room of quaking white-hooded Vrilmen, took on the terrifying form of Ayesha's enraged face.

"Tell me what has befallen my son, Master Mentith! I am feeling pain. So much PAIN!"

The terror-stricken shaman threw himself in a green heap in front of the vapour-crucible and said, "Sadly it appears he has been wounded in a duel, Your Highness."

"A duel with whom? Is it a serious wound?"

"With the Professor, Great One. Unfortunately Arnakk lost his hand but I am assured a Vril doctor has been sent for."

"I hope for your sake the doctor arrives in time. Where is the Professor now, Mentith?"

"I believe he is held prisoner of General Nicademus aboard his own underboat, Your Highness."

"Good! Then we shall kill two birds with one stone, Master Mentith! I shall pray at the feet of Taurax and mind-meet with my son to order the Professor's immediate execution. His body shall hang from the left pillar of the city gates and his spiked head on the right! You, Master Mentith, will give the order for our forces to attack. Destroy the enemies of Atlantis! And remember. I want no prisoners, only dead foes."

244

Chapter 52

The War Begins

Sam Scrivener looked up from the conning tower dome as the skies of Metronis blackened with flying machines.

One of the Houscarls standing near began laughing and pointing with his Vril staff said, "See the terrible might of She, Overworlder? Our forces go at the pleasure of She-We-Obey to wreak death on the insolent Areenee invader. There shall be no mercy."

***

In the sewer outlet control room Nikvok stared out through the observation windows. The sea beyond boiled with red Atlantean Vril canon plasma. He covered his eyes. Terrified faces stared ghost-like from the cockpit of a nearby midget sub consumed in billowing black smoke and fire. The white faces disappeared as the stricken craft slowly spiralled into the shadowy depths of an unknown abyss below.

Behind him a strident alarm sounded and a purple light flashed above the heavily-armoured door to the main sewer tunnel.

"It must be Blatvok and his detail trying to get back from the tunnel!"

245

The War Begins

Immediately, Nikvok ran to a small control console beside the door and unlocked it.

The control room's marmalade cat's back arched and he hissed at the ominous smell of burning flesh and smoke that seeped in as the door cracked open.

Nikvok's eyes stung and watered as he stared out into the smoking darkness beyond the door. The unmistakable screech of Vril staffs and screaming men floated up the iron service ladder from the sewer.

Suddenly, to his relief, Nikvok saw Blatvok doggedly clambering, hand over hand, up the ladder toward him.

A faint smile lit Blatvok's upturned face when he saw his brother's hands reaching to help him up the final rungs.

Nikvok braced himself to carry his brother's weight. Losing balance, he toppled backwards. Blatvok weighed less than a child! A sick feeling welled up from the pit of his stomach. Blatvok's legs and lower body were gone, and as Nikvok stooped to hold his brother and kiss his cold lips, Blatvok closed his eyes and died.

A jagged plasma bolt crackled and splashed the metal of a nearby wall plate into a hole and a mist of molten metal.

Wiping his eyes with the back of his sleeve, Nikvok lifted Blatvok's broken body against his chest. He backed away from the access ladder and retreated to the control room where he laid down his brother's corpse to close and lock the armoured door and await his fate.

Chapter 53

Arrival of the Witch Queen

The towering statue of Taurax frowned down on Ayesha's kneeling figure. Dressed in a diaphanous robe that showed her deceptively youthful-looking three-thousand year-old figure, she gazed up in meditation, summoning the power of Vril to allow her wounded son to hear her thoughts.

Her body felt the pain of his severed nerves, and she called out to him, "Arnakk. Arnakk. 'tis Ayesha, your mother, Arnakk."

***

In the Nautilad's conning tower, Arnakk closed his eyes involuntarily. The voice in his head was as clear. It was as if She were standing next to him.

"Aye mother, I hear you," he replied inside his mind.

"You hold prisoner the one who wounded you, Arnakk?"

"Yes, mother."

"Execute him! KILL him, Arnakk!"

"Erm…."

"Something troubles you, my brave boy?"

"He called me his son, mother."

247

"He is false! Your father died a hero in The Battle of Striding Landy. Arnakk! Cut out his lying tongue and bring me his head on a plate."

"Yes, mother. I will order Nicademus to cut...."

"NO! *Not* Nicademus! *You* must do it, Arnakk. You must cut off the wizard's head and rid me of this lying charlatan who would destroy our family and Atlantis. It is your destiny, Arnakk. His corpse must rot at the city gates as a testament to your greatness."

"Yes, mother. He will die on the dock in sight of his own underboat."

"Good. We shall come to the docks at dawn tomorrow to witness the execution."

The discourse over, Ayesha's voice disappeared but Arnakk could feel a presence, as if all-seeing eyes were watching his every move.

"Nicademus! Prepare a scaffold on the dock and take the prisoners below. They will both be executed tomorrow at dawn."

***

Neither Sam nor the Professor slept a wink. They were guarded in shifts all night and now that the sun was rising and the heat was already oppressive they were bound and led to scaffold.

In the structure's centre were a large brown-stained wooden block and basket taken from Smegeye's serpent vessel, kept to instil fear among his captives and discipline among the Sabretooths who mistreated them. Arnakk stood beside the block dressed in black. He held, with its blade inverted, a ceremonial Vril sabre specifically kept to dispatch high-ranking Xenodes or Atlantean nobility.

248

As the Professor and Sam (who was terrified) waited at the foot of the scaffold ladder, a very large and ornately-decorated golden flying machine hovered and landed a short distance away.

A wide hatch beneath its belly slowly opened and a ramp whined down to the dock. A party of slaves rolled a strip of red carpet down the ramp and along the quay, followed by a procession of priests and Atlantean dignitaries who formed parallel ranks either side of the carpet.

Last to emerge from the ship was a massive black and gold six-wheeled carriage. The carriage was manhandled by six hundred slaves who, encouraged by whips, steered it, held it from rolling away down the ramp, and then- accompanied by beating drums and fanfares- dragged it with huge hawsers along the red-carpet toward the scaffold.

Each of the entourage bowed as the triumphal car rumbled by and a fallen slave screamed beneath one of the massive front wheels as it halted a short distance in front of the scaffold.

More fanfares prompted a golden throne to rise up bearing the Witch Queen from a golden pyramid sculpted with tableaux of Atlantean battle victories from antiquity.

Ayesha stood robed in dazzling gold with a jewelled feather-plumed headdress. As she stretched out her arms the dock fell silent. She viewed the scaffold with cruelly-glittering eyes and cried, "Bring forth the prisoners!"

Lowering her arms, she signalled a slow rhythmic drum to roll.

"Get going!" snarled an armour-clad houscarl. He shoved the Professor and Sam with the butt of his Vril staff.

Sam's legs turned to jelly as slowly he climbed the ladder to the scaffold.

"Kneel!" commanded Ayesha, pointing at Sam.

The Professor laid his hand on Sam's shoulder before a guard pushed the unfortunate reporter to his knees in front of the block. A strong hand from behind forced Sam's head forward until his neck and chin rested in a carved indent in the block.

A fanfare sounded and a single drum beat signalled the start of the execution.

Chapter 54

Off With His Head

"Look!" said Mike, "The Nautilad's been taken out from inside Smegeye's ship. She looks as if she's been repaired!"

"What's that a golden flying machine, Mook?" asked Bill.

"'Tis the Witch Queen's ceremonial space barge. Something important is afoot," replied the diminutive Vril Doctor.

"And I think I can see what it is," said Lu as they approached the lines of finely dressed courtiers and the Ayesha's dazzling figure atop the pyramid throne-car.

"'Tis a beheading," said Mook Wundabuck gravely.

"NO! They're executing Sam Scrivener and the Professor!" screamed Wendy, forgetting herself and running pell-mell at the scaffold.

"STOP!" chorused Mike, Bill, Lu, Toby, and Mook Wundabuck.

It was too late. Several of the gathered noblemen ran forward and grabbed Wendy's arms. Ayesha looked down from the pyramid.

"Seize THEM!" she screamed and a phalanx of glinting Houscarls rushed out to round up Mook, Mike, Bill, Lu, Stu and Toby and the others.

"What have we here then?" said Ayesha looking down from her throne at the tattered band on the quayside.

"They are MY slaves, O-Great-One!" replied Smegeye, stepping from the ranks of Atlantean noblemen.

"The ones who came with the Professor from the Overworld?"

"Yes, Majesty," answered Arnakk from the scaffold.

"Good…In that case you shall execute them one-by-one, my son. They will be your Proving Slaves. Begin!"

Sam felt the cold sabre tickling the hairs on his neck as Arnakk gauged the cut. The drummers beat faster and faster until reaching a climax they stopped.

The sudden silence solidified spectators into statues, and in a sad flash Sam saw his mother, his father, his first love, Barkis his Labrador, and the office at Piddle Weekly.

There was a grunt from his executioner. The Vril blade whooshed through the air. The crowd gasped. Sam Scrivener clenched his fists and screwed his eyes tight shut.

Chapter 55

A Flying Machine Goes Missing

"Vell! Can you fly zis thing, Garcia? Ve might yet fly it back and snaffle ze crystal," demanded the Fat German rudely.

Casting the Fat German a withering look, the engineer slid into one of the seats in front of the now-blank control panel. He moved his palms over the panel as the boy had done. Nothing happened. He tried again. Still nothing happened.

"Third time lucky, Senor?"

But still nothing happened.

"Let me," the man with the blackened face said, stepping up to the panel. "I am The Grand Dragon of the Wallopshire Borough Council branch of the Brotherhood of the Green Dragon." He paused for effect. "And as such I am a shaman, fully-versed in the manipulation of the force of Vril. Perhaps you would vacate the driver's seat, Mr Smallpiece?"

Garcia and The Fat German's jaws dropped.

"YOU?" they chorused in disbelief.

"Let me assure you, gentlemen. There is nothing an officer of the Wallopshire Borough Council Front Line

Taskforce cannot do! Now if you would be so kind as to move over, Sir."

Closing his eyes, tilting back his head and adopting a pious expression, the Grand Dragon spread his hands over the panel and began slowly chanting, "Vril! Vril! VRIL!"

To Garcia and the Fat German's (and much to his own) surprise, the panel glimmered dimly and a hazy panorama of the outside-world flickered into view. The vision gradually became clearer and the controls of the panel brightened. In a moment the mechanical sounds of the ladder retracting and the hatch closing were heard and the floor level wobbled and with a whine, the machine began rising.

"Ach! I remember now!" exclaimed the Fat German. "Vallopshire Council. You are Herr Gray are you not?"

The whining stopped, the saucer suddenly dropped, and the panorama disintegrated into mist.

"Yes my name is Mr Gray," the blackened man answered. "I must ask you both for silence. I need complete concentration to summon and channel the force. If you interrupt me at this altitude we will surely crash! And how do you know my name is Gray?"

"Erm. Er. Your reputation precedes you Mein Herr. I read about you in the papers," garbled the Fat German, suddenly not wishing to reveal his connection with Ergolite and the council's failed investments that directly financed Garcia Smallpiece's death ray.

"I see. Perhaps we can proceed now? In silence?" replied Mr Gray. Something about the association of a fat German with a South American Indian engineer nagged in his mind like grit in an oyster shell.

A Flying Machine Goes Missing

After chanting once more they began rising again. The retracting landing legs served as a reminder to his passengers that any distractions now would probably prove fatal.

The Saucer lurched about the Atlantean sky in a seemingly-random series of climbs, dives, stalls, and banks.

Both Garcia and the Fat German could remember smoother flights - they staggered this way and that clinging desperately to control panels, crates, door posts, in fact anything that might be firmly attached - but neither chose to complain.

Their problems began when the instrument panel flashed a reading of fifty-three Grons. Nobody was completely sure quite what a Gron was, except that at fifty-three they were heading straight into an on-coming formation of Atlantean saucers that were following the distant Atlantean canal below towards the sea.

Neither Garcia nor the Fat German wanted to say anything, until the terrified faces of an oncoming saucer's crew loomed into view.

"Can we go down a beet Senor?"

Gray's eyes flicked open and immediately their saucer plummeted into the path of a *second* flying machine.

"Aaaagh!" cried the Fat German. "UP! UP! UP!"

CLANG!

"Dummkopf! You haff hit ze saucer above!"

"Well if I have it's all YOUR fault! Backseat drivers! You're both completely putting me off!" protested Gray. "This thing will probably be even harder to control if it's bent!"

A Flying Machine Goes Missing

At thirty-eight Grons they seemed to stabilise after Gray appeared to regain composure. Risking further calamity the Fat German ventured, "Look! The crystal! It's below us."

The crystal promptly disappeared from the view as the craft veered from side to side and its horizon pitched, lurched, and rolled.

"I don't want to worry you, Señores. I theenk we are being followed," declared Garcia, looking nervously at two flying machines in the rearward panorama.

A single flying machine with two red staffs protruding from its hull unleashed two red lightning bolts.

"Take evasive action, Herr Gray!"

The saucer suddenly shook as a lightning bolt found its mark. Smoke began billowing from somewhere inside.

I theenk we have been heet!" cried Garcia Smallpiece, grabbing the back of Gray's chair.

"Aaaaagh!" screamed the Fat German as the crystal suddenly filled the saucer's screen, and then with a blinding white flash....

Chapter 56

The Machine Stops

A blinding white flash bleached the Atlantean sky. A cry of pain rang out. And the smouldering hilt of the Vril Execution Sabre clattered onto the scaffold floor beside Sam's head.

Unable to believe his luck, the reporter opened his eyes, took a deep breath and then slowly rose from the bloodstained block.

The boy executioner was nursing a burnt hand and squinting beyond the scaffold with a terrified grimace.

The golden figure of Ayesha reeled backwards screaming. She reached a skinny hand towards a black billowing cloud rising from the mountain top where the temple crystal once glittered. Her youthful features were twisting into the grotesque sagging grey mask of an old witch. It seemed to Sam that she was suddenly aging, but worse than that, she now looked like a freshly-exhumed corpse. Her long flowing hair fell out in lumps and her face greyed and shrank, pulling her lips into a terrifying grin of blackening teeth. Almost bald now, she turned wide-eyed to Arnakk and tried to reach out to him with a bony claw. Her sad eyes bulged hideously from dark sockets and sinking to her knees, they shrivelled into black prunes and dropped on to her skeletal cheekbones. In an instant her body imploded leaving only a shapeless pile of golden garments and a stinking cloud of green dust that blew away with a roaring wind that suddenly blew up.

It looked to Sam as though the boy prince was waking from a dream, because he was blinking and looking himself up and down, frowning as if his clothes were suddenly alien to him. The frown turned to a look of confusion when the Professor called out to him from the other side of the scaffold with the tremulous voice of a very old man, "Rudi."

The boy was weeping and between sobs he replied, "Papa?"

In a moment father and son were embracing, reunited from different worlds after half a lifetime. Nicademus drew his Vril staff to cut the Professor down but like the execution sabre it was as lifeless as a spent firework.

Sam felt the scaffold tipping under his feet and he staggered to keep his balance.

A cry went up from nobleman and slave alike as the top of the mountain exploded. Great gobs of magma and rocks sprayed forth and sluggish steaming streams of lava ran in huge cracks that opened up in the streets swallowing people, temples, taverns, and dwellings.

Amid the unfolding destruction Podesta Blenkinsopp felt slightly dizzy. He began looking at himself, and let out a stifled a cry of joy. His pig's trotters had turned once more into human hands and feet. His trembling fingers touched his face - his nose was no longer a snub snout but sloped gently out from below the centre of his forehead to his nostrils above the grooved philtrum over his top lip. He needed a shave, but apart from that he felt human again. Sidney nodded his approval.

"Don't worry, Sidney. Perhaps you'll change back in a minute?" said the Captain.

"I do hope not, Captain Blenkinsopp. I've always been a centaur!"

***

From within the sewer outlet control room, Nikvok put down the marmalade cat and watched aghast as the murderous boiling plasma of the Atlantean Attack submarines ceased. It was as if a sympathetic god somewhere had turned off a light switch.

The tables turned, and he cheered as the surviving Areenee midget subs regrouped and counter-attacked sending the Atlantean armada spiralling out of control, flaming from their cooling vents and breather gills like fireflies in the black of the abyss.

The marmalade cat suddenly hissed and with a yowl disappeared into a crevice. The door to the sewer blew off with a bang that made Nikvok's ears ring. He looked down at his brother's poor body and tears turned to joy at the thought that in a few short moments he would be joining Blatvok in a glorious warrior's death. He unholstered his throat sickle. At least he would take one to Valdora with him.

Suicide-charging the sewer door, screaming his war cry, Nikvok was met by a bewildered man. Naked of beetle armour and wings, and carrying a black, matt, dead Vril staff, the man shrank back and held up a forearm in cringing defence. He dropped his useless weapon when Nikvok stopped in his tracks.

The confused man was soon joined by others climbing the ladder from the sewer. They too had shed their beetle armour, and as they emerged into the light and saw they were no longer beetle creatures, they began laughing and joking and clapping each other (and Nikvok) on the back.

The laughter stopped, however, the moment they saw Blatvok's body. Then their mood turned to anger. Anger at those who had turned them into murdering warrior-slaves and by manipulating their minds with Vril had forced them to fight for such a murdering evil empire.

"Revenge!" yelled the first man. "Death to the murderers of Atlantis!"

Within minutes the tool store was stripped of anything that could club, stab, or shoot, and those men with weapons led the way back into the tunnel.

Alone again, the control room cat came out of hiding and smiling began rubbing against Nikvok's legs. Nikvok stooped to stroke the cat and slowly the ringing in his ears was replaced by the cat's loud purring and the screams from somewhere deep in the sewer.

***

Master Mentith clasped both hands to his burning temples and ran when the shaking mountain cracked the lintels and columns of the white room, and its ceilings crashed down on to the gathered Vrilmen and filled the burned out vapour pit with smoking rubble.

***

In the mines of Tor, slaves reverted to their native states, some human, others Areenee, Frengling, and Lantvolken, all turning on their now-unarmed Atlantean masters, filling the lost tunnels of Atlantis with screams and blood.

Freed from the shackles of artificial long-life imposed by the experiments of Dr Grimus, many slaves grew very old very quickly, and withered into dust. The survivors, fuelled by fury at their treatment, reached the surface and ran amok through the crumbling streets of Metronis dealing death to the powerless Atlanteans.

***

"Everyone to the Nautilad!" cried the Professor as the golden flying machine collapsed under a boulder. The soldiers, their Vril weapons dead, along with Ayesha's panicking entourage took flight like rats through the rain of pumice dust and rocks.

Flying machines, with intakes blocked by volcanic dust, spiralled from the air, their final resting places pock-marking the Atlantean landscape with explosions.

Sam Scrivener and Rudi helped the Professor from the broken scaffold. Mike took Wendy's hand and Dill grabbed Lu's and Lu stretched out to hold Toby's hand. Everyone was choking in the clouds of dust and ducking to avoid the flying stones that clanged and clattered like giant hailstones on the Nautilad's hull.

They were halted at the foot of the gang-plank by a dark shape standing on the deck. The towering hulk of Smegeye the pirate loomed from the dust, drawing a massive sword.

"Did you think I'd let you steal my booty after my merry Mechaboys have restored this crate for sale, Professor?"

"Stand aside," said the Professor weakly.

"It will cost you two million Lanteens, Slave!" sneered Peabody Fiddler, appearing from behind his master's head.

"For goodness sake! Look around you. What good is money now, you fool?" screamed Wendy.

"Silence!" roared Smegeye taking a step towards them down the gangplank. Suddenly he lunged forward and grabbed Wendy's arm with a vicious claw.

"Now get to my serpent underboat, all of you, or I'll slit the pretty one's throat."

Stu slowly stooped as if attending to his boot. He picked up a fragment of shattered Vril crystal from the quayside.

"I'm gonna get you," he hissed between clenched teeth, and taking a hanky from his pocket, he made a makeshift slingshot and loaded it with the crystal shard. Smegeye looked puzzled. The sling twirled and twirled, faster and faster, and when Stu let it fly the glinting fragment hissed through the air.

Thud! Peabody Fiddler carked in shock. The crystal embedded itself smouldering in his soft temple and the instantly-dead parasite toppled from Smegeye's shoulder and swung from its fleshy umbilical. A look of pained shock distorted Smegeye's face and his head jerked back.

Dropping his sword he sank to his knees pulling Wendy down with him. Stu followed up his first shot with a second that burst the pirate's bulbous right eye. Screaming, the stricken giant released Wendy's arm and cupped his hand to cover the remains of the burning organ. After a moment's groaning, the great body slumped forward and splashed headfirst into the canal.

"Quickly, everyone. We must get away before Atlantis is buried alive," said the Professor, helping Wendy to her feet and limping along the deck.

"I'll say goodbye," said Sidney offering his hand first to Podesta Blenkinsopp and then the others.

"Aren't you coming with us?" said Toby.

"No Toby, my kin are the people of the plains. I shall strike west for Lantania."

"And what about you, Mook?" said Lu. "We owe you so much."

Mook Wundabuck smiled, "You'll just have to muddle on without me. This has been my home for as long as I can remember.... And the services of a doctor might well be in demand after the Gods have seen fit to calm the mountain."

"We'll miss you," replied Lu, stooping to kiss the small figure on the cheek.

"Ugh! Such an unhygienic human custom! Now get away all of you. That's doctor's orders!"

Rudi stood for a moment alone on the deck surveying the decimated city. The quayside deserted now, but for a lone figure walking through the dust.

"Sire! My Lord Arnakk!"

"I am not your Lord, Nicademus. I have never been your Lord."

"But you are the true king of Atlantis! Will you desert your kingdom? Will you abandon your people?"

"I am not your king, Nicademus. We have both been deceived by Queen Ayesha. Atlantis was never my home. I am a son of the Overworld and I go with my true father," cried Rudi, pointing to the Professor's stooping figure in the hatchway of the conning tower.

"Run for your life, Nicademus!" cried the Professor. "Atlantis enjoyed the gift of free energy which it chose not to share. It dies now as a consequence... Rudi! Come now or it will be too late!"

The Machine Stops

A lorry-sized boulder plunged into the canal scraping the Nautilad's hull as it sent a fifty foot plume of water into the air. The submarine rocked like a child's toy and losing balance Rudi, pitched over and skidded across the metal deck on his armoured breastplate and over the side.

"Batten the hatches we've got to leave!" crackled Podesta Blenkinsopp's voice over the submarine's intercom.

Slamming the conning tower door and spinning its locking wheel the Professor staggered back along the rolling submarine's deck to where Rudi was clinging on. The motors began vibrating through the hull as the propeller spun. The others looked down helplessly from the conning tower observation dome as the deck began disappearing beneath the waves. Leaning over the side the Professor reached down to his beleaguered son.

"Take my hand, Rudi," he cried, and when he felt the boy's fingers curling around his wrists, he pulled with all his might and lifted him on to the deck.

"Quickly!" cried the Professor and together they ran through rising water and hailing rocks to the conning tower hatch where Farouke was waiting inside with dry towels to let them in.

Chapter 57

Return to Grump Island

Austin's headlamps clicked on as the Nautilad entered the tunnel in the rock face. Podesta Blenkinsopp was sitting in Austin's driving seat taking corrective action where necessary.

They watched the blue desert canal and the disintegrating landscape of Atlantis slowly disappearing, and they held their breath as the Nautilad powered through a terrifying darkness of falling stalactites and cracking rocks clanging on the submarines trusty hull plates.

"At last," breathed Wendy, when the blue Sea of Tethys came into view through the tunnel's exit.

They were soon bathed in azure light and leaving Austin to take over, Podesta Blenkinsopp joined everybody on the conning tower deck.

"The X19 should take us back to the Arctic tunnel from here," he said.

Farouke's voice drifted up through the hatch in the conning tower floor, "Tea and coffee and roast beef served the mess. Come get it!"

"Any Tunnock's wafers?" called Toby.

"Don't be cheeky, young Effendi!"

***

Return to Grump Island

The voyage south-west was uneventful. Introductions were made and the Professor, Rudi, and Podesta Blenkinsopp were properly reunited for the first time since the Second World War.

After Farouke's roast beef dinner (cooked on the brand new cooker installed by Smegeye's mechaboys during the Nautilad's refit), that all agreed was the best they'd ever tasted, everyone was glad to spend the first night in their own comfortable bunks.

The morning was cloudy and overcast and after a full English breakfast of eggs, sausages, beans, bacon and fried bread, Bill and Toby, Rudi and Lu and Stu joined Podesta Blenkinsopp in the conning tower as Grump Island appeared for the first time in the grey distance.

"Do you really want to go back to that place, Captain?" said Lu.

"I don't think I've got much choice in the matter. I've tried to sell the Admiral Trumper, but who wants to buy a pub that nobody visits on a deserted island?"

"What is all of this?" said the Professor, climbing up through the conning tower hatch. "You must come and live with Rudi and me at Karnak House, old friend."

"Thank you, Professor. Thank you from the bottom of my heart, but what on earth would I live on? I have some savings but only a meagre sum and I could not possibly rely on anybody's charity."

The Professor clapped a firm hand on his old friend's shoulder. "We are NOT just anybody, Podesta. You are our friend! We've been shipmates. You are like one of the family."

"Is that Grump Island?" cried Wendy. She and Mike followed the voices from the conning tower and Wendy was standing looking out through binoculars.

"Yes, I shall be very glad to get home," replied the captain flatly.

Wendy took down the glasses and handed them to Podesta. Her face had dropped.

"Look, Captain."

Grump Island looked more grey and foreboding than usual.

"Oh!" exclaimed the captain. "Oh my gosh. I think I need to sit down."

"May I see?" said Mike, and he began following the island's craggy rock face down to a rock pile sticking out through the wave-beaten cliff base. The blue and gold portrait of an old naval sea lord was just visible in the gloom poking from the rubble.

"I appear to be homeless all of a sudden. The Admiral Trumper's fallen in the sea! Oh dear. What a calamity."

"Won't you come back to Karnak House with us Captain Blenkinsopp? I'd really like you to," said Rudi, shaking the old seafarer's hand.

"I know what it's like to be homeless and it ain't no fun, mate," said Stu, squinting through the glass bubble to where the sun was breaking through the clouds and shedding its pale light on Grump Island.

"Here, Stu. Would you like the binoculars," said Wendy. A lump came to her throat. Nobody had thanked Stu for releasing them from the control room in the cavern at

267

Karnak House, nor for dispatching the pirate, Smegeye and allowing them all to escape from Atlantis.

"Ta, missus. Cor, these are cool. I can almost touch them rocks."

The sun suddenly burned brightly through a break in the cloud.

"HEY! Captain! Look! Look at this!" cried Stu. He passed the binoculars to Podesta. "See?"

The captain said nothing at first.

"See what? Oh? Oh, it can't be. Is that what I think it is?"

"Ain't you pleased? Your troubles are over, mate."

"Can I see?" cried Bill, reaching for the binoculars, hardly able to contain his curiosity.

"Just a minute, Bill. Let Stu tell us all what he saw," said Wendy, raising her eyebrows and smiling encouragement to Stu. "Go on, Stu."

"I saw gold, missus. Loads of GOLD!" shouted Stu at the top of his voice. "It runs in a dirty great seam from the top of Grump Island to flippin bottom!"

"What do you think about living with us now, Podesta?" the Professor asked when the excitement of the 'Grump Island gold rush' had subsided.

"Thank you Professor. I accept your kind invitation," said the Captain and everyone -especially Rudi - cheered.

"Very good, Effendi. Perhaps now we can afford to do some decorating at last!"

"Yes Farouke," cried the Professor, "and more besides. I have big plans for Karnak House."

Chapter 58

Gunfight at the Periwinkle Estate

The Professor agreed to let Bill, Mike, and Wendy keep Austin on condition the silver box was removed from his boot.

"I think you might need welding gear to get that out," said Mike as the Professor opened Austin's boot lid. With Farouke's assistance, the Professor lifted the silver box out effortlessly.

"I think we've got company!" laughed the Professor, peering into the boot and into the face of a hedgehog, then a vole and then a mouse.

"Hey! That's my hedgehog!" said Bill.

"How did a badger get in there?" said Lu, when a black and white striped nose popped out from under a tartan blanket.

"Careful! Don't upset him. He says he is not a badger he is a skunk. And his name is Legit," said Rudi.

"That's the skunk that escaped from the zoo and ponged out your garage, Mike," said Wendy. "The animals were obviously hiding in Austin's boot and hitched a ride when we left Wishing Well Cottage to go to Karnak House."

"I think as a vet you are more qualified than me, Mike. What do you suggest we do with them?" asked the Professor, for once not knowing quite what to do next.

"Close the boot very slowly and latch it quietly. We'll release the vole, hedgehog, and mouse in my garden at Wishing Well Cottage, then I'll telephone the Bristol Zoo to pick up "Legit" to reunite him with his mate and his new family," replied Mike.

"Just a minute," said Rudi. "Do you mind if I tell them what you plan to do? They all look a bit nervous."

After Rudi reassured the animals (he didn't tell Legit about his new babies preferring to leave that as a nice surprise), everyone said their goodbyes by shaking hands, hugging, and kissing (*only polite pecks on the cheek you understand*), and the Professor issued an open invitation that if they were ever passing Tadwold-on-Sea to drop in for tea.

"But do please ring first in case I'm off on an expedition to find another lost civilisation somewhere with Rudi or Podesta."

It was a tight squeeze to fit everyone inside Austin for the journey home. Lu sat on Bill's lap and Toby took it in turns with Stu to sit rather reluctantly on each other's laps.

"Right then. We'd better get going," said Mike turning Austin's starting handle to loosen him up after the voyage.

Wendy turned on Austin's petrol tap and pulled out his choke and after a signal from Mike, Bill leaned forward to turn on the ignition switch. Mike swung the starting handle smartly and Austin's engine burst into life.

"Austin drives more like a proper Austin Seven without his silver box. Just like Justine in fact," remarked Mike as they headed back through sunny Tadwold-on-Sea with its milling holiday-makers waving at them with big smiles as they chugged along the Promenade.

Gunfight at the Periwinkle Estate

***

The Periwinkle Road estate looked every bit as gruesome as it did before Stu left. Wendy's heart sank as they stopped outside the boy's foster mother's house to drop him off.

She watched his lonely figure walk through mounds junk strewn down garden path. On reaching the shabby front door the boy glanced back longingly over his shoulder before knocking.

"Oi! You're back then?" came a nosey neighbour's voice from a window next-door. "It's no good you knockin', there's nobody 'ome. Yer mum's in prison 'cos of you!"

"It's gonna rain. Can I come in your 'ouse, missus?"

"YOU? Not flippin likely. You're nuffink but trouble. Ya little bleeder. You'd bettarh clear off before yer mum's boyfriend gets wind you're 'ere an' turns up and kills yer."

And with that the window slammed and Stu looked helplessly out to the road. Austin was pulling away but anxious faces were still looking out through the back windows at him. He waved timidly and turned away to try the side gate. It opened.

He closed the gate behind him and leant with his back against it. He was alone. He waited taking deep breaths to fight back tears. The others would be gone in a minute and he wouldn't have the shame of admitting he'd gone back to an empty house where nobody wanted him. They'd all be happy to get home. They'd all be joking and laughing and talking about the adventure together. Happy bloody families! Well good bloody luck to them that's all he could say. You're better off on your own. Don't trust no one.

***

271

"I don't like leaving Stu like this," said Wendy as they pulled out from the Periwinkle Estate onto the main road to Piddle Wallop.

"He probably lost his key, that's all," replied Mike.

"I don't care. I just don't think we should leave him locked outside. What if it rains?"

"He'll probably break in knowing Stu," laughed Bill. "Anyway, it's none of our business, is it, mum?"

"That's just the sort of narrow-minded talk that alienates that boy."

"Come on, mum. He's nothing but trouble. He plays truant. He bullies Toby, and he's a thief."

"And he shoots innocent animals with a catapult too. Don't forget that Mrs. Young," said Toby, smarmily.

"Well! I'm surprised at you both! You've got very short memories that's all I can say!" said Wendy, turning in her seat to glare at Bill and Toby. "Don't forget it was Stu who freed us when that horrible little man from Wallopshire Council left us to starve in the cavern at Karnak House. And tell me who it was who made a slingshot and rescued us from Smegeye and that revolting Peabody Fiddler? I think it's a good thing Stu is a good shot with a catapult under the circumstances, don't you?"

"For what it's worth, I think your mum's right. I think we should be grateful to Stu," said Mike.

"Yes. I'm with Mrs. Young," said Lu, "I think you're both being mean!"

"Mike! Please turn round. I'm not prepared to abandon Stu," said Wendy.

***

Gunfight at the Periwinkle Estate

Cracking open the side gate and peeking out, Stu saw that Austin was gone.

News travels fast on the Periwinkle Estate and it would be no time at all before the nosey neighbour gossiped and everybody knew Stu was back.

He had no idea where he would go as it began to rain harder, but anywhere was better than here. As the neighbour said, Wolf would soon find him and beat him up (or worse). It was only a matter of time.

He hoped nobody noticed him creeping away as he turned left at the front gate and down the street. This hope, like most of Stu's hopes, was rapidly dashed.

The air suddenly filled the deafening roar of motorcycles.

In panic Stu looked for a wall, or a bush, or an alleyway, or anywhere to hide. It was too late. In a moment he was surrounded by a dozen revving motorcycles.

The lead bike bumped up the kerb onto the pavement. The pillion rider dismounted. Then, like most of Stu's fears, this one all too soon materialised.

Wolf was blocking his path and snarling brandishing a bicycle chain.

"I wondered when you'd turn up, you little brat!" he growled, and to Stu's fleeting relief stuffed the chain into a leather jacket pocket.

"Touch me and I'll 'ave the law on yer," quaked Stu in desperation.

"Oh look boys, did you see that flyin' pig!" mocked Wolf, grabbing Stu's ear and yanking him toward the pillion seat of the lead bike. "Thought we'd seen the back of you, you little scumbag! Thought you'd disappeared off the face

273

of the earth. Still now you're back you can come with us and join a little 'welcome home' party I'm throwing in your honour."

"Leave me alone," yelled Stu kicking out at Wolf. Wolf twisted the boy's ear even harder bringing tears to his eyes.

"Quite handy you being away, really. Now nobody will miss you when I put you in concrete and make you disappear for real. It's payback time. Now get on the bike!"

Wolf mounted the pillion of the second revving machine and he was waving the pack off when Austin appeared at the corner.

"There's Stu, Mum!" cried Bill. "See? On the back of that motorbike."

Mike swerved to cut off the lead bike. Wolf dismounted and swaggered over and pounded his fist on the little car's driver's window.

"What's your game mate? Get that ****** antique out of my way!" he hissed angrily through the glass. Reaching in his pocket he took the chain and wrapped it around his gloved-fist.

Mike looked at Wendy and swallowed hard.

"Now what do we do?" he mouthed. Wendy shrugged her shoulders. Wolf flung open Austin's door and grabbing Mike's boiler suit collar, dragged him out.

"That does it! Let me out, Mrs Young! Stu isn't the only one who's a thief around here!" said Toby, pulling out a stun-gun from inside his boiler suit. "I'm afraid I stole this as a souvenir before we left the Nautilad."

"But it won't work without Vril, Toby," whispered Lu.

"*He* doesn't know that," said Toby, tipping Austin's driver's seat forward and clambering out.

"Get back in the car this instant Toby!" cried Wendy.

"No, Mrs Young. There are times when a man's gotta do what a man's gotta do."

Toby walked calmly over and looked up into Wolf's glowering eyes.

Trying his best to stifle any hint of a tremor in his voice he said, "Unhand my friends, you ruffian!"

"Ruffian?" spluttered Bill, clamping a despairing hand over his eyes.

Wolf dropped Mike, threw back his head and roared with laughter, "Watcha gonna do, Harry Potter? Blast me with your toy ray gun?"

"Look... Look I, I'm warning you!"

"Aw. Push off you little squirt," laughed Wolf, biffing Toby's shoulder playfully with the flat of his hand and almost knocking him over.

Wendy, in fact everybody, (including the other bikers) gasped gobsmacked when a blue plasma stream crackled from the "toy ray gun". Wolf was suddenly trapped in suspended animation. His lank long hair stood on end, his eyes bulged, and his mouth gaped aghast.

"Oops!" cried Toby releasing the trigger. Wolf slumped into the gutter like a rag doll in a gurgling gaga stupor.

"Come on Stu," said Toby, and with Wolf still spluttering, and his gang dumfounded and the sound of approaching police sirens, Mike pressed Austin's starter button and they drove away.

They were soon bowling along the leafy lanes of Wallopshire to Wishing Well Cottage when Toby said, "I just don't understand it. How come the stun-gun worked? It shouldn't work without Vril, should it?"

"No it shouldn't," said Mike. "I really hope nothing else funny's about to happen."

"Not now the Professor's taken Austin's silver box away, surely?" said Wendy.

"This might be the answer," said Bill, producing a softly glowing crystal from his pocket. "I dug this out of the cave wall in the mines of Tor to light our way after we left the pigmen… remember?"

"Just what we need for another adventure! You'd like another adventure, wouldn't you, Mr Stevens?" said Lu with a slightly teasing tone.

"No! No, Lu! At least, not until I've put my feet up, and had a nice cup of tea," replied Mike glancing at Lu over his shoulder.

"And some Tunnock's Wafers, Mr. Stevens?" chuckled Toby.

"Good news, Toby! There's an unopened packet of Tunnock's Wafers in the kitchen," quipped Mike returning the cheeky banter.

"I don't quite know how to tell you this, boys. The bad news is… I put the Tunnock's wafers in the freezer before we left," said Wendy.

"Looks like you can 'ave yer wafers but you can't eat 'em too, Toby!" said Stu, and with that everybody laughed.

☺ The End ☺

Check out Bill's Blog To:

Learn more about the Austin Chronicles and other books in the series.

Register to get news of book giveaways, special offers, games, and downloadable freebies.

Read about the characters and their backgrounds.

Read about the author and his real-life adventures with his own real Austin car called Yvette.

I really love to hear from my readers! And I will respond to your email personally, so why not make my day, and if you enjoyed this story please let me know what you thought by contacting me at Bill's Blog?

To visit Bill's Blog, scan the QR Code below with your mobile phone.

P.S. You might need a QR Code scanner App to do this....

x

Other Books by Stuart Taylor

These are available in Kindle and paperback versions at Amazon.co.uk

And Amazon.com

17304900R00158

Printed in Great Britain
by Amazon